Praise for Darin Bradley's *Chimpanzee*

"As with the best dystopian fiction, Chimpanzee taps into many contemporary issues and fears — in this case, everything from the surveillance state to the student-debt crisis. Chimpanzee is a post-collapse novel for those who have become numb to them, and a unique take on a subgenre in sore need of one. The book's dazzling originality not only helps overcome much of its dryness, it makes it well worth the extra homework."
— Jason Heller, *NPR Books*

"[A] disturbingly believable near-future dystopia."
— *Publishers Weekly*

"[A] densely layered novel."
— Craig Gidney,
Washington Independent Review of Books

"Excellent literary dystopia."
— Starred review, *Library Journal*

"Bradley's sophomore effort is just as ambitious as his debut, and his voice is more assured, his characters better delineated. Chimpanzee isn't cheerful stuff, but there's a revolutionary zeal, and a belief in the power of the mind to effect change in the world, that provides some light in this otherwise bleak dystopia."
— Tim Pratt, *Locus*

"Both heart-pounding and intelligent, this dystopian thriller has the best of both worlds."
— *Foreword Reviews*

Praise for Darin Bradley's *Noise*

"An exceptionally polished debut."

—*Publishers Weekly*

"Considering the nature of his dystopic fiction and the fullness of his vision, I can perhaps be forgiven for thinking that, in his debut, Darin Bradley may be The One."

—Lincoln Cho, *January Magazine*

"A cruel little knife-strike of a book, in the best possible way."

—Jeff VanderMeer,
author of the *Southern Reach* trilogy.

"Edgy and disturbing, Noise is a worthy successor to all those post-holocaust books of yesteryear."

—*Analog Magazine*

"This is a stunner of a novel, with a modernist almost poetical style, and a concept that blasts its way through the hoary old clichés....It's the best fiction book I've read this year."

—Mark Rose, *Bookgasm*

"Darin Bradley's brainy, slippery, and riveting Noise is Lord of the Flies on serious psychotropics. With narrative tendrils in the 'paper' book and online as well, Noise is deliberately speaking to a young, media-soaked audience through various texts and tricks. You watch. Noise is destined to be a milestone work for Millennial readers."

—Barth Anderson,
author of *The Patron Saint of Plagues*
and *The Magician and the Fool*

DARIN BRADLEY

TOTEM

Also by Darin Bradley

Noise
Chimpanzee

DARIN BRADLEY

TOTEM

Underland Press

This is U027, and it has an ISBN of 978-1-63023-015-9.

This book was printed in the United States of America, and it is published by Underland Press, an imprint of Resurrection House (Puyallup, WA).

I try to look like I belong, which is what we do in foreign territory.

Edited by Mark Teppo
Cover Design by Darin Bradley
Book Design by Aaron Leis
Copy Edit by Shannon Page

First trade paperback Underland Press edition: October 2016.

www.resurrectionhouse.com

For Juliet Ulman, David Pomerico, and Mark Teppo

ACKNOWLEDGMENTS

I owe a significant debt to my wife, Rima Abunasser, whose work continues to teach me about the dangerous fictions inherent to nationalist identity, particularly when those with power usurp the stories of those without.

My thanks also to my early readers, Rima, Aaron, and Leslie—and to Misti Morrison, who did project management on early parts of the book. My editor, Mark Teppo, is a patient man, and his abiding confidence in this elusive book made the entire difference in my actually finishing it.

DARIN BRADLEY

TOTEM

"First, I was the mother. Now, I'm the land. Tomorrow, undoubtedly, I'll be the symbol. Wake up, clever boy. I'm not the mother; I'm not the symbol. I'm human. I eat, drink, dream, make mistakes, wander, suffer, and talk to the wind. I'm no symbol. I'm a woman."

—Sahar Khalifeh, *Bab al-Saha*
(Quotation translated by Rima Abunasser)

1

Amn

The radiation sirens are not the real calls to prayer. But that doesn't matter.

►

The priests still sound the actual calls—those atonal bells—and the devout obey. They shuffle into the sunlight, on sidewalks or street corners, and bend themselves onto God's holy pavement. That remade stone. Their leadcloth abatement clothing folds around them by design because it's too stiff to bend, so it follows them down, that they might supplicate geometrically. It makes angles of their fleshed contours and protects them against the radiation in exoskeletal, human shapes. The abatement is regulation. They can trade up for a better fit after enough state service hours. The foreigners and tourists simply pay for it.

The abatement is sacrilege, getting in God's way like that. But the devout don't have a choice. The regulations come with the international aid. Amn thinks they look like asphalt mollusks wearing it, ribbed and unmoving as they supplicate on the solar seafloor—the tidal pool between the great, upshoved rims of Aer's excavated valley. Those outer elevations, made so anciently higher than the city center by the mining. The millennia of extraction and reconstruction. The valley's *reason to be*: God's holy stone. Amn read the phrase once in a forgotten Worldview pamphlet, carried all the way in from wherever its owner had been, learning to care about the Aeri and their plight. It was in English, but it used French and German words, like special effects or AerNet animations, to make important points. Where to send money, prayers—it had ideas about tradition and coexistence and the preservation of international treasures. *Raison d'être.* Very pretty.

But that doesn't matter. Belan had said so. Anytime someone asked him about the outside world. If they pressed him, he told them they were missing the point. Or he bit them. Once, he kissed a man for asking. Gently in the sunlight, and his acolytes followed him away.

Belan told them all to stop being something because it was getting in the way. They wrote it down.

▶

The priests still ring the prayer bells in the tower atop their common house—Amn and his brothers emerge to meet the devout around The Host or out in the streets. But the devout are few, anymore. The elder, the diseased and misshapen suffering their radiated ways to God. Amn still has to reach so many. All these meandering, revolving many. The ones who, unlike the devout, aren't ashamed to wear their leadcloth, even right there in front of him, so near The Host. And they still silently expect his blessing.

But that doesn't matter.

When the radiation sirens toss their vulgar cries across the city, the people truly emerge. It brings them from their nests in such numbers. Communal numbers. Aeri numbers. They like to pray best when they can watch each other doing it. They remember who they are, who they've been, and the breath of God in the Aeri stone feels most holy when it harms them all at once. Especially now, with God's great eye sunning radiation upon them. The outside world calls it solar maximum, and it is some astrophysical tourbillion. An inversion of magnetic fields, a bombardment of coronal ejecta. An annihilating, solar slowness, elegant and dedicated, the strength of which man has approached only in crude explosives just bright enough to burn cities. For many Aeri, maximum has accelerated the sickness, the divine touch that has, for so long, twisted them from their carnal prisons into the true presence of God. So unbearable by nature.

It's the reason they come out like this, for the rotation. To live visibly, amidst Aer's holy stone. Together. To all die this ongoing once in the stone's igneous mother-hug. Its radioactive breath that filled Father's lungs, the first Aeri, when he was nothing but dust in God's hands. When he had finished with creation, God left the stone behind to teach his children how to make themselves. He left his breath inside it so the Aeri might always be made anew. Learning to appreciate what he'd given them. As long as God maintains his grasp on the primordial dust, it will remain stone. Naturally radioactive.

Naturally.

It's what they're all doing here, the Aeri. Being something. Holding themselves together until God lets go and they become dust again themselves. Until they're done with the whole thing. It's a cosmic effort. An important one. Especially for the foreigners watching them all remotely. The donors and activists overseas. The classrooms of learning children. The organizations and governments, historians, pundits. The angry and the compassionate. The watching many.

The network is called Worldview.

It's an important effort, so the Aeri sit at café tables, drinking bitter tea and smoking imported tobacco while portable air scrubbers wheeze the pollutants from the civic smog.

The cameras aren't visible. It's important.

▶

Amn can tell they're getting ready. The radiation sirens will bleat their profanity across his beloved architecture, painting interference into every echoing corner. Vendors and street people are getting ready. They stand to make so much with the entire city emerging and rotating to new domiciles around them. Exchanging areas of radiated exposure because it's fair. Amn ignores the people around him at the bus stop, their askance existence and the unlikelinesses they imagine. Their corner-of-the-eye beliefs that Amn will bless them despite themselves.

Before the rotations began, the radiation sirens were just radiation sirens. A screaming idea that everybody ought to move along. A foreign idea. Now they only sound at regular intervals, to get everybody rotating.

Technically, they are *revolving*, in their slow, domestic paths around the city center, shifting in protracted orbits from place to place to be in a little bit of Aer at a time but never in too much of it at once. For their own safety. Amn imagines it would have been hard to sell the U.N. on a "Revolutionary Housing" program. He wonders if they even thought about it. He thinks about it, every time. He thinks Rotational Housing is a beautifully large and sacrilegious idea. The biggest the world can get against God. It thrills him.

On the bus, Amn sits as the driver announces the route. Onboard LED screens flash through a WELCOME animation from the transit authority, and a chime indicates a signal sweep. All around him, phones ring, message alerts chime, and screens embedded into headrests light up as AerNet reaches out to the newcomers. It is Aer's mitigated connection to the rest of the digital world, screening things like Worldview from the Aeri, to *preserve their way of life*. It's a better internet. The administration says so all the time.

The passengers who were already on the bus stare dumbly away from the new arrivals. They've already been through the sweep's interrogation.

Amn pulls his phone from the pocket of his vestments.

"Good morning," the operator says.

Conversations bubble around him. Diesel exhaust clouds and dissipates beyond the window.

"Good morning," Amn says.

"Thank you," the operator says. "It's evening here."

"Isn't it always?"

She drops her tone.

"Confirmation, please."

Amn pulls the phone away from his ear and thumbs the screen awake. He taps at his identification app, and it sends its secrets across the connection.

"And your abatement?"

"Exempt. I'm clergy."

"One moment please."

The connection goes flat. Check-ins could be automated, but the transit authority considers live interaction more personal. More Aeri.

"Thank you," she says. "We would like to remind you at this time that anti-radiation supplements remain available and can be expedited to your attention in the common house."

"Thank you," Amn says.

"Destination, please?"

"Exempt."

"In that case, let me remind you that there are over a dozen cafés along this line ready to serve you the breakfast of your choice. If you require assistance selecting one, please visit the transit authority on your mobile device."

"Thank you."

"Tobacco, confections, and soft drinks are available at your nearest dispensary beginning today at 11:00 AM. Premium brands will be available from 3:00-5:00."

"Thank you."

"Thank you for allowing the transit authority to serve your travel needs. Goodbye."

"Goodbye." But she was already off the line. Taking her next call.

Travel needs. The language they borrowed from airliners and trains. Outside, where people moved in long, bending lines from place to place. Where they didn't move in circles and instead let the world spin for them.

He remembers when the tobacco was a problem. When Worldview fought with the administration about paying for it. Outsiders don't smoke like Aeri. They all stopped doing it, sometime. Amn thinks the companies themselves, the cigarette people, give them away. Business losses. The Aeri don't quit doing things the way other people do.

The Net won't bother him again today, not when he moves through his favorite avenues or approaches the turnstiles back into the mound of The Host. Worldview gave them the network. They think it's too intrusive to see yourself the way the rest of the world does.

▶

There is a program on the screen in the headrest in front of him. A documentary about the international embassies and their construction. It plays on every screen in the bus, and the people stare as the program looks out the windows for them, detailing their own city.

The embassy plazas, in the program, look mostly sepia. Like re-creations. Most of their hydrogel tarps have been hidden beneath canopies of electrodeposited copper. Or annealed. Whichever. Amn isn't actually listening. The hydrogel absorbs what radiation the copper can't bounce. It's another blasphemy, but there are fewer Aeri who care anymore. It comes with the outside aid, the political momentum, the foreign subsidies that keep Aer a UNESCO World Heritage site without forcing the Aeri out of it, so their charming, ancient culture can continue cooking inside an international treasure. A cradle of civilization. The Aeri do the world a favor by anchoring it to that pre-science era that left room for miracles and things like theophanic stone. The international preservation effort gives them what they need. Subsidized food. Travel. Radiation abatement. Regular medical examinations. Because it is still their right to live here. The capital of the ancient empire, when it still was one. The rotational housing schedule keeps things moving, evening out exposure democratically. Allowing them to safely preserve their culture. Their faith. Their ways of death at their own choosing.

All that copper, bouncing dirty sunlight onto all that photocatalytic paint. The central plaza looks bronzed on the screen. Just barely postcolonial because what a charming era that was. So great for the holy stone architecture. The foreigners in the program look almost fashionable in their custom abatement wear—the Germans and Americans and Emirates phasing in and out of their embassy airlocks. The clothing reminds Amn of reinforced motorcycle clothing. Like it's only just a minute, this quick errand, and then they're back onto some café racer to a fashionable chalet or mansion or whatever.

They're just being something in Amn's way, but that doesn't matter. Because God forgives us all.

▶

This bus route, in particular, is painted onto the city itself. The depolluting paints, in their patriotic murals, appear less frequently the further the bus moves from the city center. Toward The Wall. Technically, the young men from the Belgian firm informed them, the paint is part of an ongoing experiment and is therefore exempt from the fair exposure and abatement details of the Registry Act. Their company did something with titanium. Something about nitrogen. So much smog. So many cars spinning in the roundabouts—the scooters, like symbiotes, driving in their wakes and drags. Endlessly. The Aeri reenactment, perhaps, of that solar tourbillion. Moving, like waves, without going anywhere. The traffic follows its own laws, dumb to civic mandates or common sense. It behaves like water, following the path of least resistance.

Amn doesn't mind the paint, not the way some of the others do. Air pollution is not part of God's plan. It is getting in the way, twisting bodies in ugly, choking ways.

The paint disappears, the farther they drive, marking the route by its conspicuous inability to reface the stone. Its stains.

▶

The route doesn't go directly to The Wall—Registered Aeri aren't permitted through the old gates, so the Transit Authority doesn't take them there. Not unless they rank highly enough in civic government or law enforcement. Or the clergy, which had been a provision of the Act.

Amn walks the last half mile to The Wall. The traffic disappears around him. Protesters gather in tired circles. Spinning below The Wall. Young police volunteers watch them wearily, their submachine guns heavy against their riot armor. Foreign correspondents point microphones. A beautification crew is planting ornamental shrubbery along the base of The Wall, which is made of imported concrete panels. Thirty feet tall.

Amn approaches the checkpoint. The Unregistered, in line, stare at him, hands extended for his blessing. There is no irreverence, waiting to be patted down.

A police volunteer shouts: "Priest."

Amn goes to the front of the line.

"Name?"

"Amn."

"Papers."

Papers.

"Your purpose today?"

"Exempt."

A phone call to a superior. Have a seat.

Amn watches. The police volunteers paw at the Unregistered. Squint at their papers. Make a big show of it. They pull a few aside and confiscate packs of cigarettes, tins of coffee, sachets of tea. Registry items. The international monitor steps in when they pull aside an underage girl. Her mother doesn't fight the volunteer's arm across her chest. She maintains the shuffle, with the others. Her daughter will be escorted to her on the other side.

Two young men in hazmat suits walk directly to the front of the line, up against the checkpoint gate. They have their headgear tucked under their arms, satchels over padded shoulders. One of them hands a sheet of paper to a volunteer—no older than they are. Early twenties. Younger. The volunteer laughs with them at something before examining the paper.

"Leve?" he asks one. The worker nods, eyes on his cell phone now. Something to look at.

To the other: "Belan?"

Belan points at something on the page, and leans around to examine it with the guard.

Amn stares. Belan. The holy name he gives every male infant, at every naming he's called to. He will do it again, today, on the other side of The Wall. A favor to some Unregistered with the means of getting a message to him in the common house. His patron. His *raison d'être*.

He doesn't remember which of his brethren hands out "Leve." But Amn named this young man in his hazmat suit, laughing with the volunteer in front of the Unregistered. Belan. Some time ago.

Belan glances at Amn on the way through the gate. Who cares?

Helena

Helena Villarreal would like to know what, precisely, the fuck *Aerte Dam* street is and why it's sabotaging her first Worldview link-up. She closes the translation app and reopens it one more time. *Aerte Dam* remains doggedly not English. Her navigation app believes Aerte Dam exists where Imperial Avenue should.

The Aeri brush past her on the sidewalk. A scooter gargles through the crowd, separated from its herd, and into her side. A slow collision, like glacial drift. Something that happens all the time, changing the landscape. Diastrophism for the masses.

Helena braces herself on the scooter and shoves off. The driver has a leg planted on the flagstones, as if ready to leap from the leaning machine and just be done with the headache. He gets it upright and wobbles through the foot traffic. He joins a flock trailing a bus. Helena doesn't understand the name blinking in the bus's route-display.

They're all getting ready. For the rotation. Her nav app indicates that it can still find hot spots, despite everything it won't translate for her, so she follows its pulsing icons along two-dimensional primary-colored street lines. Her leadcloth abatement makes zipping sounds, like bees, when it brushes against others in the migration. The result is a mass humming. She doesn't mind.

She finds the spot—a digital wall screen off the thoroughfare flashing the menu of grilled meats and cups of tea available from the dispensary window two meters to the right. A young man leans through that window, his forearms resting on the stone sill. She imagines it burning his arms, searing them up in direct contact. His eyelids are shadowed by the copper awning. He wears a flat white cap. A chef's smock. He watches her read the menu. She tries again, but there still isn't enough signal for a proper link. Not unless she rides the same satellite protocol twinkling her nav app. But this isn't priority enough. Bruce would bitch. She opens her press badge instead and shows the phone to the wall screen. She's only supposed to do this in critical situations, but having just arrived, she can't even get her bearings, much less evaluate the severity of a faulty app. Fuck it. She's here now. Let them sort it out back home.

There is a beep, and the animated meals dissipate from the screen. The Worldview icon appears. The resolution is too high. Too over-produced. The animated gleam on the logo's artistically metallic edges looks like some design student's semester project. Something rendered charmless and unreal by a too-high ladder of producers and art direction. Something that could make it past the board. The cook in the window is unimpressed.

A woman's face replaces the logo. Blonde, made up. People carry digital tablets through the office space behind her, busy with what they're supposed to be doing.

"Good morning," she says.

Helena can see the night through the windows behind her. That lurid glow of thousands of uncooperative lights, interested only in their own late-night offices or street corners or individual, passing cars. All of them only accidentally doing anything bright for the city.

"Villarreal 5714," Helena says.

The woman's eyes don't move. She monitors whatever non-intrusive data feed she's seeing upon Helena's face in her monitor.

"Good morning, Ms. Villarreal. State your inquiry."

"This app"—Helena shakes her phone at the face—"the PassPort, isn't working."

"Have you initialized the diagnos—"

"There isn't signal enough. I've tried."

People pass behind Helena. They move directly to the dispensary window. They don't read the menu—don't watch its interruptive blonde face. The screens all say the same thing, at every location. Even when there's some Worldview face on them. For maintenance, or announcements, or whatever.

"Yes," the woman says, "I'm unable to establish a secure link. One moment while I transfer you."

Her image digitizes away, and Bruce appears, in his office. The day's beard looks sharp in the light of his banker's lamp, which blows out the shadows under his cheekbones. He's looking at something offscreen. Reflections flash and crawl across his glasses.

"Obviously, your flight was okay," he says.

"*Flights*," she says. "All of them."

He looks at her and spreads his hands. What do you want me to do?

"Look, the PassPort app isn't working."

"What's it doing?"

"I'm supposed to be walking down Imperial Street with a hot Americano and plenty of sunshine for my first link-up."

"It couldn't find you a barista?"

"There is no *Imperial* Street."

He does something with his hands under the screen.

"That's because it's called Aerte Dam now."

"Motherfucker."

"Easy. I have to report every one of those you drop when you're public like this. Why didn't you use the phone?"

"Oh, the one without a proper signal? Yeah, totally. I just wanted to play with this direct screen in front of all these Aeri like a fucking tourist. You know."

"Okay," he says. "Okay. It's probably just another flare. They'll do signal sweeps to reconnect everything. You should watch the reports."

"I will. On the phone that can't stream them."

"They're changing the street names. Cultural initiative. Getting back to their pre-occupation roots."

"And when will I—"

"In the next update. App should have downloaded it in the hotel."

"I haven't *been* to the hotel."

"You should go. It's nice."

"For fuck's sake, Bruce."

"That's *three*."

"Goodbye."

She taps her press badge, and there's the menu again. Steady on the wall. A Bluetooth restoration of the indigenous décor. The cook leans on the sill again. On cue.

She turns. Rotating, like everything else she's seen here already.

"English?" she says.

"Sure," he says. He's younger than she is. Has big plans for those forearms. Probably beyond The Wall, if she had to bet. She could talk to him. Find a few things out. Get the jump on the real city, not these bullshit link-ups.

She knows he won't tell her anything, though. She's already played her Worldview role too well. He probably heard everything.

"Café Americano, please," she says.

He smiles. His beard is darker than Bruce's.

"'Please'," he says. He smiles it. Puts those arms to work, back in his dispensary.

The children in the link-up sit evenly behind their desks in rows and columns. They get smaller, like a trapezoid, as they stack toward the back of the room. Helena doesn't see any phones—they're paying attention, either because Helena is interesting or because the link-up frees their teacher from her job, so she can monitor their behavior. Mendoza, or something. Helena wasn't paying close attention. Miss. The woman was maybe a year out of university. Helena was working for free as an intern fact-checker at her age. A farm news desk an hour's drive from Lincoln. Helena hated Nebraska. Fuck Miss Mendoza.

It's a social studies class. They're high schoolers, soon to loose what they think they know upon the world. Their steady, upward ascension. Growing towards families of their own and full-time jobs. But how much damage can they really do wherever they are. Was it Peoria?

Social studies. So, prison:

"Aer doesn't maintain prisons," Helena says. The kid who asked the question—in row three, column two—has folded his hands upon his desk. His participation grade is a sure thing now.

Helena glances at the notes provided for her on her phone.

"Miss Mendoza tells me you're studying the Registry Act. International Tax Law."

They nod. They're distracted by the Aeri behind Helena. When she found the link-up, not far from The Host, on Imperial or whatever, the young cop scanned her press badge and smiled at her, like he might for a welcome aunt. Police service was a way into Aeri politics. He flagged down several passing Aeri and ordered them into place behind Helena. They gathered around her, around the storefront window projecting the classroom and pretended to browse its goods. To talk amongst themselves, oblivious to the students. They spoke Aeri loudly.

"Being kicked off the Registry, for offenses that would put you and me in jail, back home, is punishment enough."

"Why is that?" Miss Mendoza prompts, offscreen. She calls upon a girl in row one, column three. Her name is probably Stephanie. Or Lindsay. Candace.

Helena turns to watch the Aeri behind her. They are getting restless. The rotation is coming. There are things to do. The cop lets two go and ushers a new pair toward Helena. He makes them take off their leadcloth. The woman's gown is beautiful, traditional. Helena wants to take one like it home when she leaves. The woman's husband combs his beard.

Helena doesn't hear Candace's answer.

"The Unregistered have to work for their goods and services," Helena says.

The new couple make a show of kissing hands and cupping faces. As if they know the other Aeri around them.

"Can you tell us a bit about your assignment, Ms. Villarreal?" Mendoza says.

The police officer shoos the Aeri away. In the central plaza, beyond its great, congested roundabout, Aeri are gathering and praying below the great mound of The Host. Singing. The cop makes sure there's a view.

"I'm here to bring you information about The Wall," Helena says.

"What's behind it?" one of the students says, out of turn.

"We'll see," Helena says.

"Thank you, Ms. Villarreal," Mendoza says. "Class, thank Ms. Villarreal for the link-up."

"Thank you," Helena says. "Enjoy your observation."

The the projected classroom dissolves into a normal window display window. There is cookware and bags of rice, beans, soy—scattered casually, like a kitchen: a home, where there isn't time to put things properly away.

Helena steps out of range of the pinhole camera in the window frame. The students are gone, but they're still watching. They'll be taking notes on what they see for the next twenty minutes. There'll be a quiz.

The corner mart adjacent to Helena's hotel is as crowded as the streets. An unbroken, cycling parade of Aeri, moving inside, swimming through currents because it is easier to go along than move someplace on purpose. She watches them split into the aisles, preternaturally following the right leaders to stop and browse in sections that suddenly seem confusing. They twirl her, where she stands, bouncing their language at her as if they could sound her out of the way.

She fights her way to the clerk, and it is offensive. There are ways you're supposed to move, trying to get somewhere. What is the point of going straight there, as if your own shopping exists in some more important time than everyone else's?

The clerk wears an apron. Clean, pressed white. People hand him their cards, and he swipes them without looking at what they've bought. They aren't paying for it—simply logging their transactions. The world takes care of everything.

The clerk looks at her.

"Yes?" he says in English.

"Shampoo," she says. Hers had been too big, at the airport. Too much fluid for one woman's handling. Because she'd forgotten the transparent plastic bag in which it was to be secured.

"Fifth aisle," he says.

She watches him inspect cans and tuck them under his counter. She doesn't like the complimentary bottles of shampoo they will, no doubt, provide in her room. The feel of them, those tiny, childlike canisters, only reminds her that she is not to get completely comfortable in this place. In any place.

In aisle five, she gets her turn with the shampoo, after the women in front of her are finished handing shades of hair dye to each other. She tries to be patient. All she wants is a shower and a sandwich and that painful sleep, that jet-lag slowness, which is as unpleasant as it is restful. She could set the auto-cam in the window and sleep through the damn rotation. Let Bruce comb through the footage.

A young woman stops the flow beside Helena. Her hair is short. Except across her eyes. It's Western, but she's Aeri. Her clothes are dark and layered. She isn't wearing any abatement. Helena is suddenly conscious of her own—a leaden sack her driver provided at the airport, outside the city. Up above the valley rims, where the air isn't as toxic. Where the stones don't reach. She has a voucher for a custom fit. Later.

The young woman looks at her.

"You can't read the bottles," she says.

Helena looks again, as if only now realizing why she'd just been standing there. The realization relieves her.

"No."

The young woman has a white scar on her forehead. An old one, feathered. As if she were hit by something as a girl. Or scratched by a cat. Helena thinks she isn't much older than Miss Mendoza's high school students.

"What are you looking for?" she says.

"Tea tree," Helena says. "Just, any kind."

The woman studies the bottles with her. She chooses one and hands it to Helena.

"This," she says.

"Christ, thank you!"

She smiles. She moves. Helena learns from her how to walk in this place.

The clerk is arguing with another worker. A man in a jacket, gesturing under the counter. An older woman waits, placid, confident on the other side of the counter. This will resolve itself. Everything always does. The workers do their jobs.

The worker extracts the cans he'd been secreting under his counter.

"He is angry," the young woman says in front of Helena.

Helena looks at her, but she is watching the clerk. She has two bottles of wine tucked, like infants, into the hollow of her elbow.

"The clerk was going to purchase the cans, but he must give them to the woman."

Helena looks at the shampoo, as if he might have plans for it, too.

"You're a journalist," the young woman says.

"Yes. Helena." She extends a hand, and the young woman adjusts her bottles to accept it. Strangely. An American thing she doesn't mind doing.

"Vesse."

The clerk has given up his fight when Helena hands him her card.

"But this isn't news," Vesse says, handing over her card. Her earrings catch the light. Helena knows this woman won't be rotating. Not tonight. She has bigger plans.

Vesse's smile is a secret between them. As if they've just gotten away with something.

LEVE

Leve's mother calls with a prayer. He feels odd taking the call naked, but he knows better than to let her go to voice mail. He is a good son.

He responds to her prayer when he's supposed to, the way they do at service, the way the priests teach. Leve doesn't go to service anymore. He has it all memorized. He doesn't bother putting down his tube of cream while his mother speaks. He looks at how the foil stamp that reads ZINC glints in the overhead light. As if it is zinc itself. There are other ingredients he doesn't pay attention to. His mother intones the saints, his patron especially. Leve. He's heard it enough that he knows not to confuse the identities. She prays for his safety, for an early wife before God renders him sterile with the stone. His corpus. She gives thanks for the lump in her throat. She tells him the address of their next apartment, in the rotation schedule. He hasn't memorized his yet—it's in an envelope on the counter, with the other mail. He tells her he loves her.

He goes back into the bathroom because that's where it's appropriate to apply abatement cream to oneself. He massages it into his face, over the globes of his shoulders, and the corrugated ribs. He applies it twice to his testicles. Those especially. He has a new favorite cologne—a popular brand, and the weight of the glass container is excessive for the contents, the lid over-large.

His shoes are dirty, but he doesn't want to take the time to brush them. It'll be dark anyway.

He tucks the last of his things—the comb, the charger for his phone, the I.D. tag he wears to Central Maintenance, on Tuesdays and Thursdays, where he volunteers. It's a way into administration, and he has big plans. The rest of his things are packed into the crate. He sets his duffel on top, tucks the mail into a small outer pocket, sized for such things. Except the address. He folds it into his jacket. The administration will come for his things—a courtesy for its workers, so he doesn't have to bother. His brothers will help his father with the family crates. Not too many.

He leaves the keys on the counter. There is a new message on his phone. A text from the shift supervisor. He forgot to lock the cabinet when he replaced the medication he and Belan carried with them through The Wall, earlier. *Everything is accounted for, but be more careful.*

Leve walks out.

▶

State Radio is murmuring in the elevator. Leve stands against the wall, leaning away from the others as best he can. Older people, mostly, their eyes on the speaker in the ceiling, dutiful. They get on, off quietly, shuffling shoulders, coughing, avoiding eye contact that way you're supposed to in cramped circumstances. Participating in the many-legged beast without making too big a deal about the intimate distances between themselves—spaces usually reserved for bedrooms and doctors' offices. They're procreative, like the human amoeba: absorbing, dividing, sending bits of itself off for grand adventures in different directions through the primordial social ooze. Not much has really changed since then, except for the architecture.

Leve watches his phone, tapping away the advertisements and announcements that flash for his attention. Reminding him, inviting him. Pre-rotation motor traffic will be limited in an hour or two. He has time.

The radio reports a solar flare, from earlier in the day. His friends are joking about it—he thumbs through their posts and replies.

An animated .gif of the solar recording, filtered and colorized so people can see it without going blind. One of his friends has added an animation to it: the AerNet logo on fire.

The radio thinks the flare was many times larger than Earth itself.

▶

Leve reads his phone's interesting things as he walks through the building's parking garage. There are rows of scooters like coordinates around him that he doesn't see. Something that only requires the corner of his eye, the back of his mind. Something migratory—the hundreds of them. His phone gets no signal down here, underground in the old forum or market or bathhouse or library or statehouse or barracks or hospital or whateverthefuck it was this time, this rotation, in this changed place, this *domestic conversion*, with its retrofitted abatement and ill-fitting apartments in every repurposed corridor. It is no different from all the other repurposed, ancient buildings with their very important Old World ambiance, which they left behind, building up, up, out into the world, the empire. Back then. Exporting saints with God's voice, and his stone, into the hinterlands, whence the capital collected their grain and meat, and tributes, and concubines, and sachets of spice and oil that made everything just so much more interesting at the center of the world. If they weren't eating it or boiling it into something alcoholic enough, they were smearing it on their faces or rubbing it in blocks over withering elbows and the cancerous maps of their shoulders. Leve doesn't get a signal, so he scrolls through the posts his phone refreshed in the elevator. Thumbing through the recent past, inside the ancient, with its unwanted reverence for whoever did whatever down here back when everyone gave a shit and none of the Aeri even knew yet that there were seven other wonders of the world beyond their Host.

Leve's scooter is parked against one of the columns, his helmet tucked into a niche in the wall. He catches up on his phone. They changed the party. It'll be easier now if he just takes the bus.

He puts his phone in his pocket and looks up. There everything is.

▶

He has time.

Traffic is thinning. The old people go first, back to their homes—the most easily intimidated by the police. The most easily encouraged to keep the social order and follow instructions.

He moves into a corner dispensary. There is a video cycling on the door screen with the smiling, waving faces of an aid organization in Paris and Los Angeles, who most recently met their aid goals and funneled some number of millions into the Aeri effort. It's a pro-faith organization. Leve knows because of the nuns, who are improving their image by trying to COEXIST. He's seen the slogan on stickers, on cars, in newsfeeds entreating everyone to do so. Except, it only works in English—the little symbols that stand in for the letters in the word.

He takes two tins of minced ham. Gives the clerk his card. The clerk says something to him, but Leve doesn't hear it, so he looks up at the man. Gives him eye contact for a moment. He shrugs.

▶

He has time.

There is no one in the Christian Quarter. It isn't really a quarter—it's just an area. The missions, with their colored glass and cruciform façades, like giant treasures discovered by scientists with graph paper—*Look at this, these right angles, this discovery!*—are elegant in their emptied, flood-lit blocks. Their airlocks are closed. They're allowed to give things to the Unregistered, when they feel like it. Their exterior abatement is always new. It's imported, customized for the aesthetic task, and he and Belan have been on more than one crew that installed it.

It's how he found them.

There are three of them this time, behind the loading dock at the Catholic Center of Someone's Sacred Organ. They writhe toward him, like sidewinders, through the perimeter lighting. Like they're dizzy, or very good at being drunk. He knows they're full-grown, but their mewling still sounds infantile to him. Like they're supposed to spend their whole lives that way. They rub his ankles, and he thinks they look clean. He hopes the Catholics are giving them things.

He pulls the tins from his jacket and peels back their razor-edged lids. The cats cry more loudly now. They can smell it, and he knows they will be careful with their pink tongues on the gleaming lids. He stirs the ham with his pocketknife and shovels it into three even pyramids. Potent, smelling piles of meat.

They're going to be much further from his new apartment. From whoever brought them here in the first fucking place.

▶

It takes the phone a second to find its signal, after Leve unzips one of the outer pockets on his jacket and pulls the phone free of the abatement lining. It catches the attention of the bus's signal sweep, and he waits while the phone swaps data with the AerNet's interface. Somewhere, in one of the processing centers, the net realizes it's merely reuniting with his phone. Leve said his hellos in the morning, on the way to work. The screen animates its recognition and blinks clear. There is an indication of the exchange upon the driver's monitor up front. Something he doesn't pay attention to. Leve is the only one on the bus.

Leve thumbs open the MeetUp app, and it syncs with some other processing center, in California, where the app's welcome screen says it was developed. Another gift to the Aeri. He wonders about its encryption only long enough not to care. The app informs him that nothing has changed. The party is up along the outer rims, at the edge of the Old City—near The Wall. The bus chugs, swirling, revolving up the spiral avenues that ascend the valley. It gasps the way workers once did, dragging the stone from the deep hearts of the excavation. Or sometimes the Aeri, in carts, so they didn't have to walk themselves.

The bus sighs when its pneumatic brakes ease its bulk to rest in the turnabout, where it will begin its descent. This is as high as it goes.

The party is in a bakery. Leve wonders about that.

▶

The line is noisy, in the narrow passthrough that carried Leve up the steps from the thoroughfare below. There are no paints upon its walls. No canopies, or sheets, or scaffolds. It's warm here. The stone is dark around him, smogged and exhausted from its native blush. There aren't any police around. The girls behind Leve wear loud shoes that clap the stone as they totter awkwardly up the stairs behind him. They're laughing, and they aren't wearing any abatement—their arms are bare, emerging from their sleeveless blouses, hairless and buffed, which is the fashion. They don't swing naturally, walking up, but instead pump and jerk to maintain balance rather than momentum. Some of them chatter in line, where the climbing stops. Some are glowed by their phones, painting their attending faces pastel while their fingers move the light.

The baker's son, who logged this party on MeetUp, bares his phone's face to each in line, as he or she steps up to the door. He's younger than Leve. He smiles—this must be exciting. Leve lifts his phone in response, an ancient gesture, halting the progress of something, offering greetings, exposing a weaponless hand. The good reasons to stop and be people together for a moment.

The phones have it out between themselves, trading light and animation until they both reach the same conclusion and agree that Leve was, in fact, invited. The baker's son gestures him through the doorway, and inside the bakery is quiet and dark. Nothing is baking in the old ovens, those boxed kilns that keep the bread traditional, irradiated. The old bread suffers few infestations, unlike the loaves in the dispensaries, which have come with weevils before. There are small, framed portraits of saints above the ovens. A religious inscription over the counter. The baker is somewhere else, being reverent. He doesn't have to do this job, after all. There are more important means than bread of keeping the faith.

Leve follows the people in front of him, between the ovens and through the gaping service lid resting open in its strange geometry from its place in the floor. Down the ladder, phones become flashlights.

▶

The tarp on the old, hewn wall is tied open, and the tunnel behind it is tall enough to walk through—mostly. Leve ducks his turn through after the others. A girl behind him lays bird fingers on his shoulder, thin and clutching. She keeps her balance in her high heels, and her friend squeals behind her, not as lucky.

▶

Someone shushes the giggling from ahead, when they hug their way around the concrete pylon. It pierces their ceiling and pillars into the floor, going further down, deep enough for the task of supporting this segment of The Wall overhead. It's a tight fit, squeezing sideways, breasting dust onto his jacket pockets.

"Shit," she says behind Leve, "my shirt."

She folds her hands across her chest, and her oversized rings tap against the concrete. She turns her head sideways, as if she needs to. Leve takes her elbow and tugs her through. Why not? It's a party. She *follows* him now, instead of just walking behind him, and her teeth are brighter than his when she smiles and turns to drag her friend through the gap after her.

They curse The Wall as they move underneath it—and its pylons, the ones they added to support the crumbling sections, like this.

▶

They move like smugglers.

▶

No one really watches them when they emerge from the unfinished building's engineering room, fully beyond The Wall now, in the Unregistered Territory.

They move past the sign that alerts the Unregistered that this door admits and expels authorized personnel only. Leve follows the herd, the way Aeri do, joining up because people are moving, and they must be going somewhere. He sees a woman between partially tiled marble columns, here in the lobby. She glows in the light of her small television through a gap in her aquamarine, PVC tarp, which she has stretched between the columns to construct her home. She has things on the floor around her. She isn't stooping voluntarily. Her extension cord is taped to the floor.

The placards, on the walls beside the doors from the stairwell to the unfinished floors, say PEMCO FINANCIAL in small letters along the bottom. At least the investors got as far as floor signs, before independence robbed these buildings of their usefulness. The tax benefits of doing business in Aer evaporated with the occupation, like fairy godmothers. All this unfinished construction, at least, had been write-offs for foreign investors—may still be. Leve sees the buildings' occupants through the windows—the Unregistered in their tarped and papered shanties where accountants and data managers were supposed to hang diplomas and do their jobs. Squatters, pests—a hindrance to dead operations they can't do anything about, back home, wherever they pay taxes, with convoluted forms and professionals whose only job is to decipher that arcane financial writ.

Their twinkling televisions jitter the dark hallways.

▶

Leve helps tie yellow nylon ropes between the girders on the top floor. They create a web so no one walks off the building. It's men's work. The girls cluster in the middle of the floor, well away from the abyss as if more susceptible to *l'appell du vide*. They mix drinks, hand beers to the men who step away long enough to reach for one. Their cigarettes mask the smell of the trash fires down in the streets that the Unregistered tend beneath shutters of sheet metal to keep the light low. The smoke is difficult to see in the dark out here. It's a good time to do it.

"Lana," the girl from beneath The Wall says, offering a beer to Leve. Brave, all the way over here where he ties his bit of the web. She tucks her hair behind an ear when he takes the bottle. Her hair is too short to stay put.

"Leve."

"Come away from the edge," she says.

She knows Vesse. Walks right up to her when Leve follows her back to the roost. The women greet like chimes, trading pleasant tones with a gentle laying of hands upon cheeks and shoulders. Vesse's laugh is louder than Lana's, and her hair is long enough above her brow to stay behind her ears. Leve sees Belan at the folding table with the mixers and the bottles. He comes back with the drinks and hands a glass of wine to Vesse. She doesn't react when he slides his arm around her waist. It is a natural act. She takes her eyes off of Lana to light a cigarette, but she is still listening.

"Pain in the ass," Leve says. "Out here."

"Come on," Belan says.

"For fuck's sake," Leve says.

"You need to live a little," Belan says. "They aren't going to touch us out here."

"I'm not worried about them," Leve says. "It's just in the middle of goddamned nowhere."

"Exercise," Belan says.

"Right, because I don't walk all day."

Belan shrugs. His jacket is darker than Leve's. It's only a matter of time before the women clutch their marble arms and beg the jackets off them. Leve wore long sleeves, just in case. They will complain about the weight of the abatement lining, and they'll have to zip it out and pile it out of the way.

The music starts playing across the floor. It's traditional.

"What the hell?" Leve says. "Why are we listening to this?"

Lana brings a handful of small breads on a napkin. She offers them to Leve.

"Here we go!" Belan says.

▶

The rotation sirens echo through them, and it warps the cumulative effect. Everyone swallows the drinks, cheering. They turn up the music, and it's funny. The baker's son joins them, and he gets a good cheer. Leve can see The Host, from his place beside Lana— its great mound, the scaffolds and the sheeting that bandage its restoration like a body cast all the way up, up those heights.

They chant their prayers, down in the city, rotating, following, moving in meaningful circles. The party chants them here too. They laugh it. Lana laughs it, and she tugs on Leve's arm, as if she might pull him into the game.

JEGO

BE_DISTURBED, the lintel tells him. An efficient, square stencil stencil upon the stone maw, which is only barely capable of its original right angles—the abatement door is custom-cut to its organic shape, like a monotone scab to seal the entrance. The heaveways, Jego's father calls these—too heavy to just be *doors*.

Jego types the stenciled passphrase into his phone and waits while the device confirms it with the building's AerNet server. His mother is so excited—was when they walked in. The phrase is from one of her favorite saints. His great edict. It is a slow password, and the link is taking too long. Jego's phone has no signal, otherwise—his family's apartment is too deep into this altered building, this domestic conversion. Too inside. Too well-abated. He would have to rely on the wireless. This would be one of those fucking places.

"Jego," his father says. Elsewhere in the apartment, among its still-packed crates and shuffling possessions. Its meaningless architecture. Some ancient floorplan designed for somethingthefuckelse. Jego doesn't even know which room is his yet.

"Jego," his father says, "get the wash."

His phone establishes its link. The AerNet logo animates hesitantly.

"I'm setting up," Jego says. "Let Ad do it."

His family moves and turns and makes good use of hallways and spaces behind him. His father says something.

"What?" Jego says. He stares at the loading screen. He talks over his shoulder, back into the interior space.

His father says something again. Jego can't hear him fully, wherever he is.

"God. Fuck," Jego says. The phone begins downloading the building's updates. He turns and stomps back into the apartment, the narrow entryway doesn't echo behind him. The abatement board upon the walls and the foot-molding against the floor is stained by bodypassage at hip and shoulder heights. The reinforced metallic caulk is chipped. It does not mark Jego's passage.

His mother is standing in the kitchen, unpacking nothing. She has her fingers on the stone—the unabated square of it, in the original walls behind the boards. It is framed by the electric-red approval tape that says this stone counts among the allowable square meterage of unabated stone per domicile, preserving their religious right to be with it, upon it, as approved by the UNESCO engineers. She has her fingers on it, tracing grooves she didn't create, pressing her lips against the same dark-polished stain that brought this succor to somebody else's religiously panicked mother. She prays.

"Dad, what?" Jego calls. He stands, still in the room, his hands hanging at his sides like anchors—keeping everything in place so he can echo-locate his father here.

"Ad is too young to sign for wash," Jego's father says. In some bedroom. Jego looks at the stains on the once-white walls in here. How much work this means for him.

"Vidi can go then," Jego says. "Dad, I'm setting up."

Vidi emerges from the hallway carrying blankets, towels. She looks at Jego—those dark eyes—as if he came with the apartment. Even already he feels like this place is hers. More than the last place. She already knows its secrets and where to secure essential household things he and his father and brother will still be struggling to remember by the time they rotate again. She has that look of permission, that he may be eclipsed by her ascent in this domestic space. Those steadily elliptical hips, her breasts now that make him not want to embrace her anymore. The way she knows this—how she's teaching it to herself in preparation for the outer world.

Jego wishes he were the elder, so he would move out first.

Jego's father comes out for this. He stands for it. "You would send your sister to do this? You would send her down?"

Jego looks down. He twists his palm to check the phone, and it's all set.

"No, Father."

"Get the wash, Jego."

"All right."

"Be disturbed here, sweet," his mother says, kissing the fucking wall. Tracing her prayers into the stone.

He looks at her. It's going to take so fucking long to repaint all the board in here. There is a ledger pinned to the kitchen wall, near her reverent space, where the families have logged their rotations. And which are responsible for new wash. And his father has already signed their name in the box indicating the chore.

▶

"Water," the lobby tells him, "is the most insidious of our needs." It is a character voice—some actor's. Probably some American who took the time to learn Aeri, just so he could land these jobs. A Worldview man. There are couples—old people—staring at the murals painted into the abatement board while it was still wet. Frescoes—the Aeri version. Jego gave a report about them, last rotation, with Siou. She did most of the typing. He found all the images and coded their presentation page.

The old people listen to the building's voice. They hold Styrofoam cups of coffee. They aren't far from the folding table and the dispenser where these things are stacked. Old people are never required to do rotation maintenance. They move in fast.

The building changes voices. "Belan told us this near the end of his life, during a period of civic improvement." It is a boring man's voice.

There are lines of people around Jego—queuing for things, moving in groups, circulating presence in and out of the conversion's entryway, as if consuming and casting off sunlight. There are steady streams of them, in and out. Lifeblood.

Jego ignores the signs stenciled onto lobby's arches. He pulls up the building's map on his phone and finds the engineer's office. He shoulders past people blindly, navigating by sixth sense, watching his blue dot make its way through the phone's pastel map. Like one of his brother's games: move successfully—it's entertaining.

A message window shades over his map. It's Nedo, from last rotation.

Where in fuck did you land?

"Belan was watching a sewage leak," the building says, "in a cordoned-off avenue southwest of The Host's footstone."

Jego thumbs open the messaging app. *Third District. Inner edge. Kinda close to the ascension hospital.*

He joins the line into the engineer's office. He stands where the app tells him to stand.

No shit? Do you hear Dal's mom in there?

Shut the fuck up. Where are you?

Belan takes over for the narrator. "Water is the most insidious of our needs because it always follows the path of least resistance."

Jego moves his feet when the others do. A fired nerve. A footstep for the Aeri organism.

Still First District. Like two blocks. I'm looking at the football lot.

You fucking suck.

"Our best notes indicate that Belan then retrieved feces from the leakwater."

Dal, man, he's got a fucking Worldview lens.

Oh shit. That fucking sucks. Where?

Eleventh, man. He can see The Wall from his window. Fucking watching him move in. Somebody's going to follow them next time they go to the hospital. Listen to his mom moan.

That's fucked up.

"Even when that path is directly up," Belan says.

"Holy Belan then thew his feces high overhead to make his point," the building says.

His dad likes it. Waiting for her to ascend.

Jego drags Nedo's message into his map. It tells him they are thirty minutes apart by current route measure. There is a bus stop five minutes from Jego's current location.

Are you in the same school?

Yep. So is Siou. She's still here too.

Jego stares at the message.

"What do you need, son?"

Jego looks up. He's at the engineer's office. The map confirms this. Jego checks. He looks back at his phone.

She's in this building too, man. Saw her with her parents.

"Son?" the engineer says. There is a line behind Jego. The engineer is wearing reinforced coveralls. He has a tablet computer in one spotted hand. There is abatement cream scabbed along his white hairline.

"What do you need, son?"

Siou promised to meet him in the lot, if they received "excellent" for their report. Grades wouldn't be delivered until next week, to his new class, in this neighborhood.

Ha, whatever. You should see the girls in this building, man.

"I need two gallons of wash," Jego says. "And brushes."

"Number?"

"712."

"Name?"

"Jego."

The engineer gives the information to his tablet. He looks at Jego. Looks at Jego's phone.

"How old are you?"

"Thirteen."

Fuck yeah!

Siou's hair hangs past her elbows. She is paler than Jego. Slightly taller.

"Put your phone away," the engineer says.

Jego clicks it off and slides it into his pocket. The engineer hands him two gallons of wash and a transparent plastic bag with an assortment of brushes.

"Don't get it on the floor."

▶

Jego does his and Ad's room last. There isn't much wash left in the second gallon, and its metallic glitter keeps settling at the bottom of the can. Jego uses the cardboard dowel from an old clothes hanger to stir it. Ad lies on his back on one of the beds, tapping at his phone, a leg kicked at an odd angle. Something he does without thinking, to maintain circulation or a sense of comfort. His lips are slightly apart as he taps, his belly swelling and collapsing gently. Jego stares at him for a minute. He didn't have a phone at Ad's age. AerNet wasn't a thing. There weren't any apps. There wasn't even much Worldview. There were kind people, Westerners and Asians and sometimes Arabs, in their cleanest veils and keffiyehs giving the children pills and candies at school. Writing down their names, wearing heavy outsider clothing. Fear garments.

But there was always abatement. Always the scaffolds and tarps. He remembers when his father would paint the wash. The first time he let Jego help him. The thrill and the motion of it.

Jego sets the can down long enough to pull out his phone and skip this song. He doesn't even think about it. His headphones are wireless—tiny plastic corks in his ears. His family mouthed their things around him all afternoon, moving without making sounds, sometimes doing things in sync with the beats in his ears. He was allowed to ignore them and listen, because he was applying the wash.

There are flat rooftops outside their window. Solar panels slanting, making the city seem just so off. Just tilted, as if the panels have the better angle. Something determined by the engineers.

Ad adjusts his leg, settles his elbows akimbo by his ribcage.

A gecko shifts on their window, belly pressed against the glass, pale and filling, deflating, filling. Its limbs are at its new favorite angles. It is waiting for the sun in the overcast sky. Jego puts his phone away and stirs the wash. He watches. There is usually more than one gecko, but they weren't around when he was Ad's age either.

▶

People have written things on the walls in the closet. It isn't a closet. It's attached to his and Ad's room—it is half the size, and it's long and narrow, and it has one right turn before it ends in a wall of retrofitted shelves. It looks like a hallway. Something that went somewhere once. The overhead bulb is activated with a pullstring. The hangers, on the poles at his shoulders, are plastic, wire, and wire-with-cardboard-dowels. These last ones are for hanging pants. Vidi taught him so, when she was still fun.

Jego shoves them aside and paints. There is a stillness here. An embrace. Stone upon stone behind the milk-colored boards. There is no escape, except back into the bedroom. He thinks about putting a chair in here.

People have written things on the walls. Kids, mostly. Kid things. His is a room you share, with someone like Ad. Or a sister—if a son was born last, or two sisters, all at once, if that's how it went. Three daughters was the limit. Like his cousins, who didn't get a brother—who ran out of chances to. Two boys was the other limit, and they could cost you a daughter if you had them in a row.

He thinks about girls living in his room. What they did and thought here. The secrets they keep in rooms—how they practice knowing and having the things he wants to know and have.

One of the messages, in pencil, just says "Goodbye." A girl's handwriting. He thinks about Siou.

▶

He runs out of wash, deep in, at the shelves. The terminus. There are other things to read on the walls—names, mostly. There is a loose panel abutting the shelves, a piece of board custom-cut to accommodate the retro-fitting. He slaps the dregs from his can across it, and it wobbles in place like a café tabletop. He can see the fingerstains on one side, nearest the shelves, where it has been handled and probed. And hinged open, he learns with his palm.

The board falls from its niche. The stone is smooth behind it. Colorless, but a little warm against his hand. Clammy, like flesh. A secret exposure. He leaves his hand there for a minute, since he isn't supposed to. His mother would like it, though. His dad, too. Vidi would just look at him, and that's how he'd know if she approved or not.

There are lines on the back of the board. A drawing. A map. Here is a star for the closet, where he is. Instructions for these old hallways, throughout the building. How to get around, between the walls, with no one knowing. The way slaves did once.

▶

"*Cover me*," Ad says, in English. Slow and round, trying to flatten his vowels. "*Cover. Me.*"

Jego glances at him, across the room. Propped against the wall on his bed, working new stains into the board where his head rests against it. Their overhead light nightblacks the window and reflects the room. Jego can only see the geckos outside—four of them now—who pose like nothing for the small moths wingstopping against the glass. The geckos bend their limbs to blend in with the moths' next landings, in their efforts at reaching the light.

"*Heal. Me*," Ad says, dragging his fingers across his phone's screen.

Jego thumbs through his feed. People are complaining about their new places. New neighbors. Laments for friends from class they'll replace in another week. Siou's girlfriends have left messages and posts. She hasn't responded yet. Jego backs his app out of her profile.

"*Heal me.*"

Jego types a public message for Nedo. About the old football lot. Nothing interesting. Nothing he means.

"*I'm not. A terrorist*," Ad says.

Jego slides his jacket off the desk chair. He can hear the automatic gunfire from Ad's game, even across the room, through the headphones. Ad's headphones are large and plastic—neon yellow. They don't tuck wirelessly into his ears. The phone vibrates audibly in Ad's hands as he fires back against his enemies.

"*Suck it*," Ad says. There's headphone laughter.

▶

His parents are in their room with the door closed. Jego can hear his father talking through the jamb-light slipping into the hallway. To one of Jego's uncles, most likely—Pali, probably, who always says he needs extra help after a rotation. Because he is fat and has no sons.

▶

Vidi is on their sofa, watching the feeds. She is barefooted, wearing house-shorts. Her hair is fanned across the cushions behind her, as if she settled it that way, but she sits still, uninterested in it. Her phone is on a cushion next to her knees. Jego can see it flashing notifications at her, but she ignores it. She ignores their attention.

Two of the characters on her program are in love, but they aren't supposed to be. Jego hears them whispering and clutching about it.

Jego slides on his shoes, in the entryway, and zips his jacket. He checks, and Vidi is looking at him, knee cocked now, the same way Ad does it, and her phone has slipped under her leg. Jego looks at the kitchen, at the drying dishes, as if he's checking her work. She's still looking at him when he glances back to let her know he's seen it, that he's carving some ownership out of leaving the house without permission.

▶

The closest entrance is behind the soda machine, one floor down from his. The air is warm in the breezeway. He doesn't need his jacket, and moths bounce around the apartments' door lights. There are no geckos here, only spiders, who are better at sitting still in their webs, where they can wait for dawn's additional light to lure prey into a confusion about which way to move. Jego can hear televisions through opened windows. The dragging of crates, the smell of clouding cigarettes.

There are no lights in the stairwell, and the treads have been rounded, like old lips, upon their dark-polished risers. Steps that have been elevating and lowering Aeri in their futile movements for however long. There is no abatement upon them, and an unreadable metal sign warns Jego about something it can't remember. There is traffic and noise in the air, as usual. People honking at things, compressors harmonizing on rooftops. The clouds haven't lifted, and they return the city-glow back into the lower heights.

The soda machine has mostly Western drinks. Water. Plasti-colored, thirsty decals. Jego checks the picture of the map again on his phone, and then he side-squeezes his way past the machine, into its recessed nook. He gets dust on his ears, and this side of the machine is hot against his chest.

It's dark behind the soda machine, so he turns on his phone's flashlight. The abatement, against the back of the nook, is creased and water-stained. Jego gets his fingers under a rounded bottom corner, and it lifts like a flap, its hard inner material fractured and only still skinned together with the outer cosmetic sheeting. He gets through, and there it is—a hallway, leading nowhere useful to the residents. His flashlight reveals the seams in the masonry. The phone rings in his hand, and Jego almost drops it. Adrenaline flutters him, and the hot buzz feels like vomit in his bloodstream. It's his mother.

He steps deeper in, away from the false wall.

"Hello, Mama," he says.

He can still hear his father in the background.

"Jego, where are you?"

"Outside. I saw a post about a lot nearby. Some kids from the new class were talking about it."

"You're not going to Nedo's lot."

"No, it's right here."

"I saw your post."

"I was just trying to make him feel better. About the rotation."

"You be inside by 10:00."

"Okay."

"What's Ad doing?"

"Practicing English, on one of his game servers."

"He can't come with you."

"He's in the room, Mama."

"10:00."

"Yes, ma'am."

She clicks off. Jego mutes the phone. He'll leave it behind next time. In case she figures out how to map him through one of the apps she doesn't know how to use.

▶

There is no abatement here, deep into the old building—beyond the conversion. No wash, no tarps or scaffolds. The only heavy metals around him are the rare-Earth components in his phone and the micro-granular deposits in the stone, which may or may not have ever actually come together metallically, when the Earth was busy making stones and doing cosmic things with electromagnetic radiation and ions in the atmosphere.

When God was busy.

This stone labyrinth has been sealed from the outside, preserved in its own heatbreath, its own invisible damage. Jego wonders if the stone can actually damage itself. What graffiti Jego finds has been scratched into the masonry with paler, sharper stones. Insults about somebody's parents, somebody's sister. Words in English he doesn't recognize but which look stark and angry and carefully scratched. They say something about The Wall, and Jego doesn't think they're just insults about somebody's vagina. Somebody's tiny dick. A place to go for a good time. Somebody spent some time, in this corner, under this arch, carving something proper into the stone. An eye—just the central parts of it. The way the old Aeri carved things, everywhere. This eye is a new something for all the saints and statues staring from their posts all over the city. Outside windows and on balconies, looking for things that aren't even around anymore. Standing in for people who remade the stone and were then taken by it. There are cigarette butts and beer bottles in the dust on the floor. Jego wonders if they were the artist's or people watching him work.

His phone has no signal in here. Its connection to the network is weak.

There is room to lie down at the first hub. A central place that branches off into two new corridors. The ceiling is higher—there is a hole in the center of it. A vent, its ancient bars like prison metal, grating things in, things out. There are bright plastic squares in the dust, and Jego can hear people talking through the vent. He picks up one of the squares—it's a condom wrapper. They are all. He looks to see if any are unopened, and the vent tells him that they changed the news program to a different feed. State Radio tins its way down, through one of the hallways, leaking somewhere, and it's giving a statistic report about the rotation.

▶

There is a passage into an empty apartment. There is a sofa that is collapsing into its own center. Mops and yellow plastic buckets with pictures of slipping men. A place to squeeze out the water. There is a poster taped to a bare wall, and it takes Jego a moment to realize it's a photograph of one of the unfinished towers, on the other side of The Wall. Along the bottom, the poster says INDEPENDENCE. There is a broken radio on the floor, a too-big antenna. Wires into the ceiling.

He doesn't go in.

▶

There is a stack of pornography in a desiccated cardboard box. There are shipping labels still affixed to the sides, and Jego thinks they're in French. He wonders how he could get some of it out of here, back without Vidi or Ad noticing. The pictures aren't as good as what he's saved from the net, the adult parts his masking apps get him into, but he bends and slants the pages, getting a look by the light of his phone. Handling the images.

He hears more voices, following him from echo places. Conversations about dinner, about neighbors. Prayers and curses for football matches. They don't have anything to say about French pornography.

▶

The last place on his map is small. Smaller than the space between the soda machine and the wall. He is starting to wonder if he should have worn some abatement cream. He'll bring it with him next time. There are hand and foot niches carved into the wall here. Old carvings—ones made on purpose, back with the original architecture. They alternate up the wall—left niche, right niche—into the ceiling nine feet up, into an entrance small enough for someone his size but not much more.

Jego climbs, moves through the old ceiling, rising, like heat or smoke. It's tight moving up through the ceiling now tubed around him, like a tomb. A sarcophagus. The inside of The Host, maybe. Jego wonders why this place would have carved tubes through ceilings only large enough for children. Where did they need them to get to like this?

At the top, he crawls out onto a new standing place. There is more architecture in the stone here—something that reminds him of wooden rails and posts he's seen at the tops of stairways. It blocks a looking-over place, and Jego leans to see down. There are ten thin steps that lead down there, where the wall climbs from that floor all the way up to this ceiling. There are people painted on that wall.

There is another small archway down there, and Jego crawls, and it has vents, like the one in the corridor hub, and he wraps his hands around a pair of the waxy-feeling metal bars, and there is abatement board on the other side, but there is a gap in the joining of two panels, and the caulk needs to be replaced there, and with his forehead pressed against the bars, he can see through, and it is an apartment. A new one, a good one. The exterior light is on, on the balcony outside, behind the glassed doors in the sofa room that lead to it. The rotation crate beside the sofa hasn't been unsealed yet. Jego looks—the abatement wash on the walls is new, there are framed pictures of The Host and important buildings on the walls. No one moves or says anything inside.

Jego looks at everything. A little bit of time for each thing, back to some things more than once in no discernable pattern that he's paying attention to.

The sudden fluttering on the balcony surprises him, and he feels that sudden adrenaline sickness again. He jerks his head away from the bars, but he doesn't let go of them. His heart thunders its questions in his ears—about being caught or getting in trouble. And no one moves or says anything, so he leans back in. His blood a little smoother, his joints a little sore, and a new need to piss.

It's a bird, out there. He can't tell much of it, but it looks small and brown. It flies an unsteady two-foot orbit around the balcony light in its overhead copper awning. It flies fast, breaking orbit to move back for a better look, then back in, back around. It revolves, it keeps moving around that important central point.

Jego watches it. It doesn't stop. No one does or says anything, and he can't see a nest or a feeder or any good reason for this bird to do this. Jego presses his head harder, and he can still see the clouds behind it, the overcast shroud making everything glow slightly orange in the city's night lights.

It doesn't stop. It circles. It flaps frantically. It falters and recovers.

Jego pulls out his phone. Still no signal. Only the weak network. The bird stops on the railing, and Jego checks his browser, which won't resolve. He shares the peace with the bird for a moment. It's time to get back home.

It flies again. Around, around.

"Fuck," he says. "Fucking bird."

He thinks, thumbs through his apps. He can't think of anything else, so he taps the Worldview voluntary content icon.

The bird keeps at it. Gives it a good, old try.

The Worldview logo animates the app, and someone appears on his screen. Not Aeri. Jego thinks maybe he's Indian.

"Good evening," the man says, eyes bright in the tone of his face. He looks younger than Jego's father. His Aeri is good.

"I didn't know who else," Jego says.

The man drops his smile, and his brows come together in concern. "Is something the matter . . . Jego?"

He fucks up Jego's name.

"Are you in any trouble, Jego?"

"Just listen, okay. There's this bird, this fucking bird, and it's caught or something. It keeps flying in circles."

The man's face un-expresses. "Is the bird hurting you, Jego?"

The bird gives it a break. Another rest in its bobbing, decaying compulsion. It isn't flying well.

"No, it's a bird. It's, like, hypnotized by this balcony light. It won't stop flying around it."

"Perhaps there is a nest or a predator nearby."

"No, it's sick or something."

"One moment, Jego. Is it all right that I record our conversation?"

"I don't care. Just, what am I supposed to do?"

"I'm checking, Jego. Just stay calm."

"Hurry up. It's doing it again."

"Are you fond of animals, Jego?"

"What? Yes. It doesn't need—"

45

"Our viewers appreciate the chance to get these insights into your daily life, Jego. Learning about animals in Aer is very interesting for—"

"Hurry up."

"Okay, Jego. I'm looking at a weather report, and it tells me that it's cloudy tonight. Can you see the clouds?"

"Yeah, it's cloudy."

"Okay, I'm learning from one of our field workers that sometimes, when it's cloudy, some species of migratory songbirds can get confused. They fly by moonlight or starlight when it's easier to avoid predators. But if they can't see the moon or stars, they can become confused by city lights."

"It thinks the light is the moon?"

"Yes."

"So, what? Turn it off?"

"Yes, that should give it time to rest until the clouds clear."

"I can't, though. I can't reach the light."

"Is there an adult you can ask for help, Jego? The bird could die if—"

A door opens in the apartment. People move and laugh on their way in. A woman laughs.

Jego closes the app. He presses the phone against his chest, extinguishing its light. His heart and his limbs and his flickering eyes make him hyper-aware of being here. He doesn't see the bird moving.

A man walks up to the rotation crate and drops his wallet and jacket onto it. He isn't laughing like the woman. She comes up behind him—walking heavy, taking unbalanced steps in shoes with heels. She has her head back, looking at the ceiling as she walks. Her arms swing, and her purse has almost slid off her arm.

Jego breathes. They turn on more lights inside.

"Come on," she says. It takes her a long time to say *on*. "Where's the drink?"

The man looks at something on his phone.

"No more drink, Vesse," he says.

She lets her purse drop, and she fights her jacket off of her shoulders. She wears a sleeveless shirt, it glitters in the light. Her arms are long and smooth. Siou told him that her mother wouldn't

TOTEM

let her shave her arms yet—only her legs. The hairs were fine and dark on her arms, and the air moved them if there was a breeze.

"You said let's go drink at home."

"Because you wouldn't stop doing it there."

"Belan . . ." she whines, and it becomes laughter.

"Fuck, why did you take it anyway? Do you even know what it is?"

"It's fun," she says. She uses the toes of each foot to remove the shoe from the other.

"I don't even know that guy," he says. He looks at her, and she tilts her chin to the side.

"I told you," she says. "Marun."

"He has a fucking beard."

She shows her teeth when she smiles. "He's been abroad. It's good stuff."

"He's weird. All that about tradition. Who fucking cares? He says it while he's taking fucking shots."

She laughs again, and he leaves the room. "I have to piss."

"Belan," she says, to herself. She takes hold of her elbows and rubs them, eyes closed. She pulls her phone out of her purse on the floor and sets it on the crate. She stabs at it with her fingers until it starts playing music. She leans away from it, and the leaning nearly takes her to the floor. She pulls her shirt over her head, and her armpits are bare and marbled. Her bra is black, and she puts her hands behind her as she works its clasp, and it comes away from her shoulders in a progression of slides and dangles, and her breasts are worlds upon her chest, and her nipples are roseate suns, standing upright like solar flares, and Jego can feel himself only staring, and his heartbeat is in his throat and his ears and behind his eyes and somewhere deeper. She undoes the clasp on her pants, which don't go all the way to her ankles, and her panties are beige, almost skin-toned, and to get the pants off her legs, she has to sit on the back of the sofa, and when she slides off her underwear, thumbs beneath the band, her hips are like crescent moons, reflecting the sunlight from her chest, and when she stands back up, there is a rise between her legs, a gentle topography, and that cleft. He's only seen it online, but it has a real movement, true shadows and delineations as she turns her hips. She is stubbled where she has shaved, and there are small red blemishes to mark this.

47

The man steps back into the room, and he's holding his phone, but he's looking at her.

"Oh, shit," he says.

She turns, and her buttocks crease at the top of her legs. She wings her arms out to her sides.

"Welcome home," she says. It's funny.

The bird flutters, gets back to it, and the surprise of it wraps the woman's arms over her chest and bends her at the waist, as if that will protect what's below. She looks at the bird.

"What the fuck!"

The man moves toward it. "What the fuck is it doing?"

She follows him, and they stand at the doors, peering through the glass.

"It's stuck or something."

"Turn off the light."

Like suns dying.

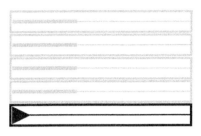

ASHA

Asha's daughter sounds like waves. He can't tell if he's awake or dreaming himself in his own bed. His own stillness and warmth. The weight and depthlessness of perception—seeing only some things, feeling only bedsheets and respiration. She has a sound like motion, rising and falling, the way she breathes when she sleeps with him on sofas or pillowed bedding, her tiny, gummed lips in the hollow of his throat, little fists perpetually clenched, ready for things years down the line. A steady, infant outrage. She sounds like movement, even and regular, learning to do things at a pace, to keep the internal clock, to measure her time and movements in the city. Asha dreams her in her crib, a few feet away in the room's bluedark morning. But he isn't fully awake, listening to waves and collapsing pasts and presents. When he looks, her crib isn't where it was, because they moved it to her own room. Middle of the last rotation. He stares at the spot where she has never slept in this room. The baby monitor makes its white noise on the bedside table, its cosmic feedback sounding itself out through the net and back. Its signals can't penetrate most walls in the city. It was designed by a firm in Stockholm—it's a gentle white sphere. Its smiling LEDs let parents know in the darkness whether or not Worldview is watching. Keeping an ear out for something they should wake up for. Helping young Aeri parents preserve as much rest as they can.

Giving them a little more time to be something other than parents. They market recorded compilations of the babies' soft sounds—the young in a cradle of death and civilization—to everyone beyond Aer's borders, all those Worldview subscribers and donors listening so closely, streaming video footage of precious, sleeping infants while the world comes together to preserve Aer—a thing they can agree on. A place, a people that can be their best effort, their connections to histories that don't require gunfire on holy grounds, or territorial disputes, or televised ideological debates. It fills him, the breadth and scope of it, amassed beyond this room, his bed, the short reach to his wife beside him—the ears of the world in his baby's room, with their fingers to their lips so he doesn't hear her unless he has to.

"Good morning," he hears beside him. It isn't his wife's voice.

He turns over to face her. The bedding requires a non-twisting negotiation. He's learned this maneuver during these years with Nisa. Without the effort, he will merely, by course of motion, torque the blankets from her, and she will be bare in the room. It happens sometimes at night. To both of them.

"Good morning," Nisa says. Her voice is thick and soft. Rested. She is holding her phone before her face, and its digital white glow marks the severity of her nose, the flattening of curls along her brow. It empurples the tributary veins in the softs of her eyes.

"Identification please," the phone says. A polite and feminine request. Service and satisfaction. He can only see a head and a desk, rendered the wrong colors by his angle of observation. A thing the screen does to preserve image fidelity in direct light and reflective situations.

Nisa thumbs her identification into the app. And the phone makes pleasant sounds as it transmits her.

"You turned Mir over to Worldview," he says, half into his pillow.

Nisa doesn't look away from the screen. The Worldview woman is quiet at her work, trying not to disturb the domestic moment. It happens all the time.

"You needed to sleep," Nisa says. She pulls a dark curl away from her face with a bent finger. The polish on her nails is full and unchipped. He wonders when she had them done last.

"Nisa," he says.

"Asha," she says, cuts an eye. "You got up three times before I turned her over. Which got *me* up three times. She didn't need anything."

"I don't like it," he says.

"You don't like it," she says.

"Please confirm your abatement and exposure schedule for today," the phone says.

A chart animates onto the screen. Nisa taps its fields, and they cycle into pleasant green confirmations. How many supplements at breakfast. How much cream for each of them in the sun. Extra today for Asha's shift.

"We'll leave it off when you aren't working," Nisa says.

He'll be downtown today, at The Host, for the display. It's his turn in the schedule for public appreciation. For the cameras and the event staff who will draft civilians into the audience and monitor their enthusiasm and humility.

"Thank you, Nisa," the phone says. "Do you need to modify tomorrow's delivery?"

"She needs more diapers," Nisa says. Cloth, as the world would have it. "Last week wasn't enough."

"Of course."

Nisa rubs her eye. "And formula—it isn't enough."

Asha groans. Nisa quiets him with an elbow.

"Are you adhering to the recommended feeding schedule?" the phone says.

"Not the fucking formula," Asha says, quietly.

"It isn't enough," Nisa says. "She's hungry, and I will feed her."

"Yes, of course. Anything else?"

"No, we're fine."

"Thank you for allowing me to assist you with this check-in. Your device is now cleared for media content."

The woman animates away. The app collapses, and Nisa's browser takes its place.

"I can't believe she likes that formula," Asha says. "It's got to be sacrilege."

"She likes it," Nisa says, thumbing for content. "It makes them stronger."

"It's against God's will," he says.

A talk program resolves on Nisa's screen—two women in armchairs. A vista of downtown and the scaffolded Host glows behind them. Their talking fills the bedspace in bassless chattertones. Asha recognizes one of the women. One of the Aeri-American actresses Nisa reads about. Keeps up with. Watches in the theater or on their sofa. She says something about the microparticulate abatement in the new baby formula. What it's doing to the next generation—strengthening their cells. Giving them a good chance. A better chance than their parents.

An icon on the screen identifies the program as suggested content. It reads Nisa's mind—her morning interaction.

"Everything is against God's will," she says.

The spokeswoman wants to talk about organic foods.

▶

Holy Asha, he prays, his palm flat against the approved exposure, the curling red tape at its limits, his lips like an instrument against the stone. Just against. Touching only so much that occasionally they aren't. The apartment is quiet behind him. Nisa is still in bed with her phone, their heavy bedroom door between them. Mir isn't done with her crib. His uniform is creased and tight upon him.

Holy Asha, may your rest be deep. May The Host preserve you. May God keep you uncorrupted. I thank God for your purity. For your brethren. For delivering you to us in pure form, unbent by his creative breath. Forgiven by the stone for your imperfect form. May your wisdom guide us who bend and twist for God's greater plan. May you be with those ascending, rendered into the better shapes, the quicker joining with God, where form does not keep us from his gaze. We thank God for your imperfect death—your exemption—to show us how we will be made better. God's hand upon you. May it remain.

We thank you for your teaching. We thank you for the principles of gathering. We thank you for your place in the progression. We thank you for the deaths of the possessed. May their blood never dry from your fingers.

We thank you for guidance as Nisa and I walk the days until our own ascension. We pray that you guide us in walking Mir towards hers.

▶

The older people, in the lobby, bow and tuck and handshake their appreciation as Asha moves through them. The younger zip their abatement wear and move around him with better places to be.

God remake you, officer, people his parents' age say.

Outside, with the movement and the populated sidewalks, and the buses and scooters migrating, people glance away. Who would want his attention? That uniform. The sun is bright upon the smog's amber glitter, and the tallest buildings wear laurels of it. His phone vibrates for his attention in his breast pocket. An Unregistered man stoops nearby in his regulation jumpsuit, with its work permit stitched to the lapel. He collects dead pigeons for the satchel over his shoulder.

It's his mother calling.

"Yes, Mama?"

"Asha. Are you working?"

"I'm on my way."

"Did you pray? How's your uniform? Where's Nisa?"

"What is it, Mama?"

"We just got a message, your father and I, on the phone."

"Do you need help? Did you get it downloaded?"

"Your father did."

"Okay."

"It was from the clinic. The World people."

"What do they want?"

"They made me go. The phone made me."

He takes a breath. He moves easily in the human hollowspace they create around him on the sidewalk.

"I know," he says. "It's okay. They make everyone go. The priests say it's okay."

She's crying.

"They found God," she says. She's happy. "Oh, Asha. In the womb. The size of a baby's fists."

He stops, and they eddy around him. He wants her happiness. Her awaited ecstasy. The long years. The divine touch. God on the move. But it smells like exhaust around him. It feels like waiting, for the first time.

"God is good," he says.

"They want to take it out," she says. "At the clinic. They gave me a form to sign. Your father says we shouldn't sign it. A World person says we don't have to."

"You shouldn't sign it," he says.

"They can't take it," she says.

"They can't take it, Mama."

"Oh, Asha. Praise Asha."

"Praise Asha. I'll come by after work. Don't sign anything."

"I won't."

"Don't sign anything. I'll come by."

"I'll get dinner downstairs. I'll have it. Bring Mir, and Nisa."

"I will."

"Bring them."

"Goodbye, Mama."

▶

"Because God has better plans than the state of men," the priest says, in English. Some of his brothers sit cross-legged on the stone around him, their backs to each other—a many-eyed beast seeing everything at once.

"And the natural state is in the way—the weak state, the state that sponges radiation and alters the fluid pressure of vital bodily treasures."

The tourists pay attention around him, earphoned, taking in the plaza by Worldview's best measure—its guidance and information app. The Host is a tower upon its mound above them, and they turn like wildlife to check it on occasion. The great scaffolding and sheeting to calm it down for human interaction. There are preservationists and Geiger counters at work. Priests in hard hats and wearing safety lines loiter with the workmen, keeping an eye on the secular task of protecting the sublime.

"The state that grows tumors and destroys valves to become something different than the inferior."

Asha eyes the observation panel—the transparent tarp exposing a great, climbing rectangle of The Host, as tall as the smaller buildings below it. The old ones. The clustered sarcophagi behind the tarp are still and angled in their placement. Amalgamated. One saint upon, around, beside the one before him, the one after. The multitudes. The holy plaster the priests use to affix each human blessing to the next is paler than the sarcophagi themselves, carved from the stone and hoisted and pulleyed and allowed to rest where God's physics deemed best. The holes in the lids, through which the holy men delivered their dying admonitions, entombed with the brothers waiting for them to quiet down and move on—the holes look like dimples, in-falling cones to amplify those important last words to the saints' clinging, rope-wearing priests, in place for death.

"The way we're born. It isn't enough. It's nothing in comparison, and God, in his mercy, will help us from our suppressive chrysalises."

The tourists snap photos, take video. They lean in to each other to see how it's going. Asha can tell the Americans by the looseness of their borrowed leadcloth, the whorls of poorly applied abatement cream. The way they pay attention in order to tolerate religiously. The priests at their feet grind their segments of stone and offer the holy dust in small vials on lanyards. There are jars for donations, confetti-filled with everyone's currency. One priest can accept donations via credit card or finance app through his phone.

Asha's coffee is too hot against his lips. The line at the dispensary across the street is too long now—he wouldn't have waited in it had it been like that for him. The foreigners look uncomfortable, learning how long to wait for the free goods and services they came all this way for.

"God promised. The saints teach us so. He created paradise—he gave us Aer, its holy stones with their invisible power. His power. Himself. A great, incubatory nursery where we can grow into terminal form."

A pair of jets roar their maneuvers high overhead, and the lampposts and trees and bench-backs blink their distraction, their camouflaged lenses readjusting for this latest interesting thing. The jets drag their sounds as they stitch the sky with their feathering contrails. Borrowed from the U.N. effort, tarmacked in the territory of one of Aer's neighbors because Aer just never has acquired its own. Which is fine with Asha. The planes tear Aer's dirty skies, its divine air with that caustic sun, burning them all so brilliantly.

Later, Aer's other neighbors, their last occupiers before independence, will fly counter-maneuvers—like stitching the rest of the shroud of international interference. Everyone has threads to contribute. Their neighbors want Aer to know they're still around.

Asha looks at the nearest café. The copper awnings haven't been polished recently. Probably due to the flare and its solar exposure regulations. He doesn't see any empty tables through the cigarette smoke and shade.

He likes the jets. He looks at the exposed swath of The Host again. Gives his tongue a controlled burn with the coffee. He hopes the jets have bombs, so some people, at least, may be lifted unto God on the wings of glowing, megaton angels.

▶

Asha stands with the others when his name is called. The applause is flat and airy, offered up to the central plaza's great space. His uniform is hot today; they aren't allowed to wear sunglasses up on the platform. The Aeri in the folding chairs stand when the event volunteers down there in the rows urge them up. They clap harder, as directed. Tourists stand beyond the ceremony's ropes, phones in hand. Some of them clap, too, following the herd. Appreciating without realizing the efforts of the city's volunteer police force— Aer's future leaders and dignitaries. Keeping order and pace and momentum in the city's daily thrum. A small quad-copter buzzes over the gathering. A gift to the department from tech developers securing funds and writing off expenses in the Worldview effort. Shaping up the company profile for paying customers in other countries. The police only have to coordinate its use for occasional high-profile public events, for the newsfeeds. It spends the rest of its time near, above, over The Wall. There should be more soon, they've been promised.

Asha and the others take their seats when the commander steps up to the podium. The officers down below gesture the audience to do likewise. A short wind stirs the bright air, and they share its push, its nudge. The avenues' sounds are distant on the air.

"Welcome, international friends," the commander says. He pauses while translation apps do their work. He is five years older than

Asha. He and his wife are still trying for their first child. They're considering medical interference because he's worried about sterility. Asha offered to introduce their wives, so Nisa could share her own thoughts about finally achieving her own pregnancy.

"We're pleased you have joined us here, this beautiful afternoon."

The commander likes his tea thinner than the other men in their office. It's a fun joke among them. Command-order humor. He has a good attitude toward it.

"Our police are the true backbone of the Aeri Renaissance."

Applause.

"Their efforts, above and beyond the civic contributions all Aeri make together, are the hallmarks of our future leadership, and we are proud to share our appreciation of their work and our anticipation for an even brighter tomorrow."

Asha thinks about his mother. He should get some flowers for her tonight. Maybe something from the Mediterranean.

"It is also with great pride that I can announce the pending opening of our new Imperial Civic Center. I invite you all to join us for a walking tour following this ceremony. The Center is just on the other side of The Host, if you're new to our city, and you'll actually be able to see the façades now that the cranes are all gone."

They laugh. Asha promised to get some pictures for Nisa to post. They've been lamenting the construction eyesore for months. Last rotation they could even see it from their balcony.

The tourists laugh shortly after, when they get the translation.

"These young officers behind me today will be among the first to welcome you into the Center as part of their regular civic contributions. A full list of schedules and services will be downloaded city-wide on opening day."

Asha's neighbor pulls his phone from his breast pocket, as if on cue. A stimulus response. Asha elbows him, and there he is, suddenly awake and surprised. He makes a *Shit!* face and puts the phone back. Asha will make fun of him afterward.

"We're especially pleased to say that the rerouting of The Wall for the rail line is also nearly complete, and the temporary structures will soon be gone.

Cheers. No one likes the temporary Wall. There's nothing Aeri about it.

"We didn't expect the surveyors' historical discovery," the commander says. "With help from the Department of Antiquities, the project's foreman has confirmed that by rerouting The Wall through additional Unregistered territory, the Civic Center has lifted a centuries-old veil from another of our beloved historical treasures. The Center reclaims an old weights and measures plaza, last used around 323 CE, where traders would have their good inspected before entering the Capitol Market."

Asha applauds along with them. Worldview is particular about Western dates in public address—he doesn't mind the accommodation. It's important that others can chart the recovery of the empire.

"Who's going to work *those* protests?" Asha's neighbor says, the tension in his jaw dropping the timbre of his voice. Something just for the two of them.

"I will," Asha says. "Gladly."

His neighbor grunts. It's important to reclaim the city. Even if people do carry signs and walk in circles to chant about Unregistered territory.

"The new Civic Center is built from compounded stone, abatement polymers, and heavy-duty sculptural resins," the commander says. "It uses natural interior lighting and solar electricity from the panel-farm on the upper plain. It's built using recycled insulation, and its new signal broadcasting tower will improve network connections within six blocks."

Genuine applause. Sincere. The officers down below aren't even prompting anyone.

Asha is full and bright, up there on the dais for this. Luck of the draw. It is a good day.

▶

The movement is slow here, in the downtown dispensary, despite its multiple clerks, its expanded lanes of egress and stations for automated check-out. There is an unsteady shuffle of movement, as if they're all learning a new dance at once, and they haven't quite got it yet—there is only the one solid idea about which way, in general, to move. Asha keeps the flowers for his mother close to his chest, so they won't be bruised and elbowed by all the crush. People carry portions of meals and errands around him—the things they will arrange or prepare for a nice evening at home. A break from the meal-windows in the alleys. None of them have everything for a whole meal, in their arms in line, but Asha sees enough. In the right combinations, he and the dozen or so people ahead of and behind him could arrange quite a party. The tourists would be responsible for the sunblock and the instant coffee.

His radio receiver blinks and fidgets on his shoulder, jumping between digital radio transmission and AerNet wireless every few seconds, depending on where he is in the city. There is a wireless bud in his left ear, and it chirps his comrades' operations. The dispatchers' guidance. Technically, he's still on patrol, keeping things orderly around The Host, but his partners will cover for him for twenty minutes. He'll be off-shift in thirty. He hears a dispatcher reporting a domestic disturbance complaint—some bad neighbors. He ignores it. They all do, and the chatter moves on. He checks his phone, and Nisa is already uploading the pictures he sent. Benefits of his position. Her friends will be suitably impressed.

▶

They move him as one of their own, along the evening sidewalk. The lights on his receiver are dark, so they know he's simply on his way now. He will be just another civilian for a day or two until his next shift comes up. There is a spice to the dinner air. Frying oil and cooking charcoal and engine exhaust. His mother will just bring something up from the window near the building. Nisa would rather prepare something, but they aren't going to have that fight again.

Asha gets a ring on his phone—it's Yewa, from the department. He answers the call and taps it through to his bud. He is now another of the gibbering masses on the move, talking around each other like ghosts. Cycling through their own space without much care for who's watching or listening. Asha wouldn't even be able to point out Worldview's closest lenses and mics. Not on this block.

Things move slowly as the mass migrates through the entryway of a glass-walled mall. Lights and music fill corners.

"Yewa," Asha says. "How are you? Off-shift yet?"

"Fuck no," Yewa says. He rarely communicates without dirtying his phrases somehow. "I have the fuck-off third rotation in Eighth District."

"God hates you," Asha says.

"Yeah, he's pretty damn clear about it."

"What's up?"

"I need you to take a call for me."

"Sorry. Off-shift."

"Fuck, Asha. Please."

Asha ebbs with the crowd. The light from a bar full of Westerners paints his arms and shadows.

"Sorry, Yewa. Important evening."

The place is named after Abao. Who taught them temperance, even during the first imperial collapse.

"I wouldn't fucking call if I didn't have to."

Classless. Asha doesn't like the downtown assignment as much as he used to, where the saints are put to bad use.

"My mother's been touched," Asha says. "There's a dinner."

"Look, it's the noise complaint."

The Westerners wear their leadcloth, even inside, past the scrubbers and the netting cast into the windows, like stitching. Only there if you see it right. Asha trails a finger along it as the sidewalk carries him past the mall. Display screens and holographic projections, and images of Worldview watchers light him goodbye.

"Yewa, you call me about a noise complaint? Ignore it. I'm headed to my mother's."

"Asha. Fuck. It's Eia's mother-in-law."

Asha doesn't remember who Eia is.

"Yewa, go yourself."

"For fuck's sake—you think I'm calling because I want you to do my job? She lives in Third District. You walk right through it."

"Yewa, you talk like trash." Asha wonders why Yewa even volunteers, what he plans for his civilian credit.

"Sorry. Listen—the woman's called every day for weeks. She's calling Eia now, who's calling me. On-shift."

Asha doesn't say anything. He waits for a bus to clear an avenue.

"Asha, please."

Abao also taught dependence. Aeri for Aeri against the coming night, in his Third Dialog.

"Yewa, you owe me."

"Oh, fuck, yes!"

Asha closes the line, and Yewa messages him the address. Asha sends a note to Nisa. Few minutes more. Have Mir ready.

▶

"I call every day," she says with him in the breezeway.

"Yes, ma'am," Asha says. "We're sorry for the delay."

"Every day since the rotation," she says.

"We get a lot of complaints," he says.

She stops a few doors away and tightens the wrap around her shoulders. It's a warm evening. She shouldn't need it. Asha stops with her, and she just points to the offending door. A taboo place she shouldn't approach. Asha reads the lines and carcinomas of her face. The anxiety for the generations behind her, following her ascension too closely for comfort.

"God remake you," she says.

He smiles. "I'll take care of it."

▶

The man who answers the door is younger than Asha. Two others stand behind him. They wear full, dark beards—Western shirts with collars. They look like bad tourists. One wears a ball cap. Asha can hear the music and the voicing behind them. It's a full party. They put on smiles.

"Good evening, sir."

Asha taps his bud thoughtlessly. An operational tic he developed. An opening gesture.

"We've gotten complaints," he says.

"Yes, sir."

"Lots of them."

They stop smiling.

"I'll need to have a look," Asha says.

"Yes, of course." They move away to make room in the entryway. It curves into the place. Some old, rounded tower, perhaps, once curving its way someplace where a right angle just wouldn't have cut it. He imagines it also probably amplifies their sound inside. Curves it through some of the retrofitted walls in this landing. Gives it right to the old woman.

The common room is full of them. Young men and women with drinks. Young men and women with cigarettes. Young men and women at casual angles on sofas, the hems of their lead-free attire cut for the new age. There is skin and fabric everywhere. A screen plays the evening news on mute. A stereo sounds music he doesn't recognize. Something in Aeri. They watch him, like a phantasm, or some interesting programming. One of the doormen turns down the stereo. When did they start wearing beards?

Asha follows the shouting into the bedroom. Past a bathroom. Light falls under its jamb, pressing and overflowing against the closed door. Its noises inside.

The shouting one is reclining on the bed. Drunk.

"Porous borders!" he shouts at the one in the reading chair by the window. He has fingers idly resting on a young woman's head. She sits on the floor with two other women, their backs against the bed. They read something to each other and laugh when the man across from them pours them liquor for their efforts.

The one in the chair stands.

"It's just life support!" the one shouts.

"Be quiet," Asha says.

They take him to mean all of them. The standing one cuts a look at his friends in the doorway behind Asha. His beard is fuller, rounder. He looks the same age as Asha. He wears a large, European watch.

"Good evening, sir."

"We've had complaints."

"Yes, sir."

"The music is probably fine, but enough shouting."

"I apologize," he says. "Belan and I had a disagreement earlier. We became too involved."

The one on the bed stares. The woman he's touching stares. Like puppetry. She has large eyes, and there is a smirk to her watching.

"No more shouting," Asha says.

"Of course."

"At least not every night."

There is a dog-eared printout on the bed beside Belan. A yellowed bundle. A copy of the Registry Act. They watch him see it. Odd choice of entertainment.

He looks at the women. "What are they reading?"

The man with the watch lights a cigarette and extends the pack to Asha.

"Usv's Tenth Dialog," he says.

Asha watches them for a minute. "You're studying chastity?"

"Trying to," the large-eyed woman says. She swallows her liquor.

Asha thinks about them. What they could be doing. He takes the cigarette.

"You'll need to find somewhere else to do this."

"Absolutely," he says. "No problem."

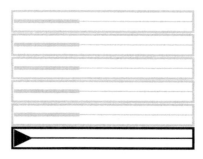

SALMI

"There's no direct translation for it in English," Sarah says. "The people there call it '*The Host*.'"

"*The. Host*," Salmi says.

"They'll be very curious about it," Sarah says. "They'll want to talk about it often. How do you feel about that?"

"Good," Salmi says. "Good."

Salmi pulls a ribbon of dark hair from her face. It lays unblended, layered, a separate thing from the rest of her hair, where it rests over her shoulders to the bottom of her ribcage.

"So, we have more of the details," Sarah says. She wraps her fingers around a brown folio on her desk. Her nails are powdered with stone and coated with clear sealant. Salmi has seen Registered women wearing them that way, through the feeds on Owi's screen.

"This is Mr. Lawton," Sarah says. He has blond hair, like Sarah, on the other side of the desk. He isn't wearing a Western tie, and his jacket looks heavy across the shoulders. Leadcloth. He's handsome, and wearing perhaps too much abatement cream. Salmi uncrosses her ankles and folds her hands on her knees.

"He is an attorney with my organization, and he's here to make sure we understand all of the details of the arrangement."

Sarah's accent still makes her Aeri sound strange, no matter how long Salmi has been hearing it. Salmi likes that she is better than Sarah at just this one thing, at least. Sounding Aeri.

"And then we can sign a few papers, and then it will all be official!" Sarah looks at Mr. Lawton. She's been here longer. She knows how to conceal her abatement cream beneath her makeup. Her eyes are slick and blue. She could be Salmi's younger sister. They could have had their lives together. She keeps Salmi's secrets, now, making up for what they've missed, all this time.

"Are you excited?" Sarah asks. She is.

"Yes," Salmi says. Yes. She is warm around the neck, and she can feel the flush where it escapes all the spaces in this blouse. Sarah's blouse. An early gift, cut with space and light in mind. She also gave Salmi a razor, for her arms and armpits. To pull the look off. Salmi feels air-conditioned, up for consideration, the inner up-thirds of her breasts awakened by the scooped collar. There they are. Salmi hasn't seen him look once.

"How're your English lessons?" Sarah says.

"Good," Salmi says. "Much better. It's fine when they talk slowly."

"*We'll talk slowly, then,*" Sarah says, switching to English. It brings Mr. Lawton into things, suddenly in the room, body and spirit. Here he is, on the case. "*So Mr. Lawton can join us.*"

He laughs. It doesn't sound like a businessman's laugh. "*Sorry,*" he says. "*I can ask for the bathroom and apologize. That's it.*"

Salmi smiles for him. Another secret skill—better than Mr. Lawton at being Aeri. "*I know how you feel,*" she says carefully. Deliberately. Intoning something. A different woman's language. Being careful with her tongue.

He has his own folio. Leaved and scripted with the details of Salmi's life. Its past and future. *He* is her present. This stumbling progression of instants under the whir of the air-conditioner, upon the condensation dampening the water glasses.

"*All right, Ms.—*" He stops himself and folds his hands on the desk. Like he's displaying them. Not up to any busy tricks. "*Is it all right if I call you Salmi?*"

Salmi doesn't understand the question. She nods her way through it.

"*Salmi, my name is Brian, and I'm an attorney—*"

"*Slow down,*" Sarah says next to him, but she's smiling at Salmi. Looking out for her.

"*Right. I'm going to explain the details behind your emigration.*"

"*Okay.*"

"*Good,*" he says. He smiles it. Salmi thinks they smile a lot. She forces one herself, just to keep up.

"*We've secured a sponsor, which helps us move you sooner.*"

"*Yes,*" Salmi says.

"*That means someone who can offer you a job, so you can emigrate legally. Becoming an American citizen takes longer, but probably not for you.*"

"He means that in high profile cases, some people become citizens faster than others," Sarah says in Aeri. She pulls the band from her hair and draws it into a fresh ponytail. Salmi watches her pull it flat beneath her palms. Roll it under her knuckles and resecure the band.

"*I understand,*" Salmi says in English. "*I will work for this person.*"

"*No,*" Brian says. He slows down to pour some more water. "*Your sponsor is a state representative in Texas. Do you know Texas?*"

"*George Bush,*" Salmi says.

He laughs. "*Yes, there's much more to Texas than George Bush, but that's good. Texas is a state where immigration is very important. The state disagrees with the government about the issue. They fight about it in court—*" he points to himself "*—where I work. Sometimes on TV.*"

"The feeds," Sarah says beside him.

Salmi nods her misunderstanding.

"*Your sponsor would like to help you because it will demonstrate immigration handled properly. Taking the time to get to know who's coming over. How it can be good for America when it follows strict rules.*"

"*I will learn these rules,*" Salmi says. Her water glass is slightly out of reach.

"*No, no,*" he says. He looks away for a minute. Trying to find his thoughts in the room.

"*No,*" he says, "*you won't have to do that. We're still breaking lots of rules, technically speaking, but that's why I'm here. I know the rules.*"

"*You're not doing anything wrong,*" Sarah says. She gives Brian a look like she would like to be the one speaking.

"*I won't work for my sponsor.*"

"That's right. Not really. You'll be on the payroll for a . . . group that works for him. That raises money and supports him. Helps him win elections."

"Is he a kind man?"

"Oh, yes! Very. We disagree on things, but he's very kind. He and his wife have hosted me and my wife for dinner. We talked about you just last week."

Salmi feels excited and nervous. She looks down at the table. She feels like she should.

"He's very excited to meet you."

"Brian."

"Yes, sorry." He goes for his folio and moves things around. *"He is from a city in Texas called Frisco. It's very near Dallas."*

"Oh."

"A good city. A strong city. You'll like it. It's the fastest growing city in the Dallas/Fort Worth metroplex. Lots of amenities."

"Okay."

"Brian, where will she live?"

"You'll have your own house," he says.

"Do you remember house?" Sarah says in Aeri.

"A lonely building," Salmi says, "for one family."

"It's a bad translation," she says. "Not 'lonely.' Alone."

"I remember, yes," Salmi says. *"My own building,"* she says to Brian.

"Exactly. Twenty-five hundred square feet on a quarter-acre lot. Place's loaded."

Loaded.

He consults more papers. Salmi feels as if he doesn't need to but does this for her anyway.

"Your father's publisher has agreed to hold his estate for you in what's called receivership."

He holds up a hand beside her. Sarah hasn't even interrupted him yet, but he keeps his eyes on Salmi.

"It just means they'll manage the money, but you will receive a monthly stipend to spend how you want."

"Okay."

"You'll be expected to give some interviews, appear on the . . . feeds, attend some rallies."

The feeds!

"*Is that okay?*"

"*Yes!*"

Sarah looks excited, too, across the table. She smiles it at Salmi and widens her eyes.

He makes notes on his papers.

"*Your government has agreed to the arrangement. Your father will be posthumously pardoned once you're in Texas.*"

Salmi doesn't care.

"*But,*" he spreads his hands, "*everyone wants something. You won't leave for a while. In that time, Worldview will provide you with some equipment on your government's behalf.*"

"*She doesn't understand.*"

"*You will need to carry a small receiver in your pocket. Very small.*" He makes a small ring with his thumb and forefinger. "*And wear an earphone in your ear. It's very small—no one will see it.*"

"*Okay.*"

"*And very small cameras will be sewn into your collars. Again, invisible. Just like Worldview everywhere else.*"

"*Why?*"

"*You're a good story for Aer. It will allow the government to show how they're cooperating with improving the lives of the Unregistered.*"

"*Does that bother you?*" Sarah says.

"*No.*"

"*I'm sorry,*" Sarah says. "*This agreement was difficult to arrange. I had to make concessions where I could.*"

Salmi smiles.

"Sister, shh," Salmi says. "I love it."

Sarah smiles. Almost just a pale Aeri across the table.

"*Programs will be assembled based on what your camera records,*" Brian says. "*You'll be asked to tell your story to a Worldview interviewer.*"

"*You just tell them everything you've told me,*" Sarah says.

"*Yes, okay.*"

"*Okay!*" Brian says. He leans back. "*Let's sign some releases.*"

►►

Some of the people worship while the workers rebuild The Wall. The partitions have already been unbolted and carried away. Workers in hard hats on scaffolds use welding torches to cut the steel lattice that framed the thousands of concrete panels into their divisive mosaic. Guy lines glow hot against the superstructure then go slack, falling like invertebrates, whipping the dust upon the ground behind the chain-link security fence. They have already reset the lower ten feet of The Wall's new contour, deeper into Unregistered territory. Police, lazy in the sun with their machine guns in the crooks of their arms, watch as the Unregistered buttress their makeshift viewing platform. They carry planks and broken scaffolds and bundles of discarded wire from the pile near the construction gate. The police let them take it, a courtesy, a way for them to keep seeing The Host, way down in the bottom of the valley, a needle through the gap. The police let them continue seeing it while construction isn't finished. The police won't let them carry any of these construction materials away from here. Not into the bowels of their repurposed towers and makeshift apartments. At first, they could see The Host from the ground, when the temporary Wall came fully down to make room for the reconstruction. Salmi watched them bend and kneel and lay upon the street—a personal gymnastics to catch God's eye. To see his piled saints in the city. Most of them were elderly. A majority of her neighbors didn't care. Never had a reason to, depending on when they were kicked off the Registry—if they were ever on it. Now, though, they need the viewing platform. Ten feet of their own, into the air, a growing edifice, with ramps and makeshift handrails. An aggregate thing, with its own strata. The believers move up and down the ramps. A few minutes each with a good view, aided by young men and boys, hanging from the structure in all places. Saints themselves, out here. Some of them probably lived in the building here, before it was blasted into itself and shoveled away by heavy machinery.

Salmi squeezes the receiver between her fingers, in her pocket. "Is that enough?" she says.

The bud is quiet in her ear. A woman with red hair is carried up the ramps on a litter. Too close to God to make it on her own.

—Let's just watch for a moment, the woman in her ear says.

Salmi thinks it's odd that the woman's hair still has so much color. Someone shouts above her, a distant voice in the air, thin against the sounds of construction. Salmi shields her eyes against the sun as she looks. A leadcloth jacket falls between clotheslines webbing the space between two towers. It bounces a few of the lines, like musical strings, flapping clothes into flags in the dun-colored air. It catches a gust and wings itself clear of the buildings, a plummeting thing out over the avenue now. Boys on the platform shout, angled incorrectly for Salmi's vision, and the jacket slaps against the street. Still. Like some alien's flayed skin. Gray and strange.

—Someone has lost some clothing.

"It's secondhand," Salmi says.

—How can you tell?

"It all is."

▶

Salmi stands in the reflection of a street-level window. It is fully glassed and stenciled with the initials of whatever agency donated it. Her hair is loose, as the woman in her ear asked her to wear it. It's uncomfortable, out in the sun, and the wind has tangled it. The charcoal she lined her eyelids with, against the sun, has dusted free of its lines at the edges of her eyes, as if she's going blurry. She has a figure beneath her plaid blouse. Khaki slacks with pleats for her waist. Not unlike abatement leggings. She looks at that figure. She doesn't make much use for it.

"Enough?" Salmi says.

—How old are you?

"Thirty-five."

—Do you have any children?

"No. One miscarriage. A long time ago."

—Were you married?

"No."

—Were you in love?

"Probably." She tucks her hair behind her ears. Watches herself do it in the window. Those lobes like amber ornaments upon her head.

—How old were you?

"I think I was twenty-two."

—Did you hope for a son?

Salmi thinks it out.

"I hoped not to be pregnant."

—Okay, that's enough.

Salmi stops looking at herself.

▶

Boys are playing football in the avenue outside the market. Too many per team. Others wait their turns to rotate in, along the sidewalk. The unlucky few wear the creams and sleeves that their mothers insist on. The radiation isn't as strong out here, beyond The Wall, but abatement habits die hard, especially if their mothers used to be Registered. Garments lay in piles against the curb, for those who would rather be unencumbered than obedient. The girls outnumber them, in clusters against the buildings, watching. Most of them are part of the problem, Salmi thinks. Born too often in the fucking and grunting for sons. Pushing the family numbers up, beyond the allowable limit. Forcing their families out here—those parents for whom infertility isn't the problem. Who wouldn't give them up to stay Registered, though plenty do—the orphanages draw more donations than anything.

Some of these have parents who speak languages other than Aeri—those who came to work before the checkpoints went up at the borders and cut off the flow. A few of the girls have phones in their hands, and their groups gather around them to prod the apps in turns, as they make their collective way through whatever they're doing, when they can catch a rogue signal from the other side of The Wall. The girls' hair ranges the neutral-toned spectrum, in braids and thicknesses depending on how long they've been growing it atop gazelle necks and the rounded crowns of their bright heads.

Salmi moves through them. Tarps and nylon ropes partition the unfinished parking garage into the market's stalls.

—Your father was Samu—

"Yes."

—Who wrote—

"Yes."

—Did you know him well?

"I knew him like a little girl. I was young when he was deported."

Salmi plays with the trade credits in her pocket. Brian gave them to her when they were done signing things—a gift from the organization. She fidgets them as she moves past folding tables and their stacks of things. She attends the strangeness of credits in her pocket.

—What was your father's occupation?

"He was a journalist."

—Before independence.

"Yes."

—Did he support the Registry Act?

It's a stupid question. An obvious one. She watches the tables as she walks with the conversation. She isn't seeing what she wants here. Most don't.

"No. That was after independence."

—Before you were born.

"No, I was little. They were still figuring out the Registry. How to feed everyone."

—And your father was critical of the plan.

"Many were."

—Are they now?

"Not as many."

—Out here?

"Who cares? Out here."

—So they deported him.

"He was active. He had his newsletters. It was more than just people talking. Too much."

She finds a table of salves and creams. Some soap. The vendor doesn't have any shampoo.

"He had guests often. Conversations and groups in our living room. It was always smoky, and my mother would sit with them, raising her voice."

—So it was a problem?

"There wasn't any AerNet. People weren't used to it like now. He had to download his information from regular newswires with a squealing modem. Until they cut the line."

—Where did they arrest him?

"In the market."

—Did you see?

"No, I was looking for something, and I couldn't find it."

—What were you looking for?

"I don't know. Something important."

The bud is quiet while Salmi moves. She keeps following instructions. They already know this story, but she performs it.

"Is that enough?"

—Let's move on.

▶

The garden is dead, on the roof. She can usually keep peppers and cilantro alive, but not lately. She stands with it until the lens in her collar is satisfied. The specter of Aeri exhaust hangs over the city down in its depression. She sees it between rectangular blocks of architecture. A few buildings out here still retain Aeri façades, cast in metals and polymers to preserve the Aeri aesthetic, after they came building all this, after independence. From everywhere. Her building was Japanese. Owi knows. He's told her. There are still Japanese characters over some of the sealed elevator doors.

—How did you find out about the organization?

"My neighbor, Owi, learned of it. He told me."

—Owi learned about it in the city?

"He has a license to work there."

—And you work for him?

"Yes. Some cooking and cleaning. The children. He has enough credits to share."

—Is it enough for you?

"Mostly."

—How do you feel about the organization?

"I love it. They have helped me so much."

—So you are excited to move to the United States?

"Oh, yes."

—Let's go inside.

She takes the stairs into the darkness, begins descending past floors. Feeds chatter, powered through borrowed and spliced lines—the programs they'll let into the jumbled and inconsistent data hubs at the edge of the Old City, where they allow outgoing lines with filters to dribble what the administration will let them see, out here. What's good for them. Tarps and discarded boards partition old offices into living rooms. People carry water past her, on their ways up.

—What happened to your mother?

"She died. Not long after."

—She ascended early?

"Yes, that's how you say it."

—Did you read your father's book?

"She died shortly after they moved us out here. They did that when he appeared on TV, about his book. It was as if she was making a point."

—You mean his appearance in Alberta.

"Sure, yes."

Salmi walks them into her small apartment. She stops so the camera can pan the room. The newsprint Owi helped her use to paper the walls. She ties the tarp in place behind her, across the doorway.

—Let's sit.

Salmi toes her shoes from her heels and sits on the cushion beneath the roped and boarded window. One of Owi's children is crying next door. Behind the plywood walls. It's probably Owia, but Nered is home with them today, so Salmi lets her cry.

▶

When the tea is ready, Salmi puts the metal cap back on the canister of gelatinized cooking fuel and slips the pot into a woven sling. She takes her flashlight from the small cabinet beside her sink. The bucket beneath it that catches the water is only half full. She'll leave it for now. It's dark in the corridor. Interior flaps glow only faintly with ephemeral feed-light from shared screens. The noise of it sounds like people living together. She takes her time in the stairwell, descending through the flat world-spaces of families laid out in grids on each floor after the other. Men smoke around lamps on tables in the lobby. Women mend clothes and pour each other tea. Officers shoo children inside from the street. She sees them escorting the volunteers and workers back toward The Wall, back into the city for a night.

—Do you have any *hobbies*?
Salmi moves into the courtyard behind the building. She is careful to stay within its fencing. There is cook-smoke and trashfire on the air. The city's nightsong is a buzzing somewhere else.
"What are '*hobbies*'?"
She settles at a table with her tea. The courtyard is empty. The adjacent streets are empty.
—Things you do to pass the time. Small activities. Regular ones.
"That's a strange idea."
—Like books. Do you enjoy books?
"Books aren't small activities."
Salmi sits with the tea.
—Do you know women who are prostitutes?
A line of people approaches the courtyard across the street. They're wearing dark clothing. They keep turning their heads to look at each other in line. To say things in the dark. Salmi looks down the avenues, but she doesn't see any police.
She lowers her voice. "Yes, of course."
They're carrying armfuls of things. They bring them into her courtyard.
—Have you ever taken credits for sex?
The head of the line swings the column toward her table. The others follow him.
"Good evening," he says. He is a little younger than she is. A full beard. Trimmed and dark in the night. It turns his teeth into stones in an expressive arch.
"Good evening," she says. She looks at the other ones. More beards. Women with bare arms and big, checking eyes. She can smell their perfume. She can see the books and bundles in their arms, clutched against their chests.
He sets an enameled box on the table. It looks like something they sell in the market. An Aeri box, like the old ones, but not at all—manufactured someplace else. He lifts the lid, and it contains cosmetics.
"Are there empty floors in this building?" he says.
Salmi looks at the box and then back at him. He has arranged his eyes into a smile. "Please," he says, "it's for you. My name is Marun."

She doesn't touch the box. There are more of them coming across the street, in their own lines.

The tea steams between them.

"The top floors," she says. "Under the garden."

"Are they safe?"

"Too high to carry enough water," she says.

He closes his eyes and bows his head. "God remake you."

One of his companions hands him another enameled box, and they move away toward the lobby.

—Who are they?

"Registered."

She imagines she can feel the camera, widening its tiny eye, taking it all in.

—What are they doing here?

She looks at the box he left behind. Another group lines into the courtyard. They look around, inside the fence. One of them sees her and moves over.

He's young. He doesn't wear a beard, and she can see him smile. He places a small satin bag on the table. He has a satchel of clanking bottles over his shoulder.

"Belan," one says behind him. A woman's harsh whisper. "Come on. He already gave her one."

He holds a finger to his lips and moves away.

Salmi's heart is beating in her throat. She drinks her tea. There are cigarettes in the bag. Some matches.

"I don't know," she says. She has a nice smoke.

2

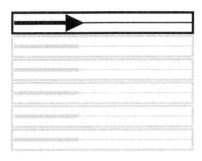

Amn

The Angel of Death is quiet. Amn isn't really hearing her. He lies in his bed, unsleeping, listening to the night sounds in the priests' common house. It is his only ailment, most nights. He can't sleep without the radio, but he keeps it quiet enough that his brothers can't hear it. It is a presence for him, enduring the night alone, and he hears it sometimes in his dreams, when he does sleep. And that's all right with him.

The traffic outside snores through the roundabout encircling the central plaza. Occasionally, the night buses bring themselves loudly into the room, growling their diesel dreams in cycles. Coming and going in precise patterns, loops without technical beginnings or endings. One moves away with a gargle. A problem for the avenue's air, interrupting the respiration. And when it's gone, the noise gets back to its breathing.

Amn hears one of his brothers out in the hallway—the latch of the bathroom door. It is probably Fado, who has gone three times already. The simple expansion and constriction of bodily parcels that is God's way of saying *Not you, my son. There's other work for you.* Fado is an Aeri, and he will die like one, as God intended, his body shed, a divine, organic failure. The release of imperfect form for his eternal mantle. There is no hope for him, for so many of them, sleeping around Amn, dreaming their prayers and memories. They will do God's work here, will give their lives to it. A saint, on the other hand, is not Aeri—is not permitted his birthright. He is seized by God, subsumed by him. He speaks not his own consciousness but God's instead. An imperfect vessel that God does not remake, that he repossesses unaltered into paradise. A gift reclaimed. A life he must keep for himself, after all. The saint dies unchanged, his body in stasis, when God has finished with him. Some few, at the ends of their lives, are regifted God's pledge, are made themselves once more and die with failing bodies after all. Their lives' work stricken from the holy dialogs. Kept from The Host. Given back humanity at the last minute. Ascension.

Those poor men. Unfit, in the end, for God's habitation. Ground into the stone like everyone else. Their bones given back to Aer, now that they're done with them. Fado has an enlarged prostate. He will not be a saint.

Insomnia is not an ailment, not according to the church. Many saints spent their nights in conversation with God, lying among candles, sharing their dialogs with sleepy acolytes over sheaves of paper. The priests used to import their paper from the forested hinterlands, where other Aeri learned to make it from the traders moving through the empire. What remains of it is in the reliquary now. When Belan offered his babbling nightspeech, they had simply noted it in secular notebooks. The priests decided later what was canonical enough to be transcribed into the dialogs. There hasn't been anyone to record since him. They pray every morning for God's next voice, who is, by measure, late in arriving. The next exams are tomorrow, and Amn thinks about them as the toilet flushes outside. The doctors, now, help the church elders more accurately determine who is a candidate. Who has God's health. Amn is a hopeful. They will begin paying more attention to him, waiting for the moment when he ceases to be himself. Just in case.

It will take a few days to process everyone's bloodwork. There are other brothers who are also now old enough for consideration.

It's odd that the Angel of Death should still be talking. It gets his attention. He increases the radio's volume on his night table. Just enough. Ordinarily, she only reports the names of the ascended. Just a few minutes' worth, and then the state's normal voices resume their programming. He knows her by her voice. It breaks at times, and she speaks like she is whispering. Soft-throated, like Mother herself, at Father's right hand upon the mountain, where he was the first to inherit God's precious breath. She had her children while he worked—her husband, partner, brother—and she was without need to scream, for they hadn't yet descended to the temptation to move beyond Aer and incur the curse she left for all her daughters.

Amn isn't sure who the Angel actually is. No one is, as far as he knows. It was decided that they shouldn't know, so she might whisper the dead unto God without some more mundane identity. So that she might be Mother herself, voiced in these modern times for them all to hear.

He listens as she reads Usv's dialogs, admonishing her daughters toward chastity. It is the state's initiative, not the church's. There would be a priest speaking these things into the night if it were the church's. She has words for the dangers of overpopulating paradise. The Aeri are God's custodians on Earth, and they mustn't let regulations and population control thrust them from the stone's bosom. God's great punishment for those who would despoil Aer with needless children. Blessed are those who let other sisters bear children and devote themselves instead to their husbands and sisters and the city itself. Blessed is she who keeps her body for Aer, who gives it succor and pride. Their great treasures. Aeri jewels. Its women and their choices.

There are clinics that can help women on this path. There are incentives for their homes. For their time on Earth. Amn thinks about women for a time, as the radio resumes its regularly scheduled programming. The saints never said anything about how many babies anyone should have.

It will be dawn sometime.

There was debate among the acolytes, when Amn was one himself, gathered upon The Host, attending Holy Belan's sepulcher. His holy stone sarcophagus, in which he'd been sealed. He asked for it. Was ready. The screamings and slatherings and poignant, enunciated meditations—they all sounded wet. Cavernous and sublime, mouthed into the world from the surety of a dying man.

Religiously suicidal, at God's request. Recalled. Masons had drilled the conical megaphone into the lid of the sarcophagus for this. It was admirable, holy work.

The acolytes heard different things when Belan stopped. When he delivered his final, holy babble. Most of the acolytes heard nonsense. Some, simply sounds. God had no use for their ears then. Probably not now either. Not all of them were accepted into the priesthood. But Amn caught it—was one of the ones. They each transcribed the same topic: disturbance. *Be disturbed*, Belan said, and the utterance became canon in his dialogs—his transcribed corpus, God's unintelligible, unknowable words, muttered and shouted and abused toward his faithful for more than fifty years, who died around him along the way. Shattered bowels and calcified lungs and failed metabolic glands. The internal geometries of cancered entrails. The pains and shapes of it, bending them into sacred posture.

Amn was disturbed. Those decades, those endless lives in the common house. Their prayers, and rituals, and obligations. Grinding stone. Grinding their meditations, like Father. Translating and interpreting and understanding the modern age around them. Helping the devout, who circled and eddied around them. An entire city, lost in understanding, uncertain what everything was coming to mean. What tradition meant as the young turned from it and returned the gaze of the world. Amn was disturbed. Everywhere and as often as possible. He followed the corpus. Devoted his life to it. He dispensed Belan's holy name to infant sons as often as he could. They all did, perpetuating patrons. Encoding Aer's holy legacy into an entire population carrying saints' names.

It was difficult, that day at The Host. Some of the older sarcophagi were loosening from their mortar. Acolytes were tucked and anchored to every open-air, sepulchral shelf, every makeshift standing corner and out-jutting funereal foothold. So high up. Amn pressed himself into a random capillary shaft—a masonic accident opened by the passage of time and the shifting of the sarcophagi from their cracked and splitting mortar, where they were stacked and piled onto each other. Only the priests themselves could slather replacement mortar to keep the saints properly agglomerated onto each other. Amn didn't even know the recipe for the mortar. How much meditation stone had to be ground into each volumetric measure of the stuff. Amn was pressed, deeper in, bodied into place in the dark heart of this uppermost sepulchral layer by his pressing brothers. State police were bullhorning down below, monitoring the crowds who were waiting for Belan's death. His terminal truth. The devout.

They were permitted this foolery by their constitutional overlords, who were still resisting the independence lobby, back then. Who were still paying to keep the Aeri alive while their holy stone city cooked them.

Amn was disturbed. Belan's mouthphone message took form in Amn's crevasse. It echoed into shape, only finally becoming anything intelligible once it touched enough stone surfaces and refracted its nonsense screamsound into a pure, refined form. They didn't hear it—those closest to the sarcophagus, but Amn did.

The doctor takes a volume of Amn's blood. Times his respiration and inspects his tongue. He inserts a finger into Amn's anus. Scries the future.

Amn can barely hear them chanting. The sound doesn't carry into the kitchens—not the way the first fathers designed the original common house to. Its hollows and arches and curving, elbowed corridors. Arced, organic—a great stone throat that sang and whispered and chanted the priests' daily noises to each other. The house had sung, once, the way the saints did—cocooned in their own sarcophagic silence, their voices warm and rich and deep in the stone's absorptive grasp—not fully aware of the nature of their projection into the outside world that would continue living beyond them. The tone and warmth and indecipherability of what they had to say. The common house megaphoned its sounds without knowing it, those many quiet generations when one could still hear things in Aer. But not anymore. There is too much to Aer to hear things like resonant hallways and singing stones.

The kitchens burned down in 1827. Old Aeri like to claim it was an effect of the war. Those cannonades and muskets. The smashing of old things in Aer's valley. But it was just a kitchen fire. A failure in a bread oven. They improved the mortar's recipe afterward. They rebuilt the rooms, but they were new, architectural. The ceilings are vaulted, barreled, tiled. The walls carry the stone's threaded striations, carrying God even into the preparing of meals and the washing of dishes. But the place is prosthetic. Tone-deaf. Ordinarily, Amn can hear the chanting through the speakers in the ceiling, which pipe in the satellite station that records the chants in real-time and beams them to subscription listeners around the world. It's just easier to stream this in the kitchen than it would be to redesign and reconstruct the walls themselves, so they can hear. So they know their brothers are voicing the dialogs while they prepare their meal. So they might think on the saints and their invectives while they consider subsistence and the necessity of being in order to understand. But there was another flare this morning. Amn heard the house's engineers running through the hallways, hurrying without saying anything to protect important systems without disturbing the priests at prayer. But Amn was disturbed. Not everything is back to full operation yet. The satellite stream isn't working. In space or down here—Amn isn't sure. The engineers try not to speak too often to the priests—try not to tell them things. They don't wear their Worldview uniforms while they work. They wear plain, black jumpsuits that are ridged and stitched with extra abatement. Amn can't even tell which dialog they're chanting. AerNet might be back up by now. His mobile phone was still seeking a network connection when he left it in his room on its charging pad. Its animated screen looked and looked for the house's wireless signal. It will do so forever, as long as Amn leaves it charging. Subsisting. It will exist for just this one, repeated task, if that's what it takes. Amn likes it.

One of his brothers collects pieces of stone bakeware from a cabinet. The pieces carry the hand-stains of their long lives. Carved whenever they were and handled and handled by priests upon priests. Their intaglio depressions and motifs patinated and made darkly glossy. The pieces work well for baking or roasting—the stone is suited to it—but not much else. They will prepare the meat first, slowly, in the cool ovens, before they fry and stew its complements for the day's last meal. Amn checks the computer tablet they keep against the wall by the light switches. The engineers mounted it there. It has a connection to AerNet. Someone has already filled in the information for the day's meals. Depending on the status of the rest of the city's servers—their connections to hubs and processing centers beyond Aer's borders—the menu is available at the common house's Worldview site. People follow their diet. There is a restaurant in Montreal that prepares Aeri cuisine, and they offer the priests' diet every day, which they collect from the site and recreate. They substitute MSG for powdered stone, when the day calls for it. The cooks came once, to Aer, and let the priests try a dish prepared with it. Amn couldn't tell any difference, but it gave some of his brothers indigestion. That restaurant donated the steel sinks and preparation tables and powered food processors. All the things stone can't handle.

The stew will need several tablespoons of stone, and they will eat it to a recitation of Ad's First Dialog on the Mountain. But they're out of table salt.

The hinges of the nursery's door need oil. They make an unpleasant sound—nothing quaint and aged and tonal; rather, the screams of something burdened beyond its time. A thing sustained. Amn will be sure to add it to tomorrow's duty sheet. The cry of the angry metal chokes off his brothers' chanting, and Amn is alone in the golden quiet of the nursery's coiled walkway. The stone is arched around him as it curves him through the spiral corridor. He is short enough to walk upright, to keep his shoulders squared. Not all of his brethren can traverse the coil so easily. Fado, for one. Amn cannot hear Aer in here. The small hollows bored into the stone over his head admit only cones of mote-filling light, which they plunge through feet of exterior stone in the ancients' strange pattern of inverted cone hollows, which eat the world's sounds. It doesn't bother Amn that the faithful call it the nursery. That had been Holy Leve's doing, who thought calling it the Conversational was insufficient to the purpose. Some of Amn's brothers, though, still prefer the old name, but it doesn't matter much. Very few of the devout still step inside the chamber's exterior sarcophagi and cone their questions through the phonic holes. So they might hear God's direction from the priests, entombed like their saints, a talking death, for a little while. Leve's heresy inverted the place. The devout didn't step into a tomb, he held, when they closed themselves into the cramped speaking compartments—instead, they were climbing back into God's womb, the grasp of him here on Earth, in a claustrophobic, stone standing-place. Not a place to die, but to truly live, to approach re-creation and inhale his divine breath.

One of Amn's brothers sits on the stool in the heart of the coil, the passageway suddenly open, like the interior cathedral of some mollusk, hiding from the world inside the corridors of itself. Amn can't tell which of his brothers it is, reading in the weak light. The room is silent. And it will stay so. They can only speak when voices come through the walls, seeking God's interference in their lives. The light is scattered on crushed stone underfoot. Small, pink geckos sit cool in the shadows. Biding their time until larger things can't see them and they can emerge to hunt the moths in their nightly pilgrimages to the house's exterior floodlights.

Eventually, everybody decided Leve wasn't a heretic. The changes stuck. It was a revolutionary time; it was good of the fathers to accommodate Leve's following. Better to adapt than be torn asunder, especially then.

Amn's footsteps crunch upon the stone. He moves to the back of the room, where an engineer sits in his soundproofed, Plexiglas shell. Cables climb the wall behind it, disappearing through holes drilled into the ceiling, which they accomplished with power tools instead of hand-drills. The engineer's face glows in the light of his equipment. He thumbs things on his phone, slouched in his swivel chair.

Amn steps inside as quietly as he can. When the door seals itself back into place, the engineer looks up and smiles.

"Hello" he says.

"Hello."

"Ready for your shift?"

Amn opens a smaller door, to a smaller Plexiglas bubble. The engineer isn't permitted to hear what people ask or what Amn says in response.

"Have there been many today?"

"No," the engineer says. "Before you, he got maybe five or six connections. Three of them closed themselves out as soon as his face resolved on the line."

"Do you think the flare—"

"No, I don't think so. It was just somebody closing out the connection. Didn't like what they saw. Or just bored, maybe."

"Well, I'm sure the connection traces will discourage more abuse," Amn says.

"Couldn't trace them," the engineer says. "Masked. Strangest thing."

"Indeed."

Amn closes the door and takes his seat. The light falls upon his face, and the small speakers behind his head sizzle as the engineer activates them. Amn looks at the stack of dialogs at his feet. Perhaps he will read more Usv while he waits. Perhaps God was the inspiration behind the Angel of Death's recitations last night. It bears further meditation. The camera blinks its readiness, waiting for a connection. The priests agreed to let the nursery app record their faces while they spoke, so the devout know for sure there is a priest on the other end of their questions. Especially the older ones, who have trouble getting to the actual nursery anymore. Who were reluctant to make use of the app instead, when they introduced it.

Anymore, most people prefer the app. Amn doesn't mind. It's important to answer questions.

▶

"God remake you," Amn says.

"God remake you." A woman's voice. A young one.

The digital display next to the camera begins counting down. A corona of LEDs around the lens brightens Amn's face, rendering him just a golden head in the dim light. She will already have been made to watch the common house's short, introductory animation when she made the connection. Amn has seen it.

"Questions are the basis of God on Earth," he intones. "What has God for you today?"

"What is your name?" she says.

Not a question he expected.

"Amn."

"I have two cousins named Amn," she says.

"What is your name?" he says.

"Vesse."

"My mother was named Vesse," he says. He looks at Usv's dialog in his lap. Vesse, the young wife of Usv's imperial ruler. Known for her chastity and purity. Never had children and ascended young. Beloved of saints and sinners alike. A pure and fragile thing in the face of her husband's bloody conquests.

"I wish to hear Ad's Second Dialog on the Mountain," Vesse says.

Amn knows that Vesse, this call, is for him—not her. He knows it's God's doing—the coincidental. They all know this—his brothers. They are trained to know it. The Angel of Death. Holy Usv. The Dialog on the Mountain and tonight's dinner recitation of same. The salt he would go into the city to retrieve for it, after his time in the nursery. His importance.

He looks at the timer. He closes his eyes.

"Usv tells us in the Second Dialog how Father brought God's paradise to Earth. How he and Mother, carved of God's holy stone flesh, inhaled his divine breath and moved upon Aer. Father worked by day upon the mountain, grinding fragments of God against each other, and the wind carried the dust to the reaches of the Earth, so that we might walk there, too. And by night, he and Mother made children, so there might be people to ponder the face of God and the cosmos he created in the First Dialog to bring form unto the darkness, light unto the void. So that the universe might have consciousness to think upon itself. And Father worked for eons bringing down the mountain, bringing Aer down, grinding stone against stone in his meditations upon creation, and when the Earth had been filled with the soft places for his children, Mother gathered the dust and fed it to her daughters, so they might know creation themselves. And in his work, Father came to understand the whole of the cosmos, and everything that would befall the Earth and the Aeri upon it. And when the mountain was no more—"

The timer chimes in the darkness. Amn opens his eyes. Vesse's time is up. The app must leave time for others.

"Your time is almost upon us," Amn says. "You may re-enter the queue if you would like me to finish—"

"Thank you, Amn," she says.

"God remake you."

"And you, Amn."

▶

"Any problems?" the engineer asks.

"Not many connections," Amn says.

The engineer nods.

"The flare? Do you think people are having trouble?"

"Not by now."

"Perhaps the mask, from before, the repeat connections?"

The engineer shakes his head. "Your first connection was masked, too. It wouldn't still be happening."

The engineer's phone chimes an alert, and he taps the screen to awaken it. "I guess they must've found what they were looking for."

"God remake you," Amn says.

The engineer taps his screen. "You too."

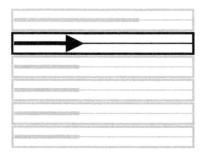

HELENA

The corpses remind Helena of her grandmother's wind chimes. They swing gently from their nooses in a breeze Helena can't feel, gallowed into the execution poles protruding from the aqueduct. The bells tied to their feet tone gently, something to accompany suburban lawns, hushed by the occasional passage of some commuter sedan, out in the neighborhood on its way somewhere more leisurely, disturbing squirrels and outdoor cats with primary-colored collars. The corpses' arms are stiff at their sides, taut. Gravity does its best to make of them inexpensive copper tubes, things that swing, in the wind. Helena bought the wind chimes for her grandmother at a home improvement store, which also sold lawn fertilizer and plumbing supplies. The aqueduct still carries most of Aer's water.

She watches the one whose feet occasionally brush the boughs of a pair of trees beneath him. The animation is incredible. Something she would see in a summer film that cost millions in production and marketing.

She pulls the content glasses away from her eyes, and the corpses disappear. The bells go quiet through the tiny buds in her ears when she tucks the glasses in her handbag. Of course, there weren't trees when they executed men here—they would have obstructed the public view. Helena doesn't know what kind of trees they are—crowns of tight branches and slender, desperate leaves. What kind of life and personal interests does it take to be able to identify trees on sight? She's glad to be out. It took Bruce four days to reestablish her connection protocols with the satellites after the latest flare. Four days of nothing but filtered AerNet and imported reruns in the hotel. Nice, but decidedly pointless.

The phone blinks a number of alternating Worldview panels at her, offering links, reports, and other historical re-creations about the aqueduct. The image of the columned building across the plaza, on the other side of the aqueduct, bears some imperial military insignia upon its façade. Which isn't what it's called, but architecture is as arcane as tree-ology. Who can be bothered with all its secrets? It's something for a coffee table book. The insignia isn't decipherable anymore on the real building.

The phone tells her that this plaza hosted a significant independence riot. There are a few old photos available with only a tap of the screen.

Aeri brush past her in the sunlight, their voices bright and tonal. The condemned were adorned with bells to draw observers, to learn the lesson. An early twentieth-century composer worked them into one of his scores, borrowed from the historical society charged with dusting the bells' display cases and polishing their museum placards.

Helena isn't interested in her phone's suggestions anymore. She rarely browses user-side Worldview. They tell her she should, and her phone defaults to it if she isn't doing anything. She did her part; she tried the augmented reality program. Enough. Pretty cool, but she already knows the story. Every Worldview reporter knows every story and every way it's been done. There's nothing new under the Aeri sun.

The Aeri around her don't stop to look at the aqueduct. They can't see the augmented reality even if they want to. AerNet screens Worldview's geo-tags. They were deemed too intrusive: their own history with the world's commentary forcing itself into their phones and wearables wherever they went. Helena agrees with the practice. It's one thing to be watched, another to watch yourself— your routines, your regular places when all you want is a walk, or a coffee, or to get to your new place in the rotation.

But she has a job to do. Helena brings up the access window and enters her PIN. The phone thinks it over with the satellites, then brings up the columns of user-generated tags for the aqueduct and the plaza. She watches some tags blink immediately away. Moderators at work, keeping the unsavory content from the discourse channel. Kids use this app, after all. Families. Helena just wants to know what the current interest in the aqueduct is. The new angle on this story, which comes up like every other story every now and then in the content cycle. She doesn't need the bots and their promises of Aeri porn. She doesn't need any jingoistic, isolationist tirades either—Worldview already owns another network that caters to those interests. The anger and invectives about taxpayer dollars and domestic politics. Wherever.

She messages Bruce.

I'm dying here. Place has been done to death.

She shouldn't even be covering this. She should be at The Wall, giving the people something new, finding a way to talk about what's taboo. Bringing the news to the world. But Bruce keeps sending her around the city. Back where the users go, where they tag their questions and bits of shared information. Where they can chat about the city as they mouse their ways through it or have a quick watch over dinner. She's already covered most every major landmark. Adding new content to the pile. Contributing nothing.

She watches the Aeri around her while she waits for Bruce's response. Her neck sweats beneath her leadcloth collar. It isn't as high as the smock they gave her when she first arrived—this one is tailored and fashionable. Something she could wear in the fall, back home, but right now it's hot as fuck.

Bruce responds. *So what's your angle?*

The satellite connection dips and climbs. She waits for its status bar to steady itself. A pair of police volunteers move along the graveled walk under the trees. There are abatement workers walking behind them, talking casually. One is dragging a small cart packed with what looks like tin foil. None of them are in a hurry.

I'm asking you*! Aren't you supposed to* produce?

A bus drags itself around the avenue at the edge of the plaza. It's been imaged, along its huge rectangular side, with the faces of young women. Some wearing traditional Aeri hairstyles, some

Western. They're smiling, and the block of text reads SISTERS FIRST! One of the women, at the far edge, against the back of the bus, where an exhaust grille distorts the lines of her face, has a baby on her hip, its face up against her shoulder. It looks confused, and its mother stands a bit apart from the others.

Helena should be covering *that* bullshit. For fuck's sake.

What about the trees? Bruce messages. *Water quality up on the plain?*

Helena watches a pair of young women cross the plaza. Their hair is short. They wear dark tank tops, one with arms like bronze and the other marble white. Their skirts are soft in the sun, luminescent white. They gleam, that confident pout beneath overlarge sunglasses. Handbags. The police see them, and Helena watches. They're all the same age, as far as she can tell. One of the women touches something on her forehead, and they stop when the police reach them. One taps his ear and looks away to say something. The other speaks with his hands, gesturing in fluid movements. The abatement workers shuffle behind them. One of the girls crosses her arms. The workers pull two foil packages out of their cart when prompted. They hand them over to the police and stand dumbly. The women step back when the police offer them the packages. The women start shouting. Pointing. Taking pictures with their phones when the police unfold the packages, and Helena realizes they are metallic blankets. Like the emergency Mylar sheets in first aid kits, back home. The police try again, and the women run. The police grab one woman each, and they are screaming, screaming. One woman falls, and the officer goes to the ground with her. They wrestle them out of the plaza, wrapped in metal, those elbows and shoulder blades now bright knobs beneath the shining blankets. Only one screams now. An old man walks by, smoking. It gets quiet.

Definitely the trees, Bruce messages. *I'll send you a file.*

"Merry Christmas, Dad," Helena says, interrupting.

"And they said it today—" he isn't fazed "—*today*, that there was a bombing in Geneva. They used a rental car."

Helena can hear *White Christmas* playing on the screen at her parents' house. The scene when Betty leaves for New York. Helena has it on the screen in the hotel room, too—muted. Bob is only just now calling Ed Harrison in her version. They always watch it, at some point in the day, which is almost as good as it was when she was little, watching it together. It's as good as it can be. Her father doesn't even like it. He's always hated musicals, but he watched along with Helena and her mother anyway. He holds his phone at arm's length, aimed at his face, and he isn't very steady about it. Helena can see pieces of Mom's china in the hutch behind him.

"Dad," Helena says, "Geneva isn't—"

"Which means the *private sector* is absorbing the costs of terrorism," he says. "That car, that company's stock in trade, is the fallout of geopolitics."

"Dad, they can write it off—"

"So I don't *even* understand why taxpayer dollars are involved over there. Just, on principle—"

"Dad." Helena is exasperated. She dodges this conversation four out of five times, when she calls, but it's Christmas. "Aer is a mediating international presence in a resource-rich region that—"

"And where are those resources? Do we see them here?"

"It isn't that simple. Aer's neighbors were once its territories. The empire—"

"But they conquered it! I saw just yesterday—"

"Yes, so they have that in common. You want to talk about the private sector and geopolitics? Aer is the one commonality between—"

"But in Geneva—"

"Dad." Helena holds her hand up to the phone. Time out. "I love you, Dad. Merry Christmas."

He looks around the edges of the phone, as if he has lost something. "Oh, Helena. Merry Christmas."

"Where's Mom?"

He lays the phone on the table. Helena can only see their dining room light fixture, which needs a new bulb in one of the sockets. The direct light blows out the image, and it darkens.

"Carmen!" he shouts in the next room. "Helena is . . ." His voice becomes unintelligible. Helena listens to the movie in her parents' house. It's nearly dark outside her window. Aer is assuming its amber blush, that evening overglow from lights of many colors.

There is a whirling of color as her mother picks the phone up off the table. Underwater sounds. She steadies it and taps the screen adroitly, setting her preferences. She is a better student of the thing than Helena's father.

"Merry Christmas, Mom."

"Merry Christmas to you," she says. An accusation. "Did your father tell you about Geneva?"

"Mom—" It stops her. "I know ... of course I know about Geneva." Have you ever even understood what I do?

"It killed some people."

"Geneva is a long way—"

"What time is it there? You aren't going out, are you?"

"It's almost 9:00. Aeri go out late."

"Oh, Helena—you should stay in. Are you watching *White Christmas*?"

Helena turns her phone to show her. "Of course, Mom."

"So small! That's your room? Isn't there something bigger? There's a Marriott at the airport. Your father—"

"The buildings are old, Mom. It's a nice place—I like it."

"Do they have that metal on the walls? Are you wearing that cream?"

"Merry Christmas, Mom."

▶

On Independence Avenue (or Aerte Ambe) the Christians from the mission are singing carols at the World War II aviators' monument. One of Aer's neighbors maneuvered flak cannons onto part of the upper plain without Aer's occupiers—who had been remaining neutral—taking much notice. The cannons brought down a few Allied bombers on a new route. The Allies were hoping for the element of surprise, and were unprepared for resistance in the area. One bomber came down just outside the Old City wall, before there was anything there to destroy. The Aeri pulled the crew from the wreckage and gave them amnesty. They sealed the city gates and repelled the Axis for two days before their occupiers took notice and chased the assault away. The U.S. government donated the monument, but it really celebrates the crew—their names and hometowns—more than it does their Aeri saviors. The Christians sing "White Christmas," and Helena thinks it's a funny coincidence. The Christians surround the monument, smiling at the pinhole cameras bored into the sculpture of the bomber. Smiling at the trees with their ambient lenses—the same species as the trees beneath the aqueduct, Helena knows now: crape myrtle. Donated by the government of China. They produce beautiful crimson flowers in the spring.

Helena moves through the crowd standing around the Christians. Most people are recording them with their phones. They will announce a massive donation to the Aeri effort when they are done. They do this every year. They raise a lot of money for the cause— all those checkbooks across Christendom bringing the light of the season to their Aeri brothers and sisters. Helena watched the telethons as a little girl. Before everything was just crowdfunded online or called for from the pulpit. She saw U2 for the first time on a Christian Life Network "Hope for the Aeri" telethon. They played their part in a live stadium. Helena's mother bought the DVD. Outdoor screens along the shop-way on Independence list trending topics on AerNet's social hub. CHRISTIANS is one. The screens cycle through user-uploaded video of the carolers. Helena looks for herself in the recordings, but she sees only the carolers' faces as some AerNet producer cuts between recordings. The sidewalk is slow with smoking traffic. Men in blazers and sandals argue as they move, hands on each other's shoulders, debating things Socratically. Things that make them laugh, mostly. Helena sees women in groups, moving in hurried knots through tight spaces in the crowd. Like the faces Helena keeps seeing on the buses. SISTERS FIRST! Helena wonders if they've been given some incentive to get out and do this. A bigger place in the next rotation? Updated television screen? Maybe something imported? A way to have a good time from someplace else?

Helena makes her way toward Imperial (or Aerte Dam). The scooters are out in their swarms. Some have strings of Christmas lights wound around their license plates. Drivers in Santa hats. Even some of the shops have lights in their windows. It's popular with the internationals and the Worldview users. The government pays to put up the decorations. The buses shudder the air in their routes, and the sidewalk smells of coffee and dispensary foods. The lights on the hydrogel sheeting—like sails capturing winds in hot zones— have been changed to green and red. They are festive, geometric planes, stretched between poles overhead, slick with flypapered radiation. The Host is a shining stone thumb in the night, and the mound below it moves with Aeri and tourists alike. The traffic in the great roundabout is worse than Helena's ever seen. Young people are drinking in the street. Getting ready for a good night. Helena sees women without sleeves, and it almost stops her. She's *almost* an activist, but reporter enough to keep moving. Let them do what they do. Take good notes.

The work lights are burning on the side of the new Civic Center. A team of German street artists is creating a photocatalytic mural. They received the most online votes. Helena helped report the story.

There's no one in line when she reaches the Hem's window. She gets a break from the gentle herd movements that migrated her here. A knot of boys are playing football in the small courtyard at the end of the alley.

Hem leans on his forearms on the windowsill. His skin gleams in the kitchen's fluorescent blue light. He looks purple. Almost black. The menu screen animates through its offerings against the wall. He has a twelve-inch Christmas tree on the sill with multicolored LEDs and a tiny apex star. He smiles at Helena and points at it.

"Happy Christmas," he says.

Helena exhales. She's been keeping a brisk pace without thinking of it.

"But I'm not British," she says. She unzips her jacket a bit. Just some air.

"What?"

"'Happy.' It's what the Brits say."

"What do you say?"

"I say café Americano, please."

He frowns. His coworkers collide and converse at the stove-tops behind him. "But *how* do you say it?"

"*Merry* Christmas."

This makes sense to him. He gestures it. "Like the virgin. Christ-mass. I get it."

"Christ, Hem."

"Christ."

"Coffee? Come on, you're killing me."

"I have something better," he says. "Just for you."

"And those chicken rolls," she calls to his back. She looks at the menu to see how they're pronounced.

He's got it in a mug. One hand on the handle, the other cupping the rim against spillage or foreign invasion or whatever one protects drinks against.

"What is it?" Helena says.

"I made it for you."

She takes it from him, and it's weird to her when the mug is cold. She smells it. Vanilla? "What?"

"Mary Christmas," he says.

She drinks it, and it tastes like Pine-Sol and cream. She swallows it, and her stomach debates with a sudden grip whether it will cooperate.

"Does it taste right?" Hem says.

"What is it supposed to taste like?"

"Eggnog."

"Does it taste right to you?"

"It's good! We all tried it."

She forces another drink, and the boys shout at their game in the courtyard.

"I still want an Americano," she says.

"I know, beloved. It takes a minute!"

Beloved. A word that manages to mean nothing. In any language. A thing to say to anyone who stops long enough for a conversation. He started saying it the first time she came back. Keeps at it.

"Can you bring it out?" she says.

He waves at her, and she moves away from the menu screen— from the Worldview hot spot. Aeri pop in, pop out of view as they move past the alleyway, out on the street. They're like some picture book. An album of comings and goings. Old people, children. Lovers, rivals. Cops and young women. People with cancers like watercolors upon their faces. People praying even as they walk, trailing their fingers along God's stone and picking it back up when they reach the other side. Helena can hear dance music and an emergency vehicle siren.

Hem steps out of the door recessed into the stone beside his window. He brings her the coffee where she is hiding from Worldview. He takes the eggnog in trade and downs it.

"I need to ask you something," she says.

He turns and looks at the menu, then back at her. She doubts he knew it was a Worldview location, before she accessed it, that first day.

"Okay," he says, "beloved."

She blows on the Americano. "I need you to get me through The Wall."

He looks at her. His eyes are dark, looking.

"Okay," he says.

"Okay?"

"Sure."

"Just . . . like that?"

He smiles, and she runs her hand over her hair without thinking about it.

"Anything for you, beloved."

"I thought it would be a bigger deal."

He shrugs. "Sometimes. When they crack down. But only sometimes."

"Christ, I should have asked you sooner."

He doesn't say anything.

"It's important to my work."

"Okay."

"Press aren't supposed to go beyond."

"Then should you go?"

"Yes!"

"Okay."

"It's important, Hem."

"Okay."

"You know a way?"

"Give me your phone."

She pulls it from her handbag and unlocks the screen. He pulls up her nav app with a series of deft thumb-taps and scrolls the tiny streets and roundabouts out of his way. He finds what he's looking for, taps a flag into it, and hands her back her phone.

"My window closes at midnight," he says.

"Thank you, Hem."

"Mary Christmas!"

▶

The rain opens on the city like a watering. Unannounced and thorough. It is immediately a riveleted course upon the streets, making deltas of oil-stained cobblestones and causeways of cracked pavement around drain sewers like old dentured jaws. There are sheets of it like slicks down the architecture, like sweat on statuary, and the Aeri emerge into it, spilling from bars and living rooms and cafés, duty bound, newly wet in the refracted orange light, and they make sure to get it upon them. The sound of rain in Aer is laughter, as if they're collectively getting away with something.

Helena stays beneath the awning, under the timpani of drops on its overhead copper, and pulls her phone from her handbag. Her AerNet app is bright with notifications from nearby users streaming videos to the social hub. Worldview isn't watching yet, so she taps it awake, activates her administrative access, and pulls up her camera. She watches an old woman in the street, abatement-free, praying on her knees, the smog's sulfur dioxide become acid in the rain, upon her skin like some chemical treatment—some peel or wash in a younger woman's salon. Something to fight the ages. The air will be clear tomorrow, after the rain—the Aeri made clean by its poisons. Its ablutions and baptisms. The old woman prays, and puts her lips upon the stone, and the traffic moves carefully around everyone in the streets.

▶

"I didn't even know it was going to rain," Helena says.

Hem smiles. He lets the rain fall upon him. "Don't you have a weather app?"

"I have two."

This makes sense to him. "You knew it was going to rain."

She has her jacket's liner over her head, a makeshift veil with its sleeves around her throat. The leadcloth is raw against her skin without it. The stones run with smog and water under the arches of her kitten heels.

"Shouldn't we hurry?" she says.

He looks around. The traffic is thin this high up, so close to The Wall. Everything seems to be headed downward, to the city center.

"The curfew will be lax tonight," he says. "Harder to tell in the rain who doesn't belong."

Helena saw Unregistered queued dutifully at the last gate. Standing in the floodlight rain, silhouettes commuting home.

"Your feet are getting wet," he says. It amuses him.

"I told you I didn't know it was going to rain."

"Nice shoes."

"Well, it's Christmas."

▶

Hem moves Helena further away from The Wall, deeper back into the Old City, away from his blinking flag on her navigation app. She follows on her toes across the broken cobbles between buildings. A window planter has fallen, from however far up, and its soil bleeds into the runoff. Plants like wet ribbons are splayed upon the stones, their thin roots cleansed and exposed around them, like something forensic. Hem kicks the ceramic fragments out of their way. Old fire escapes stitch the walls overhead, awkwardly bolted into the buildings' ornaments and stringcourses and old cultural projections. Hem chooses one of the escapes. Its access ladder is limp, low and broken. It stands out, like a mandible in the desert or a lock of bleached hair. Things that could be talismans or garbage. Hem leaps in the rain, and he grabs the lowest rung. It creaks with him to ground level, and it sounds appropriate to the rain—another sloughing of old things in the water, like planters and radioactive dust.

Helena steps up behind Hem as he shakes the ladder, checking its stability. He looks up the escape, into the rain, and squints at nothing for a time.

"Ladies first," he says.

He holds the ladder in place while she settles onto it.

"I'm not wearing a skirt, you know."

He could be smiling.

"Up," he says.

"To get to The Wall?"

"Yes."

Helena thinks about what she's doing. She thinks about being caught. About how few rights she has here. About which ones Hem has. How far she should take this. How loud the rain is around them, and how he is in her way, if she wanted to back out.

"Up."

▶

"You should turn off your phone," he says.

Inside, on the landing, her makeshift veil clings to her neck like artificial skin. Something for burn victims and cancer patients. The rain sounds machined outside the old windows, six stories up.

"You're pretty close to The Wall," he says.

"Not close enough."

She pulls her phone out of her handbag and thumbs it off. It powers down and animates itself into an inert panel. Helena is pretty sure they can still track her, if they really want to. Worldview can, at least. Most likely. She can't remember if rain interferes with satellite signals.

His teeth show when he smiles, dim in the light.

"You're tired?" he says.

"No."

"Nice shoes, wrong night."

"What is this place?"

"Pumphouse."

"A six-story pumphouse?"

"Just one really tall story," he says.

"To pump *what*?"

"Aer floods, beloved. Water must be forced to flow up, when we need it to. Have you read Belan?"

"But six stories tall?"

"One large, available story, back when they installed the machinery," he says.

They are standing on a metallic catwalk. Helena sees inactive lights in hanging sconces with protective grilles across the bulbs. They are points of darker space in the darkness. Silhouettes, playing at ideas of light. There is a sound of space below the catwalk. Room for their voices to carry.

"Come on," he says. He walks. They reverse their ascent with another stairway, affixed to the wall across the void. Helena feels a sense of giant contours upon the wall. Some sort of historic artwork. The significant lines of a face or a battle or a scene that requires feet upon feet of surface area. Something to consume the heights.

"What was it? Before?"

"Storehouse. For grains." He makes a broad gesture with one hand. He grasps the insufficient railing with his other. "The people on the walls indicated volume. Depending how much of them you could see. Tributes became necessary each time an entire person was revealed."

▶

The pumps look old to Helena. They have the curves and geometries of her grandfather's farming equipment, before he died and Grandmother came into the city. They are square and rounded simultaneously. The components carry different tones of the same industrial enamel. A color she can't decipher in the darkness but something softer and smoother than bare steel. It's how assembly lines are humanized. How it makes them innocent and disinterested when they maim careless workers or claim fingers like tributes for their continued operation. It is something they can't help, taking flesh from the weary, their keepers. Like livestock or gods. People still die for the common good.

▶

There are empty fuel cans near the pumps—the smell of spirited diesel, its evaporation and old ideas. Pipes run from the pumps and disappear along the floor that Helena can barely see. They look too small for the task—the size of her thigh, maybe.

The pumps' intake valves are open. Helena thinks this is so they don't seize in place from disuse, rendered useless and inconvenient to replace in a hurry, which is usually how vital components are changed out. A problem made worse without foresight. The flesh from the weary.

The intake valves are as tall as she is. So much larger than the pipes that will carry everything away—what these man-sized gullets can swallow. Helena looks into the pumps as she squeezes through the intake after Hem. She sees only darkness, and she thinks about industrial accidents.

▶

The water slips just over her ankles in the tunnel. The light on Hem's phone turns him dark as he points it in front of him. He has no face when he turns around to check her stride. The walls are straight and dry, bricked into an arch just over Hem's head. It doesn't look like the stone on the surface. The water makes gentle sounds.

▶

"I need to be recording this," Helena says.

"You're the one to record this?" Hem says.

"What is it you think we're doing here? Wading through acid rainwater, underground, on Christmas night?"

He doesn't turn around. She plants a hand on his shoulder when her heel catches a seam in the masonry.

"Trespassing," he says.

"These aren't drainage tunnels," she says.

He stops, and the corridor goes black in front of him when he turns his phone's light on her. He sweeps it across the water and laughs. He points at the water with his off hand.

"I'm not kidding," she says. "Look at them. They're vaulted. High enough for a man. And the paving doesn't feel water-worn."

She stomps a foot demonstratively. "It's flat. Pretty sure that breaks the rules of Drainage 101."

"You wanted to see The Wall," he says.

She pulls a damp tendril of hair from her cheek.

"The other *side* of The Wall," she says.

He shrugs. He stands there.

"Unbelievable," she says.

"Come on, beloved."

"Why hasn't Worldview done this story?"

"Come on."

▶

The corridor ends with an abrupt wall. A worn stone stairway leading up and away at 90 degrees. Hem stands a few steps up, working at unsealing some hatch, his phone in one hand, a multi-tool in the other. Helena looks at the pipes retrofitted into the base of the stone terminus. Pale cement seals them in place—artificial and alien upon the masonry. A scar. The forced couplings between the pipes and the corridor are no higher than her knees. The valves are locked open. Service plates with numbers and Aeri script have oxidized and gone to green. Like placards in some ancient museum.

Hem is watching her when she looks up.

"They are notes from the workmen," he says. "Service dates. It's a good way to know when they'll be back."

Helena points at the hatch. "What's the problem?"

He smiles. "No problem, beloved." He turns back to the work.

Helena fidgets. She wonders what updates she's missing on her phone.

"Hem?"

"Yes, beloved?"

"Why aren't you on the Register?"

It's a bad question. One they teach them not to ask in the cultural preparation program, before shipping out for an Aeri tour. Like asking a woman her age or about someone's personal relationship with Jesus Christ.

He keeps working. "My father was Registered, my mother was not. Use your imagination."

The water is shallower here. Helena's feet feel more wet now that they are no longer submerged. Perhaps the rain has let up.

"Why do you stay?" she says.

"Are you interviewing me, beloved? For Worldview?"

"Sorry."

"It's all right."

He puts his tool in his pocket and hands her his phone. He points at the hatch, and she directs the light.

"The radiation will kill you," she says.

There is a grinding sound as he hinges the hatch up.

"Certainly."

"Do you have symptoms?"

"Everyone has symptoms."

He reaches out for the phone.

"You are worried about me, beloved?"

"Christ, Hem."

He studies her with his light.

"How is your Aeri?" he says.

"*Getting better*," she says.

"They should teach you to speak it before you come."

"It takes too long," she says.

It amuses him. He lifts a finger from the phone and points it at her. "By the time you speak it all, you won't need answers for these questions."

She doesn't say anything. Just endures the examination.

"Come on," he says. "Up, beloved."

▶

Hem sits on a stone slab running the length of the chamber. There are niches and shelves worked into the masonry above and around him. Cement patches along the ceiling. He spreads his arms. "Inside The Wall!"

The loose dirt on the floor muds her toes. There are empty beer bottles and cigarette butts everywhere. Burn marks on the walls.

"What is this?" she says.

He shrugs. "Parties. Registered come sometimes, when they get bored. Young ones, mostly."

"That's allowed?" she says. "I mean, they built *rooms* into The Wall?"

"The police chase them out. Eventually."

"Why are we sitting here, Hem?"

He leans back against the stone. "People have sat here for millennia."

"*Inside* The Wall?"

"Of course. They lived here."

Helena walks the room, examines the design. The new graffiti.

"Who lived here?"

"Slaves."

She turns on him. "Bullshit."

"What is your phrase: out of sight, out of mind?"

"The tunnels," she says.

He points at her. "They had to get to work somehow."

"You're making this up," she says. She sits next to him. "Worldview has never covered this."

"There's probably a reason."

"Holy shit, Hem." She looks at her knees. "You have no idea what this could do for me."

"I'm not an idiot, Helena."

▶

He leads her slowly through a steel doorway. The gooseneck light mounted overhead, outside, isn't shining. There are tangles of frayed wires beside the doorframe, where she puts her hand to brace her way through. There is no handle on the outside of the door, only a lock. Hem uses a stone to hold the door open.

Helena looks at the shanties and towers with their dim lights in the rain. She can hear children shouting down an avenue. The nearest structures are at least a hundred feet from The Wall. Someone has stenciled graffiti flowers along its base.

"Look, beloved." He hands Helena his phone. There is a priest's face on it, shaking and occasionally flashing as the phone's signal buffers.

"What is this?" she says.

"I don't know," he says. "It isn't AerNet."

"What is it?" She beholds the screen like an artifact, as if they stand in a dig site.

The signal fails, and Hem's screen reports that it has detected a new network and is connecting.

The priest on the screen says, "Usv tells us in the Second Dialog how Father brought God's paradise to Earth. How he and Mother, carved of God's holy stone flesh, inhaled his divine breath and moved upon Aer. Father worked by day upon the mountain, grinding fragments of God against each other, and the wind carried the dust to the reaches of the Earth, so that we might walk there, too. And by night, he and Mother made children, so there might be people to ponder the face of God—"

The signal fails again. The phone finds another network.

"How is it doing that?" Helena says. "We aren't moving."

"Beloved," he says, "I think the networks are."

"—So that the universe might have consciousness to think upon itself. And Father worked for eons bringing down the mountain, bringing Aer down, grinding stone against stone in his meditations upon creation, and when the Earth had been filled with the soft places for his children, Mother gathered the dust and fed it to her daughters, so they might know creation themselves. And in his work, Father came to understand the whole of the cosmos, and everything that would befall the Earth and the Aeri upon it—"

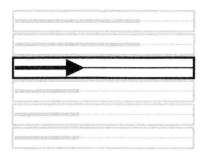

LEVE

Still life with girlfriend. Leve stands at the threshold in his jockey shorts, as if he shouldn't disturb the scene—a real-world time capsule of Lana's last waking moments in the bathroom. Last night, before she found him in bed and fell asleep smiling. She came into the bedroom wearing only a pair of two-toned panties. Semi-transparent mesh, except for the crotch, which was sewn of sterner stuff. Leve looked at them in the night's amber window light, but he didn't do anything about it. He folded her arm across his chest and let the softer places dampen between them in the still air. Lana was too drunk to do much. She made vowel sounds slowly in her throat, eyes closed, until she was just breath in the dark. Leve doesn't like to do much when she is drunk, unless he is, too. Vesse hadn't been any better, and she and Belan were still drinking when Leve and Lana left. Were still at it with Marun.

It's Tuesday morning. Belan will have a rough shift.

Leve regards the bathroom. The hand towel gone askew. The discarded bra that matches Lana's panties, one cup overturned like a supplicant's vessel. Hairbrush, a tracery of stolen follicles lost to the sink. A handprint on the mirror. Leve's comb and razor sit in a brown ceramic mug in the corner of the countertop. He steps into the tableau. A piece of something himself now. He likes having Lana around. It's better than when she wasn't.

▶

On the bus, Leve's phone says GOOD MORNING, LEVE. He moves closer to the window when someone sits next to him—makes more room. His abatement suit is thicker than standard leadcloth, bulkier. He tries to be conscientious about it in public. He doesn't look up to see who has taken the seat. The bus hums in its lane at the stop. Its systems move air and fuel through pipes and vents—an entirely forced system of least resistance. A way to tame the saints' fascination with how things move naturally. How to turn a bus into one of God's creatures. It vibrates Leve's own arrangement, his own pockets of fluid and air, busy with the work of keeping him alive in his seat.

People shuffle and cough in the aisle, taking their seats. The AerNet sweep chimes through LED screens and handhelds.

GOOD MORNING, LEVE.

He thumbs his municipal app open. It's how he prefers to deal with check-ins.

Morning.

PLEASE IDENTIFY YOUR DESTINATION.

Central Maintenance and Routing.

ONE MOMENT.

Your capslock is on.

HAVE YOU APPLIED BOTH REGULATION CREAMS FOR YOUR SHIFT TODAY?

Yes.

EXTRA RADIATION TABLETS WILL BE AVAILABLE AT CENTRAL MAINTENANCE.

I know.

THERE ARE TWO CAFÉS AND A DISPENSARY WITHIN FIVE BLOCKS OF CENTRAL MAINTENANCE. PLEASE ENJOY A FULL MEAL PRIOR TO YOUR SHIFT.

I will, thanks.

ENJOY YOUR DAY. THANK YOU FOR ALLOWING THE TRANSIT AUTHORITY TO SERVE YOUR TRAVEL NEEDS. GOD REMAKE YOU.

The app folds itself out of Leve's way, and the media window blinks awake, cleared now for content. The window plays an advertisement for abatement hats and headscarves. He looks up, and a few people are already in on the trend. Hats with brims like plates, and women with their heads covered. Leve thinks about it. He has no opinion on headwear.

▶

Leve pulls up his video library. There are two new recordings. Lana's phone died midway through the most recent party, last night. Most nights. He surrendered his phone to her when she interrupted one of his conversations for it, her eyes bright with the look of needing something to make the good times even better. She kissed him when he handed it to her. She tasted like cigarettes and some sort of fruit vodka. He watched her try to move quickly in her heels, back to the gap-toothed opening where she'd been on the floor with Vesse and a few others. The American kid was with them again. He had his laptop before him. Vesse was holding a microphone plugged into the jack. She sat cross-legged, facing Leve, an overflowing ashtray in front of her, a bouquet of brown and lipstick-stained stems. She unfolded her ankles to get her feet beneath her to hand Lana a shot of liquor. Leve turned away from the glimpse of what this motion did to her skirt.

He taps the first video file, and the buds in his ears hiss incoming sound. The image is loud when it jitters onto his screen. They're laughing and drunk-shouting over each other. The din of the others at the party is steady around them. Vesse has the microphone at her mouth. She's facing Lana, but she has her eyes cut to stare at the American kid. She glances at the camera and winks, then looks back.

"Shh!" Lana says. "Shut up!"

Someone laughs nearby, one of the other women, and it reports loudly in Leve's ears.

"Okay. Okay," someone else says.

"Shh."

A braceleted arm hands Vesse a piece of paper. Vesse wears a wry smile as she takes it. She is the only one of them that is good at this. Last time, when Marun first introduced the American kid—some computer activist from beyond The Wall, before the checkpoints went up and foreigners could no longer set up camp—and they'd played this game, calling the nursery at the common house through his computer, the kid had to close the connection several times. No one could keep from laughing. They were drunk. Vesse was the only one who kept a straight face. The rest of them kept quiet for her. But they weren't quiet when the kid broadcast the recording into the Unregistered web—whatever he had called it. Everyone's phones lit up, hot with the active, roaming connections, and the priest told his story. They laughed and squealed and clapped along with him.

"Okay, Vesse," the kid says in the video.

The image bobs gently. As if Lana is recording this at sea. Vesse clears her throat girlishly and starts reading.

"The traditions of the Aeri—today and henceforth—are the superlative concern of every citizen in our nation."

The Registry Act. The kid's computer is doing something to Vesse's voice. It makes it digital, unrecognizable. It sounds as if she's harmonizing with herself through the speakers on his laptop.

"But what we know now is that they disservice our independence, traitors for the world's eye. Perverted for—"

Definitely not the Registry Act anymore.

Lana drops the phone. Faces swirl to ribbons as it falls. There is a clack and darkness.

"Lana!"

"Fuck!"

"Hold on."

The video ends. Leve checks the phone for cracks. He pulls up the second recording.

They are louder than before. Drunker. Vesse's face fills more of the screen. A cigarette, unseen, curls smoke across her eyes. The hollows of her throat are flushed. She is angry.

"—tell you," she says, "the next time some motherfucking cop puts his cocksucking hands on me, I will tear his fucking eyes out—" she brandishes stone-manicured nails too close to the lens "—and pull those fucking metal blankets out of his groping, fat-fucked hands, and fucking . . ." she thinks, closes her eyes to meditate it out "*strangle* him with it. *I have fucking rights.*"

She takes a drink from a beer. She swats her hair from her face. "Where are Belan and Marun? I want to . . . talk to them."

Vesse gets up, and Lana turns the lens on her own face. She makes a comical *oh shit* expression, and the video ends.

Leve decides he'll keep these recordings.

▶

"It's called donor fatigue," Belan says. His voice is full of circulating air inside Leve's headgear, from the small breathing unit on his back. They communicate cyclonically—he and Belan—standing in independent airstreams that move things like sound and respiration in predictable, measured patterns. Good air this way, bad air that. Leve's mask fogs under his eyes when he bends for the nozzle and brings his nose too near the visor. He is his own weather system. The breathing unit vibrates his spine—a massaging sensation doing harmonic things to valves and fluid streams behind his ribcage. The soft places beneath all this abatement.

"Marun says it happens all over the world," Belan says. "Rich people grown exhausted with the plights they pay to forget."

Leve maneuvers the hose nozzle away from them. He has to lift it over Belan's shoulder. The scaffold doesn't leave much room, and Belan isn't watching him closely enough to see he's in the way. Belan fumbles with his own nozzle, attached to the de-ionized water-line. The two hoses slap their disturbance in wave motions against the building beneath the scaffold, and it causes a chugging sound in the pumps on the ground. Twelve stories below. Their coworkers are tiny, moving down below to check the pressure gauges. There isn't a good way to hoist the pumps up the side of the building with the workers. It's easier to just get longer hoses.

The maintenance cones in the street are diverting traffic into only one lane. The vehicles make their own chugging sounds, compacting their noise into a slower, condensed movement. Decidedly not the path of least resistance.

Belan situates the nozzle and palms it between his gloves. He looks over at Leve.

"Clear?"

Leve nods. "Go ahead."

Belan opens the spray on the building. It blasts congealed smog in shiny flakes from the stone, which winks its natural flesh tones under the slick. Leve tries to slow his breathing. They're supposed to take it easy when they disturb the stone—for all kinds of reasons.

Belan finishes and palms the nozzle closed.

Leve lifts his own hose, and the scaffold sways with it. It's thicker than Belan's water line. A heavy, reinforced canvas vein. Like they're fighting fires up here.

"Don't get it on your mask this time," Leve says.

"Fuck you." There's a squawk as the communicator accommodates his rise in volume.

Leve opens the line, and the force of it sets his shoulders back an inch. The radiotrophic fungal spores jet forth in their dark slurry, slapping and sticking to the now-clean, now-wet stone. Leve coats the stone until it's as scabbed and granular as blood sausage. It bubbles and settles in the bright day. It will dry pale later—a second skin. An ecosystem that eats the stone's radiation. Central maintenance received it from a firm that handles reactor disasters.

Leve stops the flow, and the pumps calm to a purr, and Belan activates the lift. They climb slowly past their handiwork.

"Donor fatigue," Leve says. As if he's trying out the term.

"There's a lot of profit in charity," Belan says. "Funds allocated for only one thing, like fridges for refugees. They don't have any fucking electricity, but people in Ottawa and Kansas are buying them fucking fridges."

There's a commotion on the street. Cars are honking, and their coworkers are hurrying.

"Marun tell you that?" Leve says.

Belan shakes his headgear. The motion is stiff, Frankensteinian.

"I have the fucking net," Belan says. "Same as you, asshole."

"You listen to Marun too much."

"That motherfucker."

"You do."

"He has to be right about everything."

"Well?"

"Well." Belan shrugs his huge shoulders. "What else is there to do?"

Leve hears a muffled thud. He looks, and it takes a moment to get his neck angled upward. The support line beside him, along the building, is whipping against the stone.

"Stop!"

Belan stops the lift.

Smoke plumes weakly away from the roofline, three stories up. Someone leans over, waving some cloth or banner. Leve can't hear what he's saying.

"What the fuck is happening down there?" Belan says, leaning over the railing.

"The fucking lines!"

Belan pivots, and the roofline thuds again, and smoke puffs immediately away. The line next to Belan begins its own spastic movements.

"Motherfuck—"

"The hoses, Belan. Hurry!"

Leve winds his hose behind the protruding pipes of the building's drainage line. It is bolted to a stringcourse just above them. The scaffold line snaps and whips to the street. The scaffold drops with it and jerks when the hose cinches against a bracket. A rupture splits the canvas hose, and dark fungus showers them.

The sun goes away behind the gathering slurry while Belan ties his hose, and they fall and jerk again.

▶

It is a while before the slurry stops hemorrhaging from its hose. Leve isn't sure if the tank has emptied, down in the pump on the street, or if one of his coworkers noticed the pressure alarm and shut it off. If the former, then the plume of fungus would have showered the workers and pedestrians, would've rained dark upon windshields and helmet visors. The slurry isn't as dangerous as the fungus in its unengineered, native state, but it's still toxic until it has cured. The street would now be a hazardous cleanup site.

Just like the scaffold. Like Leve and Belan themselves. Their reinforced abatement will protect them, until it can be hosed and chiseled free in a contained clean room. They are as dangerous to public health now as the stone itself. Aer's great threat, humanized. Pinpricks of sunlight wink through the paste smothering his visor like constellations of slurry-free suns, burning through dark matter. Leve thinks of the light. How it traveled millions of miles, dodging planets and debris to reach its final destination against his helmet, where the spores will devour it. A life cycle. A strangeness he fixates upon as the scaffold sways in the wind, clacking gently against the architecture. He lies unmoving, subject to forces greater than himself, staring into the dark.

Aer's first astronaut.

▶

"Who was it?" Belan says.

"I don't know."

"But you saw?"

"Yeah."

Their respirators create wind across the communication link.

"What did you see?"

"Smoke. Someone . . . blew the mooring grapples."

"Someone?"

"A man. He had some sort of flag. Or something."

"Fuck."

"Yeah, fuck."

They listen to themselves for a time.

"So, we're somebody's political statement, or whatever."

Leve laughs into the link.

"Life's great journey. To end up in the sky, covered in goop. Terminal punctuation."

"People die for all sorts of reasons."

▶

"My phone's ringing," Belan says. "Keeps happening."

"Can you reach your communicator?"

"Yeah, but I can't see it."

"If you try . . ."

"If I switch channels, I might not find this one again."

Leve thinks about it. The two of them grasping at sounds. Alone together on this platform. Too scared to jostle it. Locked in.

"Just leave it," Leve says.

▶

"How much battery do you think is left?"
  "Six hours maybe."
  "It's getting darker."
  "Relax. It always gets darker."

▶

Leve's phone rings, too. Over and over.
  "Fuck. Signal's good up here."

▶

"How's Vesse? Since the aqueduct?"
  "How's Lana?"
  "Doesn't talk about it. I don't think she really cares."
  "Fuck. Vesse does."
  "No shit. I saw the video."
  "Which video?"
  "The ones they made the other night, with the American kid."
  They breathe at each other.
  "Yeah, that," Belan says.
  "Kinda weird. For that dark web or whatever."
  "Yeah," Belan says.
  He waits a moment.
  "Yeah," he says again. "She's more and more into it. I don't know.
She thinks I shouldn't be doing this anymore."
  "No shit."
  "She worries about something happening. Like this."
  "Women's intuition," Leve says.
  "Something like that. Sex is good though, when she's pissed."
  "Well, that's something."

▶

Leve feels the helicopter. The basso hammering, disturbing the air.
Thundering against his ribs. The feeling disappears from above,
eclipsed by the edge of the invisible building. There are no more
stars to see through the visor.

He feels them, when they take hold of the scaffold. It bangs against the building, and the hose slides away, snaking against his leg. One of them touches down steadily at his feet.

A moon landing.

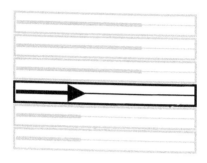

JEGO

Jego thinks it's weird, seeing two worlds at once. He takes hold of the augmented reality glasses' earpiece between his thumb and forefinger and hitches them up off the bridge of his nose. Aer is different before his naked eyes. And also the same. People around him, standing in line. Light off the building-tops. Traffic and its sounds in the avenue behind. He lets the glasses back down, and tiny electronics whir beneath his fingers, busy in their circuited lines inside the earpiece. The buds in his ears switch back to their sounds. No one has moved, but they aren't the same, wearing different clothes and having different hair and being different sexes. He watches when they shuffle forward and the real-time map in the bottom of his field of vision tracks them like a bird's eye. Keeping Jego situated among the real people around him, even if the glasses are swapping them out for this fantasy.

The glasses arrived last week, for the family. Handed over by a smiling man in a polo with something monogrammed over his heart. He didn't say anything. Just smiled and pushed the package at Jego's mother. The international monitor standing with him watched, making sure, like all the rest, that he didn't do whatever it was that would disturb their fragile culture. Jego's mother unwrapped the package and inspected the glasses dully. She looked at the icons and the images in the instruction manual and handed everything immediately to Ad, who would figure them out faster than any of the rest of the family. Today is the first time Ad let Jego leave the house with them. They are too big. They look like an adult's sunglasses.

He moves with the augmented reality. The people in the program are somewhere in America, Ad said. The glasses read and reinterpret the world, he said. It gets the Aeri out—a little tourism of their own. America has a blue sky, like he's seen in the feeds. People wear bright, primary colors. Mostly blue, as if they're all players on the same football team. Many of them have the same words spelled out across their jerseys between their shoulders. The same numbers. Jego knows the American numbers. They have hats with silly bills for the eyes. There's a building ahead, as big as the new Civic Center with flags from its peaks. Jego watches the flags move in the wind. There has been so much about flags in the feeds lately, especially the ones his dad watches. The same flags, in grainy footage, over and over. That man on the street with a flag, stabbing the abatement worker. Stabbing and stabbing in repeated motion while people whose faces take up the whole screen blink in and out of view to talk about it. And the man on the roof, waving the same tiny flag, while the men on the scaffold huddle against falling, and dark fluid sprays over them, like someone stabbed the building.

The flags on this building are the same color as all the jerseys. Jego listens to them babble in American, and he shuffles ahead in the line, getting closer to the gate. Ad said this game is called baseball. Jego thinks it's pretty boring. So far. He gets to the ticket taker at the gate, and everything smells like fried food and there is a thunder of feet and music and architecture overhead.

"Take off your glasses," the unreal ticker taker doesn't say, in Aeri.

Jego pulls the glasses back onto his forehead. The man in front of him wears a police uniform. He has his palm out at Jego's chest level to indicate he may not pass. There are men behind this one in combat armor holding assault weapons in the crooks of their arms like dozing infants.

"Identification," the man says.

Jego pulls his phone from his pocket and thumbs the ID awake. He hands it over. Jego doesn't see any international monitors, but the men with the guns don't look Aeri.

His phone comes back to him, and he slides it back into his pocket, and he raises his arms and spreads his legs like they show on the feeds. The man pats his arms and legs. Looks through his school bag. He turns and pulls a pin out of a bucket of them on the table behind him, where his half-emptied water bottle sits and sweats in the sun—a beaded terrarium without anything to grow. He attaches the pin to Jego's chest.

"Wear this."

The Aeri flag. Jego still thinks there's too much red in it. He likes the old imperial flag. The white one.

He lets Jego through.

"Go straight to school."

"Yes, sir."

When Jego moves up the ramp into the stadium, the baseball diamond is huge and green and dizzying, and Jego likes the feeling of falling into it.

▶

Jego watches Vesse read on her couch. Her T-shirt says something in English. Her shorts have bright yellow stripes along the sides, as if she might wear them to a race. He thinks her hair is unwashed. It looks the way Vidi's does, on the third day, before she washes it, occupying the bathroom for too long a time. Their father tells Jego not to complain about such things when he and Ad get impatient. Vesse's hair is much shorter than Vidi's—Jego can't imagine his mother brushing it the way she does Vidi's. He wonders how old they are when they do things like cut their hair short and move away from their mothers' brushes.

Jego stole one of his mother's kerchiefs and folded it on top of the narrow stone ledge where he rests his chin to see into the apartment. He carried his abatement cream out with him and rubbed it into his face and neck, like he's seen his father do after he shaves and before he goes out to meet other fathers in the cafés, or to attend to family business. Jego waited until he was past the drink machine and in the corridor. He left his phone on the family table, beside a half-finished bottle of water. He left the chair askew. Things believably forgotten.

Vesse looks like she's reading the dialogs. She has a large, bound volume, like his mother's, back on the shelf over the screen in the family room. But Vesse has a stack of papers beside her on the cushion, and she lifts one to compare against something in the book. She takes a picture of the page with her phone.

Her phone chimes, and she puts the reading down to acknowledge it. Jego watches her consume its message. A note, or a picture from someone else's phone. A social post. She nudges its content with her thumb, then takes hold of the phone with both hands and types. Her fingernails aren't painted.

Jego holds his breath when she unfolds her legs and steps off the couch. A stick-like movement. Swift and long-lined. She walks heavily. Not like Vidi, who makes a point of being slow, like she's careful with her shape or maybe afraid of it. Jego hates when they all walk somewhere together, moving at Vidi's pace. Vesse isn't shaped like Vidi—narrow and flatter in places where Vidi isn't. Vesse is shaped the way Vidi was when she would still play football with him, or go to the dispensary for ice cream and things to throw at the buses.

Vesse does something on the counter on the other side of the wall. He is up high enough to see a scar on her forehead, like a tiny piece of moon, crescent-shaped.

She moves in the same fashion back to the couch when she is finished.

▶

Belan walks in, and she sits back up on the couch, lets an arm fall over the back so she can turn to see him. He's wearing an abatement worker's uniform, not like the one he wore before he got trapped on that scaffold, and he starts the process of removing it into the closet by the door. They don't say anything. He comes over and puts his hand on hers. She wanted him to stop putting on abatement suits at all, but he still does.

"Did you find out?" she says.

"Midnight," he says.

"What? That's too fucking early."

"Even earlier for kids."

She takes her hand back and turns around to look away from him. Crosses her arms about it.

"They say it's temporary," he says.

She doesn't say anything.

"They'll announce it tomorrow," he says.

She stares at the light through the door to their balcony.

"They're not calling it a curfew," he says. "'Domestic Return' instead. So we'll properly enjoy what we have with our families at home. Especially our mothers and sisters and daughters. Our wives."

"Bullshit," she says.

"Bullshit," he says.

"I can't believe you're still doing this shit," she says.

He leans over her.

"This 'shit' is how I find these things out."

He kisses her on the forehead. Jego wonders if he uses her scar like a target. Something to go by, like the moon.

▶

You're coming today? Nedo messages.

Jego steps out of the line into the classroom, which was once a café. Street-level along the avenue coiling this level of storefronts and apartments up the Aeri spiral. The façade is plain, heavily abated. It looks plastic in the sunlight. So many layers of photocatalytic paints and leaded polymers. Things they make them all know, in each classroom.

After class, Jego messages. The attendance app bobs for his attention in the corner of his phone's screen. He is close enough to the classroom router that it has detected him through the rectangular windows, now rounded with their age and paint. He can't see through the UV film coating the inside of the glass. It looks like a green and purple mirror to him.

Fuck this place, he messages.

Jego is the youngest in this classroom. Ad goes to another one. Vidi is already inside. Jego didn't walk with her.

We could cut, Nedo messages. *Do a few routes on the buses. Hit the lot when everybody else gets out. Maybe go downtown.*

Jego isn't in the way, standing out of the line into the classroom. But one of the older kids bumps him anyway.

"Move," he says.

Jego doesn't know this one's name. He doesn't want to know it. He gets back in line, back into the hierarchy, and tries to walk and message at the same time.

See you later, he messages.

Inside, he taps the attendance app, standing beside the teacher's desk. It animates through its operations, then auto-populates his presence to the teacher's screen, who thumbs it away without looking up. He's as old as Jego's father.

Jego moves to a desk in the back. Vidi doesn't look at him. She talks to another girl, their heads together, their headscarves two different patterns of a similar violet. They wear headscarves now. Jego doesn't like the hats some of the other boys wear.

He watches from the back of the room. It gleams in here. In every classroom, everywhere—each one of them an achievement in white. Brilliant, safe, clean places. There is never any exposed stone inside them, not even for the devout. Classrooms are culturally bleached, an ongoing mandate from someone Jego is supposed to remember, from Registry Studies. Not Worldview. Probably some government.

The big red flag is on the wall behind the teacher, to remind them in this nothing place that they're still in Aer. Jego remembers classrooms that had marker boards there. Now it's probably all flags.

They don't say much around him, tossing data and content at each other.

The lesson arrives in the classroom app, and the phones go quiet, socially dead until the lesson is learned. Jego puts his buds in his ears and taps the first feed in the lesson. He's doing geology today, following a man in khaki shorts with a British lilt to his Aeri as he hikes into some canyon, with important words about rocks for the camera following him.

The screen freezes when a message comes from the teacher. His grades have arrived from the last classroom. The project with Siou. ACCEPTABLE.

Jego looks up. The teacher is busy with his computer screen.

Jego watches the feed when it resumes, and he learns nothing, pondering the semantics of ACCEPTABLE when one wants to say EXCELLENT.

▶

Going through checkpoints on the bus is faster than walking through them. One officer stands beside the driver, his hands on his gun. The other swipes and taps a tablet, and it pings all the devices on the bus. Jego watches as it displaces his social app and awakens his identification. He stares at his own photo on the phone. His updated district and address. It blinks away, and the police step off the bus, and the traffic barricade swings out of the driver's way.

Piece of cake.

Ad learned the phrase last night, through his game server's English app. He said it for hours while Jego tried to read about schist and alkalinity and other things he didn't want to try to remember about geology.

He sees a flag draped from the Civic Center. A huge one, covering one exterior wall. It covers a portion of the mural the Germans painted.

Piece of cake.

▶

The bus expels Jego into his old neighborhood with an exhausted hiss from its pneumatic brakes. It smells the way it's supposed to smell here. His abatement feels heavy on his shoulders. It's too hot to be wearing it, but there are police around, looking for it. Jego saw a few through the window along the route.

His phone finds Nedo for him, and Jego stops at a café window for two sodas—the most they'll give an unaccompanied kid at one time. He holds the bottles by their slender necks in one hand. Glass, so he and Nedo can do something with them after.

Some of the buildings are fuzzed with the new abatement fungus. There haven't been any more scaffolds on the news since they started the checkpoints.

A state broadcast takes over his screen, and Jego can't get rid of it. It's a woman's voice, and she's talking about the Domestic Return. Jego has heard his parents talk about her. They know her name. People stand frozen on the sidewalks, staring at their phones. Some still walk while they watch it. Jego sees the broadcast in store windows-turned-content-screens, their transparencies replaced by the gentle footage of Aer from above, filmed with one of Worldview's new drones, Jego assumes. The glass will be a regular-looking window again soon. He hears the woman's voice from speakers he can't see.

The rules, the reasons for the Return—be home by midnight. Ten for people his age. Jego keeps walking and lets his phone show the broadcast to itself in his pocket. He isn't the only one ignoring her.

Jego reaches the lot, and Nedo is there, and so is Dal and a bunch of kids Jego doesn't recognize. They're already in the game, and half of them aren't wearing shirts, and none of them are wearing abatement, and their phones are piled against the wall of one of the buildings enclosing the lot, flashing the state broadcast dumbly to each other. There's already a collection of soda bottles lined up, some still full, most empty.

"*Motherfucker!*" Nedo shouts at him in English. "Come on!"

Jego sets his bottles with the others and drops his phone into the pile. The message is over, and the screens twinkle again with social notifications and messages from parents and apps tracking things relevant to their owners' particular interests.

Nedo is on the team not wearing shirts. Jego looks, and there are knots of girls at the far end of the lot, looking at each other's phones and not at the boys. Some of them wear headscarves, dyed and inlaid with tiny mirrors and bits of stone that turn their dappled heads into constellations. Jego thinks about metamorphic rocks.

A few of the girls smoke. Jego thinks they're older than he is. There are older boys in the game, too. He takes off his shirt and joins the chase for the ball.

▶

The police volunteer looks at them while they eat, but mostly he ⁻ tches the workers inside the dispensary window. He watches them cook and slice bread and pour coffee from the dispensers. He made Dal move, who'd been holding the table while Jego and Nedo stood in line for their food. An older couple needed to sit. No one said anything when they collected their meal and stepped out of line. They just joined Dal on the ground across from the window—their backs against the adjacent wall. The pavement is warm with the day's long heat. Radiant, even now that shadows have taken over the plaza. It glitters. It doesn't look like the stone, though he can see the ground bits of it that were mixed in. The amount of it they allow, pouring the stuff over the old cobbles—a plaza, a street, a lot at a time. It's gray. An unbroken clastic skin, like a callus, across the whole of the plaza. Jego learned the term from the geologist, but he doesn't think he's got it right. He isn't worried; the test is later. They haven't paved over the stones in the avenue yet. The traffic growls with the tires and the unevenness and the vibration of it all.

"I'll bet they spit in it," Nedo says.

Dal looks at the food. He has grease on his fingers. It permeates the bread.

"You watched them make it," Dal says.

Nedo shrugs. "I was looking at the police. They probably noticed and took the chance."

Dal looks at the food again. "Jego, did they spit?"

Jego puts another potato in his mouth. "Maybe. I've heard of it."

"Unregistered fucks," Nedo says.

Dal inspects the layers of his meal.

"I heard of one in Eighth District that got caught with semen."

"No you didn't," Dal says.

"Fuck you I didn't!" Nedo says.

Jego sees Siou on the walkway outside the plaza. She walks with two older girls. They're wearing headscarves. Siou isn't, but her dress is red, like the flag. Jego sees red on many of the pedestrians, passing them by, and then he doesn't see Siou anymore, lost to the motion of the traffic.

He jumps up. "Shit. Siou."

He runs across the plaza, and Nedo shouts something, and he doesn't hear it, and he puts himself into the foot traffic and looks for Siou's uncovered head somewhere further along. He looks for her hair that reaches her elbows, and when he hurries to where she might be, she isn't.

"Shit."

He pulls out his phone, and he moves with the mass while he thumbs her number out of his directory. She gave it to him for their assignment, but he just followed her to her apartment after classes, and her mother made him sweet tea while they put together their presentation.

He sets the buds into his ears and calls her. Beyond him there are the noises of Aer—its state voices, and exterior speakers, and the horns and squeals of the cars, and music from the places where the tourists eat, and it is difficult to hear clearly.

"Hello?" she says. There is as much noise around her there as there is here.

"Siou, it's Jego."

"Oh, hello."

"I saw you."

"Where?"

"Walking past the plaza on Faad Street. I was with Nedo and Dal."

"Oh."

"Did you see us?"

"No, I didn't."

"You were with two older girls."

"They're my neighbors. We're going to the rally. Are you going?"

"I didn't see you at the lot today."

"You were there?"

"Yeah, I took the bus after class. Did Nedo tell you?"

"No."

"Oh. What rally?"

"They announced it earlier, after the broadcast. Didn't you hear it?"

"I was playing football."

"It's in the central plaza, for the Domestic Return. About safety."

"You're going there?"

"Yeah."

"Can I go with you?"

"Okay. Where are you?"

"Still on Faad Street. I can hurry."

"I'll wait for you at Wol."

"Okay."

"Bye."

"Bye."

Jego runs into the street and between the parked cars, and he passes the slower people on the walkway, and a police volunteer shouts at him when he stops staring for a moment at whatever he's supposed to be monitoring, and Jego gets back on the walkway, but he still runs, and he has to stutter-step in place when slower groups block him. He sees so much red clothing, so many red flags, and there are more police out this evening than normal.

Siou stands as upright as the crossing signal on its pole beside her. The other girls are gone, and she taps her phone. A man wearing content-glasses doesn't see Jego and gets in his way. Jego wonders what exists in his place in whatever program the man is running in his glasses, and then he reaches Siou.

"Hey," he says. He exaggerates his breathing. The desperateness of it that comes from running.

Siou looks up, and she creates a half smile for him, and she tucks her hair behind her ear with one hand and slides her phone into her handbag with the other.

"Hi," she says.

Jego looks around and sees only people everywhere.

"Do you want to walk?" he says.

"Sure."

He moves slower now, with the flow of the people, among families and strangers sharing the walkway. Coiling, all of them, down Aer's roadways to its pure and busy city center. A whirlpool condensation, growing dense so they might spiral back outward later, filled with the state's central energy. Jego should message his parents, but he leaves the phone in his pocket.

"So, there's a rally," he says.

He thinks he sees her nod out of the corner of his eye. Her shoes are a different shade of red than her dress, and they make clapping sounds on the pavement. Her dress reacts to her steps with heavy, fluid motions, structured by the hard lines of its inner leadcloth. It covers her arms. She is taller than Jego.

"Yeah," she says.

They stop at a traffic crossing.

"For safety?" he says.

"Yeah. Against terrorism."

"Oh," he says. "That's good."

They move when the crossing light tells them to, and there are Aeri flags drooping from vestibules and entrance canopies as they move down the street.

"Did they always have all these flags?" he says.

"I don't know."

They pass dispensaries and cafés.

"Do you want anything?" he says.

"No thanks."

Police divert traffic down adjacent avenues with barricades and hand signals. Jego and Siou move into the street itself, which is reserved now only for all of them, like a rotation.

"Do you like your new class?" Siou says.

"It's okay," he says. "My sister is in my class now. She's an idiot."

She smiles. "My sister is too."

There are no cars or buses or scooters in the city center. People walk slowly around the great roundabout, circling The Host and its garish red floodlights. Jego can't tell if they actually changed the colors of all the scaffolds and abatement sheeting and reconstruction tarps, or if it's just the light. A band plays in the central plaza, and drones and quadcopters hover in circles, drawn to the light like the moths outside his window. Worldview reporters stand in the crowd, their faces lit for their cameras by lights on poles.

Jego isn't sure where to go, so he moves into the rotating crowd. Siou grips his elbow and is forced to walk behind him. She finally comes abreast of him when they come upon circles of priests, cross-legged on the stone and grinding out their dust. Forcing the crowd to move around. Jego and Siou watch them for a while, and then they move onto the mound and sit beneath the lowest of The Host's scaffolding, where others are sitting and smoking and drinking tea or coffee or bottled sodas, and they all watch the spinning crowd and hear the come-and-go music and try to listen to the speeches through PA systems that mumble through the air unevenly about terrorism and international allies and support and taking back the nights for our wives and daughters in the homes of our families and renewed pride in the face of threats to the Aeri way of life. And the cameras watch them back, blinking in the waning light with the unclosing eyes of everywhere else in the world. Someone pleads for donations through a microphone Jego can't locate.

Siou tightens her dress over her knees, and she looks at Jego when she holds his hand, and he feels inside out. Pressure in instead of pressure out, and he watches police in formation marching through the roundabout and the people applauding and praying and bending to the stone around them.

"I'm sorry we got 'acceptable,'" he says.

"It's okay," she says.

He climbs onto his knees so he is high enough and concentrates on her forehead, where she has no orienting scar, and he places his lips on her skin there, his first kiss, and her eyes are closed when he stops, and he can hear the hovering camera behind his head, not far, floating in its place, making a sound like it's breathing at him, which is what he imagines Siou would sound like if he were close enough to hear her instead.

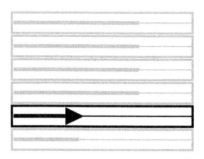

Asha

The security consultants wave the van through the checkpoint, and they stop on the other side of The Wall where U.N. peacekeepers check in with Asha's commander through the driver's window. They're new—the U.N. and the consultants, on loan after the rally to keep an eye on whatever's happening with all the Aeri flags and the security plots his commander has mentioned but can't discuss in any detail.

People stand in line beside the van, waiting their turns through The Wall in both directions. The line leaving the Old City into the Unregistered territory moves much faster, with pat-downs for licensed Aeri with business beyond The Wall reduced, at times, to handshakes and exchanged greetings. The Unregistered wait longer for their laying-on of hands, to get into the city for whatever work they're being allowed to do. They stand in the sun in their secondhand abatement, being still. They know better than to get impatient. A few are looking at phones in their palms, and Asha wonders what they could be watching. He looks at his own phone, and the AerNet signal is already failing. The other officers on the benches in the van around him get what final use out of the signal that they can, or they stare out the windows. The receivers on their shoulders chirp back and forth into and out of the radio network, getting ready to keep them connected when the AerNet responders' channel dies for them completely.

Asha looks at an old woman getting to her knees before The Wall, just outside the yellow security stripe on the old pavement that she's not supposed to cross. Asha's phone chimes in his palm, and he looks at it while its automated signal sweep wakes up to a connection. Asha doesn't recognize the network. A weak one. Its name is a jumble of Aeri script and English letters. He looks at his neighbor, on the other side of the bench, who sits unmoving, staring at nothing. The phone establishes its connection, then loses it and makes it again. His media app begins autostreaming an AerNet feed: a program detailing a new Worldview initiative to bring live recordings of Aeri and their counselors to the watching nations. A way for them to know the individual struggle over the larger, Aeri one. The program details the incentives for participation, for those who see counselors and therapists regularly enough. Asha saw the program this morning because Nisa watched it on their screen while she drank her coffee.

The connection collapses again. Asha looks around. He looks at the Unregistered with phones in line. He looks at the old woman, and she gets up from her prayer, staring through The Wall at the Host she can't see, and she walks deliberately, painfully back into the towers and shanties, and the phone chimes to him that it's lost all available networks.

▶

The van moves through the Unregistered as if cast from hydrophobic metal. They ebb and stream out of its way, moving out of the avenues that don't normally see vehicles, the roads they walk and work and sometimes sleep on. People pull each other aside, and tables of goods are lifted from the roadway and settled on the sidewalks, their vendors clutching them like young, waiting on the predators to pass so they can be safe in their original nests once again. There is a wake of Unregistered behind the van, reclaiming the roadspace they think is theirs. The commander doesn't have to use the siren, and Asha watches the multicolored PVC tarps and dimpled metal sheeting of the Unregistered architecture blink past. The tarps remind him of the advertising screens that flash in the city center, along its avenues into the upper districts. These tarps, though, offer only primary colors and snapshots like abstract paintings.

Asha prefers black and white photography over weird paintings. Nisa gives him a photograph every year for their walls. Black frames and generous white mats. His favorite is from beneath the Eiffel Tower looking up.

The commander pulls the van along the New Wall. Asha was only a teenager when they started building it, cutting the Unregistered territory like a severed limb to make way for the train from the airport. It isn't finished. They don't talk about it on the news feeds anymore. People still take buses from the airport, up on the outer plain. The landing strips still aren't large enough for large jets. Regional carriers with small craft have contracts with the administration for bringing visitors in and out.

They pull up to other dark vans, and Asha sees more international consultants. These aren't carrying assault rifles. They have tablets in their hands that they tap and study while they survey what looks like a construction accident in the New Wall. Asha has seen them doing the same thing with their tablets in the dispatch office. They have a wing of the building now for their own use.

Groups of Unregistered watch from the shade of the buildings that were spared from the easement the engineers cleared alongside the construction, presumably for the vehicles and heavy machinery required to erect the prefabricated concrete panels. One of the pedestrian bridges—a caged thing for their own protection—spanning the railway between the walls is in pieces on the tracks.

"Let's set up a perimeter fifteen meters from the van," the commander says. He opens his door. "Authorized personnel only."

Asha watches the Unregistered while he waits to file out. They aren't even within thirty meters. None of them have stepped into the bright easement.

▶

Asha stands in his position watching anything that can hold his interest. Mostly it's his fellow officers, the nearest of which are five meters or more away from him on either side. He watches his commander talk to another volunteer over by the broken wall. Consultants and engineers either crawl across the debris taking measurements and samples or they wait their turns for something important, standing as still as Asha. A few talk to each other around a field unit of some kind they've set up on a folding table.

Asha checks the Unregistered—they cycle through newcomers and those who grow bored and abandon the crowd for more interesting affairs. His phone chimes its signal search in his breast pocket, and he pulls it out to check, but the network disappears, its nonsense name digitized free of his network listings. He puts it away when he hears someone approach from the site.

"Stay off your phone, Asha," the commander says. This one is the same age as Asha, but he volunteers four times a week instead of two.

"Sorry, sir. It's just . . . it keeps picking up networks. I think it's broken."

"It's not broken," he says. "They're all over. We think the Unregistered are carrying them around to pick up AerNet."

Asha just stares through his sunglasses. He didn't know networks could move.

The commander points at the consultants. "They think it's how the explosion was detonated. Through a mobile network."

"Detonated?"

The sergeant stares at him. "What did you think this was?"

"An accident."

"Do you see any construction equipment here? The new segments are kilometers away."

Asha looks down the length of the New Wall, as if he might see it in the vanishing perspective of the easement.

"The Unregistered have bombs?" Asha says.

"Something like. Somebody got them in."

"And built networks?"

"They're getting help."

"Now what?" Asha says.

"We'll have to build a new fucking bridge here. It's in the funding mandates."

The commander lights a cigarette and looks at the next officer down the line.

"Not a word," he says. "To anybody."

"Aer Together," the announcers say on the screen, "is the new rotation."

Asha thinks it's an odd thing for them to say, calling the football match.

"Now, if you're unmarried without a service record, the rotation will give you more of your important years with your parents, your brothers and sisters."

Asha feels strangely aware of how he is hearing without listening, still on the sofa with Mir in her sleeper on the floor. He feels himself not move. He sees images like concepts with his eyes closed.

"Women under thirty and men under twenty-five can now avoid rotation licensing of their own and help preserve their families until they start their own. And women can look forward to new sister-roommates once they do register as part of Sisters First! with new incentives for those who stay child-free, for a newer, more exciting way to spend your thirties and beyond!"

Asha hears it like he's saying it to himself, and when he realizes he isn't fully awake, the knowing of it wakes him up.

The apartment is still filled with the day—the sun hasn't dropped below the city's rims. The match is no longer playing on the screen. The ticker at the bottom of the feed reads 2 – 0 FINAL, and men in suits sit before a windowed vista of the stadium as it empties of fans. They say nothing while talking—Asha muted it earlier so Mir would sleep. She moves her lips while she sleeps, and her blanket has slipped off her shoulders. The beer he opened is only half-empty, on the table beside the remote.

"Aer Together is your new future!"

It's Nisa's web radio. Asha hears it from the bathroom, and he can feel damp from the shower in the air. Nisa must have just only finished.

"The new regulations will take effect this rotation. Learn more at Together.aer."

He hears the State Radio bumper, and someone begins discussing the traffic.

"Asha, you need to get ready," Nisa says from the bathroom.

He gets up quietly, studying Mir for signs of waking, and moves to the bathroom. Nisa is rubbing cream into her face, a towel cinched around her, and another entombing her hair.

"Shh," he says. "You'll wake Mir."

She doesn't look at him. She works carefully on an eyelid she has stretched with an uplifted brow.

"She's slept enough," Nisa says. "She won't sleep tonight."

Asha watches her, and he thinks about the towel's tucked cinching.

Nisa looks at him in the mirror.

"Don't even think about it," she says. "We don't have enough time."

Asha crosses his arms. "There isn't time when we have it!"

"Don't be crude," she says. "Take a shower."

"Why so early?" he says. "There's plenty of time."

"No, I want to take the car."

"What? Downtown? We'll have to park it."

"Exactly," she says. "Shower."

"But the bus—"

"I don't want to take the bus."

"It's better for Mir. The air filtration is twice as good as—"

She pulls her fingers from her face and turns to fully regard him in the mirror.

"I'm not taking the bus for a nice evening," she says. "You think there isn't enough sex around here? How about nights out? I'm here every day, Asha. I want to take the car."

He thinks about how much time she spends with her friends. The cafés and salons and strollers in plazas under reinforced polymer sheeting and sunlit hydrogel tarps.

He undresses for the shower, and the water is loud enough to drown out the speaker.

▶

Asha stands helpless in the conversion's garage. The models of the cars in their spaces vary only by their years of issue and the limited palette of available colors. He doesn't know where theirs is parked. Nisa stops with him, and they stand for a moment, her hands on

Mir's stroller, knuckles pale and buffed. She's pretty, standing there beside him, Asha knows, in her makeup and dark headscarf. He doesn't even have to look to know it.

He uses the car's security clicker to honk the horn, and he hears it one level up. He looks at Nisa, and she rolls her eyes, but he smiles hopefully, and it makes her laugh. She slaps his arm and turns the stroller around. Asha takes it so she won't have to push it up the ramp, and she lets him have it, and she grips her skirt between her fingertips on the outsides of her thighs and pulls the material just up over her ankles and concentrates on walking uphill in shoes Asha knows have small, uplifting heels.

Their car is newer, bigger, because of his service, and Mir's seat fits easily inside it.

▶

The day is copper around them, and The Host looks taller without its floodlights. The sun is behind the city's rims, but there are still people around them in the central plaza wearing their sunglasses and hats. Nisa sits on the bench. She is hunched over her crossed legs with her phone in her hands. Asha stands with the stroller, watching Mir slap at the tiny content screen in the roof of her stroller. An amber LED wakes up at the other end, upon the forward rim above Mir's feet. It is nested in a smooth black dome the size of Asha's thumbnail.

He sighs.

"The camera is on again," he says.

Nisa doesn't look up.

"It's a public zone," she says.

"I know, but doesn't it seem like it comes on *too* often?" he says.

"No."

"I'm serious."

"No." She looks up. "I'm out with it every day, and it hardly comes on. You just think it's often."

He stares at it, wondering if anyone is staring back. He's heard how Worldview feeds and listings work, but he's never seen the menus himself. He doesn't know anyone who has. Just because it's on, is someone watching, or is there simply some algorithm waking cameras up across the city center with its programming for a world that doesn't always care?

"Well, I still don't like it," he says.

"You don't like it," Nisa says.

Are they watching The Host or Mir, on the other end of that lens? Are they scrolling the panorama in circles, bored someplace, his daughter rotating in and out of the image like something celestial? An orbit to keep an eye on. It's the first time Asha imagines the view from the center of the sun.

"Besides," Nisa says, "it's probably just on for the lights."

He watches The Host on its mound. Its onlookers and supplicants and observers with camera phones. It's a few minutes before the floodlights come on, but then they cascade awake, blinking on and back off in climbing waves before they settle their crimson gaze unblinking. People applaud.

"See?" Nisa says.

"Where are they already?" he says.

▶

Asha sees his parents walk out of the common house, but he doubts they will see him over here.

"There they are," he says.

Nisa taps her phone out of its app and stands up. She slides it into her handbag and situates the strap over her shoulder. He walks the stroller quickly, before his parents wander off in a fruitless search elsewhere. Nisa falls slightly behind, but they aren't far.

"Dad!"

His dad turns, and he waves at Asha across the meters. He stops his wife with a hand on her elbow and points. She turns, and it takes her a second, and she waves.

"Hello, son," his father says. He extends a hand across the stroller, and Asha shakes it. His dad isn't wearing a tie, and his throat looks polished in the plaza's lights. His blazer is too heavy for the weather, Asha thinks. Nisa catches up to him, and his mother goes for her first.

"Hello, my daughter," his mother says.

Nisa kisses her. "Hello, Mother."

139

"Uncover your head," his mother says. "So close to the Host."

Nisa pulls the scarf off of her head without a word and settles it across her shoulders. Asha looks at the wave of her hair. She didn't iron it straight today.

His mother turns her attention on Mir, whose face gleams in her overhead-screen-light. She throws her arms about her when his mother puts a hand on her head. His mother reaches out with her other hand to cover the lens at the end of the stroller.

"Little star," she says, and bends her face over Mir's.

Asha steps around and pulls her hand off the lens.

"Mama, don't. We'll get in trouble."

"Trouble," she says. As if she's trying it out. "Silly cameras on babies."

"*You get what you pay for,*" his father says in English. Asha doesn't know where he learned it, but he remembers it at home, growing up, never certain if the phrase made sense the way his father wanted it to.

"The ones without cameras aren't any good," Nisa says. "I think Mir is popular. They like her."

His mother ignores her and coos at Mir.

"Did they sign it?" Asha says.

His father pulls a folded paper from his jacket pocket and brandishes it. "All signed," he says. "We'll take it to the clinic tomorrow."

"Praise Asha," his mother says.

"Praise Asha," they say.

▶

The café is loud around them. Asha feels people brush his shoulders when they move past, between the tables. Except the waitress. She is small and silent bringing what they need back and forth. Asha hasn't noticed how old she looks.

"When will you transfer to clerk?" his father says.

Nisa shows his mother something on the phone. Their faces glow together in its light, looking at it.

"I don't know," Asha says. He arranges his meat in its sauce.

"It's time," his father says.

"I know."

"I called the office this week. There are openings. I can still get you in."

"That's good."

"Policing was just to start, Asha. It isn't good work."

"I know, Dad."

"It isn't easy to clerk. There are wait lists."

"You told me, Dad."

"But I still have pull, son."

"I know, Dad. Thank you."

"You're lucky I could get the policing. There are so many who want—"

"Dad."

"It isn't good work."

Asha checks his watch. There is still an hour before the Domestic Return, but already tourists are filing from cafés and bars, moving the wrong direction along the walkway, swimming back upstream to their hotel rooms and guest houses. He's been lingering in full view of the windows at Abao's for twenty minutes, sending the message without actually asking anyone to leave. The Aeri will wait until the moment is upon them, then he'll have to argue every one of them back home, and it will be two hours past by the time he's done and finally back home and will have a few minutes with the feeds on the couch before he joins Nisa, who will already be asleep with her phone still in her hand.

He watches a road construction crew standing back from the avenue, smoking lazily under a sodium lamp between two cafés. Their reflective construction vests shine gold in the light. Their trucks and safety cones and heavy equipment are situated in the street against the curb. Asha imagines someone has already checked their papers, so he doesn't bother. They'll work after everyone's gone home to keep from disrupting traffic during normal hours. He's glad he won't have to stand as their escort all night. He wonders how well the administration treats construction volunteers.

His receiver chirrups a conversation in codes and procedures between another officer and dispatch. Some unruly drunk who needs to be sent home early.

He feels his phone vibrate in his breast pocket, and he ignores it. He stands, an eye on anyone moving along. Nods and smiles for confused tourists. The phone buzzes again, persistent for his attention. He steps away from Abao's windows, and an advertisement for coffee starts playing on an exterior screen. He ignores it. The message is from Nisa. It's a picture of Mir with his tablet. She has smeared something across the screen—drool, maybe?—and is looking at Nisa's camera.

FINGERPAINTING, the caption reads.

His receiver barks for his attention, and it's now a conversation with more than one officer, and they are loud asking for backup and repeating "assault." They are three blocks from Asha, and he's running and decides it's better to clutch the phone in his hand than to try to put it back in his pocket, and he adds his responding voice to the dispatcher's tangled conversation.

▶

The crowd isn't too close when Asha runs through them, moving shoulders out of his way. The dispatcher reports a van on the way. There is a woman, not much younger than Asha, standing in the street with an abatement sheet around her shoulders. Her hair and makeup look disturbed, and she looks confused, talking to an officer. She keeps looking back to the walkway, where another woman her age sits against a wall. This one's abatement sheet has been tied around her with a cord, and one officer has a hand firmly on her shoulder, and he anchors her to the pavement as she bucks and tries to stand, shouting about her rights and the fucking tourists. She looks familiar.

Asha finds an officer milling between activities.

"What's the situation?" Asha says.

The officer turns. Asha recognizes him, but he doesn't know his name. They usually volunteer different days.

The officer gestures at the woman against the wall. "Attacked a pair of tourists. Clearly drunk—probably some drugs, too."

"Unprovoked?"

"The calm one," he points to the woman standing in the street, "claims she was protecting an old woman. Someone praying to the building. Said she was confused about the time of day and the direction of The Host."

"Where's the old woman?" Asha says.

He shrugs. "Gone when I got here."

"Were they harassing the old woman?"

"Who?"

"The tourists."

"They were taking her picture."

Asha looks further down the walkway, where he sees a pair of foreigners talking to someone out of uniform. They're older, but not elderly. He can't tell where they're from.

"She assaulted them?"

"No, she tried to kick Imal in the balls when he got here. She missed."

A woman shoves through the crowd, and she lights up the street with a Worldview camera, pointed at the woman under restraint.

"Turn that off," the officer beside Asha says.

She doesn't look away from the viewfinder. "I don't have to. Review and Approval will go over the recording. I can cover whatever I want."

"Let me see your clearance," Asha says.

She tugs a plastic ID card on a lanyard out from under her abatement jacket. Asha takes the flashlight from his belt and examines the card. American. Villarreal. He just makes a show of having a look.

"Just stay out of the way," he says.

She makes a thumbs-up and steps aside.

The van arrives, and the driver turns on its lights, and the crowd parts, and the woman on the walkway gets hysterical, and Asha remembers her now. The plaza under the aqueduct. The abatement. The way she screamed when he touched her.

"Shit," he says. "I know her."

"Who?"

"The screamer."

"A friend?"

"No. Repeat offender."

The officer claps a hand on Asha's shoulder. "Well, have fun filing this one."

Asha helps put her in the van, and she isn't strong enough to really resist two of them, and she screams at her friend to call some boyfriend or other, and the reporter follows alongside asking questions about Sisters First! and police protection.

Asha doesn't reply to either woman.

▶

Asha hands his report to his commander, who still prefers them printed out. The commander takes it without looking and sets it on his desk. He turns his monitor so Asha can see it.

"This her?"

The screamer.

"Yes."

The commander readjusts the monitor.

"The consultants are looking into some things," he says. "Data sniffers must've found something weird."

"Weird?" Asha says.

The commander tightens his lips. "Something about those signals beyond The Wall. They want police presence, to corroborate some things. Over in the Civic Center."

"There?"

"Sub-levels. Medical and outbreak—that kind of thing. File says they built it in case there's ever some kind of health emergency."

"Okay."

"No need to bring anyone else in on this," the commander says. "You're it. Come in tomorrow for it. You can have Thursday off."

"Yes, sir."

"Not a word, Asha."

Asha stands in a viewing room with people holding tablets, wearing ties and imported jackets.

She is restrained on a table, but not sedated. Asha can hear her shouting, but the glass is too thick. It sounds like something in a dream.

A person in a lab coat, on the other side of the window, approaches the viewing room and activates an intercom, and now Asha can hear her, and she is pleading behind him to know where she is.

"Subject analysis for . . ." the lab technician looks at his tablet ". . . Sisters First! and Aer Together. Aberrancy and risk assessment?" It's a question.

A man at the other end of the viewing room actives this side of the intercom.

"Yes, that's correct."

The technician nods and taps data into his tablet. Asha is the youngest person in the room.

They gag her with something they tie around her head. Asha watches them draw blood from her arm.

"Bloodwork analysis for pathogens and damage to the liver," another technician says into the air. The intercom collects his voice for them in the observation room.

The first technician comes at her with hair clippers and shaves her head. They collect her hair in a steel bowl. "Follicle analysis will be for narcotics and other contraband."

Asha's neighbors tick boxes on their tablets. Checking up on someone else's work. Like him, for whatever reason. He wonders how many times they've done this before.

He watches them work on her in the other room. He turns away without intending to when they pull her gown up over her hips.

"What are they doing now?" Asha says.

His neighbor looks at him. A shorter man with smoothly parted hair. A clerk somewhere.

"Checking for venereal disease," he says. "We need baseline data to track the new family initiatives."

The clerk looks confused, as if Asha should already know this.

"We need to see if they improve," the clerk says.

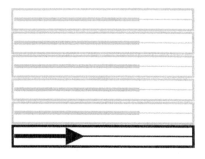

Salmi

—Good morning, Salmi.

"Good morning."

—Did you sleep well?

She laid awake while Owia cried through an ear infection. The volunteer clinic gave Nered drops for it, but she is sometimes very good at sleeping through her children's unhappiness. Salmi used credits that Sarah gave her to pay for a rushed appointment at the clinic.

"Yes, very well."

Salmi hummed lullabies through the dark, willing Owia to hear them upon her burning eardrums, which seemed to inflame about every two months. Owi has heard of the same problem with Registered children. The unlucky ones. He saves credits for a surgical procedure.

Salmi expects the woman in her earpiece to say more, but she doesn't. Salmi lies on her mattress and listens to neighbors with morning business move past her doorway. They try to do it quietly, to keep their noise out of tarped and papered apartments, but the footsteps and the coughing of their passage are the noises of closeness to Salmi. She looks at her shirts, with their unseeable lenses, folded atop her cushion, and she brings her fingertips to the scooped exposure of her nightgown. She plays her fingers across the fabric's absence, along her collarbone, where the lenses like to be, and she listens to them step past her in the hallway, less than a meter away, where they only can't see her because of fragile and permeable architecture. She thinks the lenses in her collars, over there on her cushion, are much farther from her exposed skin than the people in the hall.

▶▶

—Good morning, Salmi.
"Good morning."
—Did you sleep well?
"Yes. Did you?"
—Yes, thank you. Where are you taking us today?
"We're going to the apartment I used to share with my mother, after my father."
—Are you ready to talk about your mother?
Salmi shrugs. The man behind the folding table in front of her thinks the gesture's for him. He looks at his stacks of paperbacks and magazines, as if there might be something he can do about it all, for Salmi. She pays him for a magazine in English, from two months ago. She thinks it might be British.
"Sure," Salmi says. She walks the conversation away from the vendor and his magazines. Off the avenue, she moves between buildings, frozen in their states of construction. Some have exterior walls, glass, fire escapes—they're festooned with lines and canopies of habitation. Others are mere suggestions: metal and concrete cages with their outer tarps rolled up for air, exposing Aeri on the furniture they've worked or traded for, from the carpenters who can make it. They lounge or sit within implied walls, accepting breezes and currents to keep their air moving. Down below, Registered workers in abatement hand things to children as they move in and out of the building, collecting whatever it is the workers are dispensing, like it's candy. Something to hoard. Something useless in other contexts.
There is an empty lot beside this building. An expanse without avenues or edifices. They brought in construction equipment at some point, long before Salmi would have noticed. They moved

it inside the chain link fencing surrounding the lot with its aged green slats, which provide privacy but only in half-effective vertical strips. Salmi sees children on the hard-packed dirt inside, its surface blasted stone-like by the constant sun and the unforgiving stone it eroded from. The children play on a bulldozer, which hasn't moved since it demolished the last of what was here. An actual house, some say.

—Let's go in here.

Salmi moves through the gates. She has never seen them closed. Women beat laundry against a machine with a massive, scooping arm, dull and clean with a slight orange memory of its original paint. Salmi leans against the fence where there is shade.

—Did you come to this place before it was flattened?

"No, I was too young. It's been this way since I came."

—There isn't any Worldview data on this plaza.

"You think this is a plaza?"

—What more do you know?

"They don't destroy things without a reason."

—Do they still?

"When they want more land, yes."

—That construction equipment looks about as old as independence.

"That would make sense."

—Why?

"There must've been something here that was bad for independence. They left the machines like public sculpture and locked The Wall to the foreigners. Some kind of reminder."

The earpiece goes quiet. Salmi watches them in their plaza, splashing in sand like water, in reflecting pools of dirt that intone the old Aeri threat: premature destruction. Erasure. Like the first Unregistered, who just needed work. The first ones at the gates of paradise. Their vast, recordless existence. There's nothing of them left on this dirt.

Salmi looks at things—tries to see them some new way. She is Worldview having a look behind The Wall, paying attention for the rest of the world. She thinks about the foreigners that will see her life here—the rest of it that remains. She wants to tell everyone here to stay away from her, from the things she sees, but she lets them beat their laundry and dodge boys with footballs and run into each other in the bright day to exchange embraces and stories about the samenesses of their family lives. She likes the feeling though, moving like a predator with her unseen lens, stealing things and people for the rest of the world without anyone noticing.

She looks at her magazine, and there is an article about how the global Aeri effort is preparing the world for extraplanetary operations. She reads it slowly. Shared costs, pooled resources. Global innovation to preserve life in an inhospitable environment. Aer will take them all to the stars.

▶

"My father took me to the rock garden many times. Once when I was little, they had just finished restoring the outland saints. The last of them were gifts from international friends, he told me, returning the sarcophagi from the days when the empire held their lands and exported stone shrines and saints to carry Aer out of the capital. Everyone was giving them back to the Ministry of Antiquities. Thousands of them, all together for the first time. Each on its own pedestal, with its own anchoring wires and ready-angled floodlights. The outland saints would be given their own resting places, but not upon The Host. They were filling the entire rock garden. So many of them."

—How long ago?

"Thirty years? More?"

—Where did they move them?

"I don't know. Underground maybe? Nowhere public. Someplace with room for them. My father took me so I would see the old imperial reach, before the empire collapsed, before any of the territories retaliated, but he was there to meet someone and exchange some papers. He told me the story of the saints, and then he was gone, and I was there with the other families, who had their kids. It was bright, and the sarcophagi had been cleaned, and I remember that their stone looked like skin. Some of the sarcophagi no longer held their men, and these were open or had been bored through so everyone could see in, and they were the size of vans to me. Most of the kids played around a popular few sarcophagi, and there were people there with food carts and ice cream freezers, and the adults mostly sat on stone benches near the entrance, or strolled in couples down the unending rows, holding hands, and some people were there on their knees and bellies, praying to this holy man or that. People with old lineages outside of the capital that eventually drew them in.

"Is this story okay? I can tell something else."

—Go on, please.

"I met a little boy named Eswi, who was there because his mother wanted to put her lips upon the sarcophagus of her son's patron, who had left Aer after he became holy and had traveled to die someplace else. There were reasons for this, but I don't remember them. Things his mother told me later, in their apartment."

—You went home with Eswi?

"My father was not around, and it was time for dinner."

—Did you play together?

"We wandered to the furthest rows, where we could no longer hear the buses or the claps and shouts of the other children. We pretended—we believed—the saints were watching us inside their tombs, and we found one empty, and its lid was bored through at the feet. It stood upright, like the rest of them, but it didn't need cables to anchor it in place. We climbed through the hole, wiggling and bracing ourselves inside. I remember it hurt my shoulders, and I thought about this place the first time I saw one of the geckos lose its tail, and it made me cry."

—What was it like inside?

"It was empty. We wanted to talk to him, so we decided that we were saints, too, and Eswi said they put the saints inside without clothes, so we took ours off into little piles with fabric-worn knees and elbows in the dust."

—Did you look at him?

"Yes, I remember the stone-colored finger of his penis. And we stayed that way for a time, feeling what I thought was holy. Then we got dressed and squeezed out. I remember the dust on my skin under my clothes, and it was a cold feeling that was nice in the sun. We played some other game—I don't remember, and then we were with his parents, and the floodlights were coming on because of the evening, and his mother took me with them. Eswi took a bath first, and his mother brushed my hair and told me it was good that I came—that Salmi had been alive the same time as Eswi, and that she had argued with him in a plaza, and he stayed her arrest for it because God was done with using his sons to call out things he thought were wrong and was ready to use his daughters now, too. This woman had only Eswi—no other children, and she helped me in the bath, and the water was cloudy with my dust, then we ate rolls with salted meat."

—How long did you stay?

"She took me back to the garden after dinner, and my father was there, and he thanked her for taking me. That was the Aeri idea, back then, and it wasn't odd."

—Did you see Eswi again?

"No. We returned home, and my mother was smoking on the couch, reading magazines, and my father was having a friend over later, so she made me go with her to the café to *make* a meal—what she called it. Like it was a chore or some service. I read something while they ate, and their friends came to shout and laugh."

—Salmi, what are they doing over there?

"Those children?"

—Yes.

Salmi gives the building beside her a good look. She squints against the sun, and the black around her eyes shifts, like falling plaster, and small segments of it will now blow away in the next breeze.

"They're playing a game."

—With the suicide nets?

"Yes, no one has used them for that in a long time. The nets deter it."

—What game are they playing?

"Suicide."

▶

"This is my old neighborhood. When my mother was alive."

—Where is your building?

"There."

—So far from The Wall.

"Yes, the settlers camps aren't far from here."

—Who settled?

"Anyone. People looking for work after independence. Some stayed after the Registry Act, walking out of these towers and into their shacks. Maintenance staff mostly. The checkpoints coming in from the outer plain weren't around yet."

—Anyone could join the Unregistered.

"There is no identity to being Unregistered. That is its only thing."

—But not any longer.

"No, there are checkpoints coming from the airport. They haven't been there long."

—Do you go to the settlements?

"No, I don't speak all those languages. Owi says it isn't safe."

—Is it safe here?

"Safer than it was."

—Not as many choose to live here.

"Not as many. We didn't choose."

—Someone chose for you?

"They did. This area was where they contained deviants and homosexuals, after they kicked them off the Registry—for being the 'wrong' kind of Aeri. Like criminals."

—Did someone monitor your confinement?

"Yes, in disguises. They looked Unregistered, but we could see them. Mother didn't have any heart for trying to move anywhere else."

—I'm sorry.

"They do what they want. They stayed in places out here, which they kept for things and disallowed any of us from going inside."

—Did you experience any violence here?

"I fell in love. Got pregnant in the end. After Mother died, they stopped paying attention to me."

—And your father never came here?

"No, he was deported entirely. They didn't want him talking out here. That's what people on the feeds say his book says."

—Yes.

"They weren't executing anyone anymore. Everyone was paying too much attention, at the U.N. At embassies downtown. They had no choice."

—Have you read your father's book?

"No."

—You sound very much like him.

"Okay."

▶

Salmi looks at the tower's old office floor, from the stairwell doors. Steel doors with intact windows that swing easily for her. There is only open space out on the floor.

—It was open like this?

Salmi walks into the expanse, trying to remember by footstep how far in she lived.

"There were walls."

—It's been cleared.

"They've been here."

Salmi walks across the empty idea of what might have been her old apartment.

"Mother died here." She stops walking, and there is street dust on the toes of her shoes, and the floor beneath her has been swept.

—What did you do?

"I had a kind neighbor. He arranged people for her. She died angrier at Father than she was at Aer. It was easier."

—What did she die of?

"Some disease."

▶

—Salmi, be careful.

Salmi pulls away the translucent sheeting. There is an apartment of it—the only one on this floor. Four sheeted walls taped to the concrete and the ceiling. Almost just another Unregistered dwelling. Inside is a metal table, and a metal tub, and before she sees everything else, there are men on the floor now, and they're walking across the clean expanse, and they have a woman with them, and she stares with Unregistered eyes, but Salmi can tell she isn't. They shaved her head. Her scalp is too pale for it—a recent paleness.

"Are you supposed to be here?" one of the men says to Salmi.

"I was once," she says.

One of them has a large PVC barrel on a hand truck. There is a hose curled on top of it, and he has a dispensary bag filled with bottle shapes hooked over his wrist. Salmi stares at them, and they aren't all that interested in her.

"Go back out and get a signal," the central one says. "See if anyone cares about this." He makes a gesture with his hand that could mean Salmi or the plastic sheeting or even the entire building. Salmi thinks about her own signal—Worldview's satellites are better than Aer's, she considers. She can hear silent line noise, like pressure, from the tiny speaker in her ear.

"In the meantime," he says to Salmi, "be useful." He takes the dispensary bag from the other man and hands it to her. The other wheels the barrel through the plastic sheeting, and he is a silhouette in there, whatever he's doing, setting the barrel in its place.

Salmi looks in the bag, and it is body wash and shampoo and an artificial loofah sponge. Nicer things than she takes with her to her floor's wash room.

He pulls the shaven woman forward by the wrist and hands her to Salmi. There's nothing in his eyes. Nothing in the woman's. They all stand for a moment, doing what they're told.

▶

"The water is cold," Salmi says, which he interprets as an invitation to leave them alone. He disappears through the plastic sheeting.

—Who is she?

Salmi doesn't want to talk to herself in front of this woman. She looks at the rest of the things inside the sheeting. The table with restraints. The metal tub. A bucket with a toilet seat upon its opening. The cot is low and has only a blanket. She continues draining water from the PVC barrel with the hose. It takes a while to get enough of it into the tub to be of any use. Salmi wonders how they got it up the stairs. She didn't see them outside, and she hasn't been here long. Another entrance? With a powered lift, maybe.

She stops the hose, and then looks up at the woman who is standing beside her. Her hands hang at her sides, and she just stares at things. Salmi has an arm draped over her leg, kneeling beside the woman.

"It's cold," Salmi says.

She looks Aeri. Salmi wonders.

"*It's cold*," Salmi says in English.

The woman looks at her then.

"Fuck you," the woman says.

"What are you even doing here?" Salmi says.

"I don't know."

Salmi thinks about that. "Take off your clothes. Get in."

"I can clean myself."

"They don't want you to, I think."

She just stands there. Salmi imagines it's because she doesn't want to take off her teal jumpsuit, so Salmi undoes the buttons and takes it from her. She pulls elastic bands away from their tasks, and walks her into the tub.

"Please," the woman says.

"I'm Salmi."

Salmi sees the effects of the cold water on the woman's body, how skin takes shape and remakes itself for warmth. But she sits in it and looks at Salmi with large eyes. She has a scar on her forehead, and it is vivid in the light of her scalp. She wraps her arms around her knees.

"Vesse."

►

It is near dark outside the tower. The one of them who walked out earlier, to get a signal, stands behind Salmi in the doorway to the street. Salmi looks back at the building, at its functional doorways, architectural repairs. Upkeep.

"Don't come back here," he says.

She looks at him. He sweats slightly in the evening's leather-hued light. There isn't a breeze to do anything for him.

"I used to live here," she says.

"It's condemned," he says.

Salmi looks at the building.

"What about the girl?" she says. "Do you need me to come back tomorrow?"

"No," he says. "There is no girl anymore."

Salmi turns around and walks away. The settlers have generators, out in their tents and shanties beyond the buildings, and she hears them attempting their work, like clearing throats. Aer sells them fuel, too. It's humanitarian.

"What will you do with this recording?" Salmi says.

—I don't know. It isn't my decision.

"Will you let people see it?"

—I don't know.

"If you give it to Aer before I leave, they may get angry."

—We won't do that.

There is an American smoking against a retaining wall along her sidewalk. This little part of the territory that belongs more to him than it does to any Aeri. The lens makes her feel larger than him. Older.

He watches her approach, but he doesn't say anything. Salmi stops. She thinks about what the lens wants. The way it wants things to unfold for her story. She knows he's American because she looks at photos of Americans as often as she can. It is more difficult to find pictures specifically of Texans. She regards him, forcing him to have something to say.

"Hello," he says. His accent is practiced.

"Yes?" she says.

"What do you need?" he says.

"You're American."

"Yes."

"Texas?"

"Wisconsin."

He smokes, and she waits him out. Waits on his reason to smoke in the gathering dark away from the settlements.

"Do you want some credits?" he says.

She studies the prospect of him. "I have some."

"More is always better."

Salmi thinks about the lens. About her silent companion, and what they're doing together. Taking the Unregistered territory for themselves. Laying claim to it and all the things it permits in the light and the dust. The world she's making here for everyone outside of Aer.

"Okay," she says.

He lifts a brow. "Okay?"

"Yes."

He has a satchel on the pavement by his feet. He reaches into it and withdraws a plastic-looking rectangular panel. The size of a used paperback on a street vendor's table. He turns it over and manipulates its switches until its LEDs glow the way he wants them to.

"Just carry this with you," he says. "When the battery dies, just bring it back. I'm around."

Salmi stares at it in his extended hand. She examines him again and takes the device.

"There is a woman in that tower named Vesse," she says. "A Registered woman imprisoned alone by some men. Her body is not her own anymore, and I imagine someone in the city would like to know."

"Who?" he says. He lowers his arm. "Why are you telling *me*?"

Salmi thinks about the lens in her collar, the recording of her part in this. What she's done with everything that's happened to her. The territory after Worldview does what it will do with these recordings. After she's gone and erased from the dust. Condemned, like her father.

"It's not about you," she says.

3

AMN

They tell Amn after lunch that Lido, one of the other hopefuls to take up God's mantle as a saint, has developed moderate hypertension. God has other work for Lido, and he must continue the desperate tasks of the priesthood. He will maintain the honor, like his brothers, of overseeing the devout, helping them walk their lives through God's metamorphic embrace and into final, perfected form. Lido is no longer a hopeful for sainthood, and thank God that they get to keep him at his important tasks, and Amn agrees that Lido will enjoy a special honor indeed, continuing God's great work in the city.

They tell Amn after lunch that he and Eod are the remaining two hopefuls, and they will now wear appropriate vestments for this appointment until God shall decide through which of them he will speak. Amn keeps his hands still in the dishwater when they tell him that there will be acolytes, who they've selected, to be with him now and keep the record of his days and utterances, should God choose Amn's voice for his own. And Amn understands, except for the part where he must also wear some piece of technology for the task.

He finishes washing the dishes, while his brothers move through their personal hours or recitations or conversations out on the grounds, depending.

There are three of them. One of Dal's rules. There must always be at least three. There will be more, of their own volition once God takes his ownership of the saint. They will follow in their numbers as Amn wanders and talks and observes and teaches them what it means *right now* to be Aeri. That is the way, and they will leave just as gently, like a natural sloughing, if God ever takes his hands from a saint and renders him back to the Aeri. It happens, sometimes—he allows them back into the Aeri tide to become something better than themselves. *Better living through cancer.* Amn has seen that joke on the feeds.

But they start as three. Their hair trimmed, their vestments soft and permeable and woven of space to let God between the fibers. Dal said there should be at least three because Aer was at war then, during his lifetime, and the fighting was close to the capital, and the rebels liked going after priests. If one was injured, one other could stop to aid him, and the third could continue on as tasked. It's just a holy idea now—a way of doing things, but Amn likes its secret meaning. He likes the truth of things.

The technician finishes typing something at his workstation, and he removes the machine's cable tether from a pair of thin, plastic spectacles. He hands them to Amn without speaking. He has some sort of powder—burn powder, Amn thinks—on a reddened swath of his dark arm. Something his skin is doing. The short sleeves of his black polo shirt show some bruising around the veins of his upper arms.

Amn takes the spectacles.

"Doesn't this send the wrong message?" he says. "A hopeful saint with defective eyes?"

The tech doesn't say anything. He goes back to his work at the computer, monitoring the lines and systems threading from his workstation to all the distant digital points of the modern common house.

"It's so the others can hear and see," one of the acolytes says. Amn hasn't learned their names yet. "Just like the nursery—through AerNet."

"Everyone knows it's not for vision," another says.

Amn puts the spectacles on. He doesn't see anything special.

"They aren't functioning," Amn says to the tech.

He ignores Amn.

"He isn't allowed to speak to you anymore, Amn," one of them says. "Here, let me see them. And your phone."

Amn surrenders his things, and the acolyte gets the spectacles to communicate with the data feed in Amn's phone. When Amn puts them back on, his field of vision is alight with clocks and tasks and a map for his guidance. There is an information feed, if whoever needs to send him some directive. He can see that it will take his calls and messages and load the net from his phone.

"You've turned me into a mobile phone," Amn says.

"It's what Aer needs," one says.

One of them is always writing what Amn says. He remembers that from his own time as an acolyte, following Belan. The importance of it.

"Won't the glasses record everything?" Amn says to him. "Do you have to write it?"

The acolyte looks up. "What if they break?"

There's humor to the young man's worry—the technological innocence of it. Amn smiles at it.

"Everything breaks," Amn says.

All three of them write that down.

▶▶

He escapes them, when they are praying, by leaving his hopeful's vestments in the bathroom and running undressed to his room and donning his old priestly garb. He puts the phone and the glasses on his bed, because they can track them, and he slips through the evening doors.

When he reaches the base of The Host's mound, the central plaza opens up, and he sees them gathering, and the rotation sirens bleat their sounds, and the city of them begins the rotation.

Amn moves with them, another Aeri in the streets—their packages and parcels on wheels and strapped in place and some things moved by van services with state dispensation to move at pedestrian speeds through the great mass. Amn doesn't leave the roundabout around the plaza. He stays with the cyclonic stepping as everyone around him shuffles out to their exit avenues, radiating like wind-bent whips from the central plaza. They spend only as much time in the great congestion as they have to, but Amn keeps to it. He isn't supposed to, and it's okay when some people—fewer than usual—entreat him for blessings, and he is mostly praying as he walks, but sometimes the whole of it breaks his concentration, and mundane thoughts enter the dialog. He doesn't get any bad feeling from God about it.

▶

For a time, the massed shuffling carries him near a troop of young women. They move with their arms locked to resist the crowd's shearing forces. They have signs hanging around their necks and across the backs of their shoulders.

WE WERE ALREADY SISTERS
INCENTIVIZE YOURSELF
MY UTERUS IS NOT AERI

He isn't sure what the last one means, but they're chanting together and sometimes laughing, and they lose the rhythm and have to start over. They wear abatement. A few even have their heads covered with pastel scarves. Amn thinks of them this close to The Host, covered up like that, following enough rules not to get arrested. At least until the police care enough to move into the current and shut them up with their machine guns. He and his brothers don't talk about the arrests very much. The devout don't get arrested.

One of the women's signs reads

WOMEN ARE PRIESTS TOO

She wears a camouflaged headscarf, and her jacket, which is cut high and doesn't reach quite to her hips, is fashionable. She has stone bracelets on her wrists, and he imagines her identity: young and frustrated. Bored enough to walk the rotation with her signs from some home that gave her enough Aeri sense that she's still comfortable with the stone, at least as jewelry. That makes sense to her. He imagines her parents answering the call to prayer, when they hear it, hoping she outgrows her twenties sooner rather than later. Amn thinks about the things he thinks he knows about her. About women back during the revolution. How this woman reminds him of them, with their hair unbound, short, flashing in the daylight. In the demonstrations. Fighting and bleeding and making those screams against the occupiers. The thoughts he had about them, trying to ponder God. Before he knew how to be disturbed. Before Belan even thought it was important, dying in a stone box.

He isn't supposed to hope for sainthood. It's better to serve the people. To see to their needs.

He shoulders through the crowd, shuffling in little steps, listening to hymns upon the pedestrian buzz, picked up here and there by people he can't pick out of the crowds. Mostly, he sees mobile phones and people murmuring into their collars and the flashing of the screens and lights beyond the roundabout, along the storefronts, and the glitter of the massive screen on the far side of the central plaza. When did they install that? It's at least ten meters high. And a woman's face is upon it, and what she is saying isn't clear over the multiform drone of the people—their low, buzzing vowel. The sound of things heard in larger contexts.

He reaches the woman with the camouflage headscarf, and he pulls at her shoulder. She glances at him, and then she unhooks an elbow from her neighbor, who looks too, and Amn wonders about her name. Individual needs. Dreams and aspirations and future children or empty womb, and he feels only empty himself. A vessel.

He pulls a handful of meditation dust from his pocket—as much as he can clench—and with his other hand, he opens her palm and packs the handful into it. He closes her fingers over the cascading grains, and it falls in ribbons at its own slow pace. Time suspended by rotation air, for all of them here, doing this slowly because it is the natural pace—the enforced pace—that the whole of them make together.

She looks at her leaking handful of dust, and she is wearing makeup, and there is an irregular mole on her tanned neck, like an uncut gem.

▶▶

His new room has a better view. The window is larger, and it reveals more of The Host and the ascending city districts on the slopes climbing up and away from it. This room has beds for all four of them. They confiscated his standard vestments. He reads Belan's dialogs in a wooden chair facing the window, and it is already night here, in the city center. The districts create their own topaz light, and he can still see the slow curtain of dusk pulling its colors from the outer rim, offering The Wall's old watch towers the last of the sun's thoughts about what's going on in Aer.

Two of the acolytes read Belan around him. Looking for a better idea of what to expect from him, Amn thinks. The other one is in the nursery. Rotations always generate more calls, most of them insincere. Drunk and unimportant. Like it's always some party. Especially the young people. Which, Amn supposes, it is. He remembers hiding alcohol, back during the occupation, since it was contraband. It made them gather in drunken numbers and pick fights with soldiers in the street, which annoyed them. And the only conflict Amn ever joined earned him a comrade's thrown stone to his back. It was an accident, but Amn took it to mean he would enjoy the soldiers' batons even less. He left the fighting to his drunk friends and thought about God instead. He was always thinking about God. It was his greatest interest because it marked superlative experience. There was no perfect flower but for God had created it. No best dream. No woman's flesh. No unreadable map of cancers and birth defects but for God's destination coded therein. Amn stole a kid's crutch when he was a schoolboy because he was jealous of the deformity that required it.

Those calling the nursery tonight will be held accountable tomorrow. AerNet will restrict their bandwidth.

His spectacles crawl with notifications. Topics and conversations among the people that might interest him. Rotation reports. The notifications move like insects, and he's too distracted to read Belan. He should focus.

And then suddenly she's standing in his room—a perfect idea about how a woman might look, visiting this chamber. He saw her face on the large new screen in the central plaza. And then on smaller screens out beyond the roundabout. A woman in her forties, with manicured hair falling on her shoulders, which are exposed, as if to collect the light and the heat. He doesn't see any abatement upon her, and when he slides the spectacles off, she disappears from her place, and she return when he replaces them, with a softness of traditional music behind her.

Amn sees the acolytes pull out their phones as one. Something's got their interest, too.

"Good evening," she says. She stands in a modest skirt that reaches below her knees. Her hands are folded primly over her abdomen.

Amn waits a minute. Is she talking to him specifically?

"Can you hear me?" she says. Her tapered eyebrows lift in the center of her brow, and it creases her forehead.

"Yes," Amn says.

"Oh, good." She smiles and relaxes. Her voice is full and clear. The bones in her face are symmetrical, attractive in that way he liked when he was finally old enough to know it and caught himself looking at women like his friends' mothers or older sisters, trying not to be noticed.

"Sometimes these connections aren't the most stable," she says.

"Are you seeking the priesthood?" Amn says. "You shouldn't contact me on this device."

"No, no," she says, and her smile warms. She wears makeup in a Western style. More subtle than Aeri trends. "My name is Suva, and I am an announcement from the administration. I'm seeking everyone, not just the priesthood. Are you a priest?"

"Yes. You're calling everyone?"

She tilts her head just perceptibly, and it alters the lines of her hair in their clustered filaments. She looks patient to him.

"No, this isn't a call—it's an announcement. Some people are receiving it via their phones. Others are watching on the civic screen in the central plaza. Some, even, are just listening to me on the radio."

"You're a part of this device?" He points at his glasses.

"Yes." He's pleased her by understanding. Her hands come away from her abdomen and rest at her sides. A light he can't see points new wedges of brightness across her dark skirt and her shining blouse, the color of slightly darker skin.

"The software is quite advanced, for wearable interaction. We can talk about whatever you like."

"You're new?" he says.

"No." Her tone makes him uncomfortable. There shouldn't be anyone in this room, and he doesn't like thinking about her. "We just haven't spoken yet through your device. If you're a priest, that doesn't surprise me. My name is Suva, and I'm the director of Home and Family Life."

"What's that?"

She bobs her head a little bit, to make the light play, and to show him she thinks it's all a bit much at once, too.

"It's a new program. I report to the Ministry of Health, and I will be coordinating with State Radio and the church. My team will concentrate on improving domestic living for all of us."

"You're real?"

The acolytes are done with watching whatever version of this came over their phones. Now, they watch him. Amn makes himself be used to it.

"Of course." She gestures with her hands. "This is just a way for me to talk to more people at once."

Another new program. He thinks of the young woman in the rotation, with her hands full of his dust. What the people need.

"We don't need more programs," he says. "People know how to live. We teach them."

"Of course!" she says. She moves herself with the saying of it, but she stays in one place, even if he turns his head.

"Of course," she says. "I'm only here to help. My team will coordinate closely with the church."

"To do what?"

"All of Aer's social programs will finally be in the care of one office: Sisters First!, Aer Together, the Domestic Return—and our new initiative, Faith and Family, which we're rolling out tonight."

"Family used to mean faith," Amn says. "It wasn't programmed."

She laughs. "Oh, I know! Faith and Family will try to get us back to that Aeri idea. We don't all believe the same way we used to in Aer, and it's important to understand how we can share the same values despite this. Now that families are stronger because of Aer Together and the Domestic Return, we think it's time that we take back the purity of the Aeri body."

"That's sacrilege. Only God brings purity to the body."

"Exactly!" she says. "These days, impure bodies get in the way of God's plan. Faith and Family will ensure that it is God's will that changes people's health and not secular poisons like STDs or blood-borne pathogens. By requiring STD examinations for marriage licenses, we can ensure that only those couples ready for God's will can create the new Aer. Clean, they can be ready to be remade, or whatever their paths may hold."

"*Or whatever their paths may hold,*" he says. "More sacrilege."

"Please," she says. "Ask me anything you like."

"I won't ask a piece of propaganda about God."

He pulls the spectacles off. His acolytes are writing and looking at him.

One of the acolytes comes back from the dispensary window for all three of them, following Dal's edicts in reverse. The other two still sit with notepads on their knees, staring at Amn when they remember to. When the boredom of waiting doesn't steal their attention.

The third one brings drinks in pure white cups with cardboard sleeves to insulate the fingers against the contents. There is chill enough, at this hour, that the cups' respiration hangs in the air—tiny cloudribbons climbing from the perforated lids. Like stab wounds in the snow, as Dal described them, on the outer plain, when he watched soldiers die instead of helping them, after the battle, so he could learn what he was seeing. So they all could—those following him around and recording his holy observations. In their too-thin vestments for that time of year. Thin and spindly men, broken men, dying men—men ascending, standing in observation of the soldiers taken early from God's plan, from his hopes for each of them. God has a plan, and men usually get in the way.

The acolytes stare at Amn as he stares at them. These days, they wear windbreakers.

Amn thinks of his mother, searching for the sun, the way she did. Looking up through Aer's haze, even back then, when the occupation trucked trailers and troop transports and officers' cars in loud, blacksmoke conveyances. When the architecture became tanned from such industrial exhalations and God's flesh lost its rosy blush for the bronze it wears now. Or was it a trick of the light? His memory, lighting stones?

She followed the sun, his mother, tracking it around the lip of Aer's valley from the paned window in their kitchen, and she was fond of Western music, which was coming in now through the radio—those bits of it their leaders thought were an okay pacifier. It occurs to Amn that the radio is impartial—an incorporeal voice in the smog. It sings for any state, and his mother never got to hear State Radio when the term meant what it was supposed to.

Amn tries to think of the saints. He tries to summon lines from the dialogs, from the catalog of Amn's lifetime reading—over and over until the bank of words at his cognitive disposal is largely the saints' and not his.

But he doesn't want to, standing in his mother's old kitchen, his new acolytes huddled into the alcove where the old refrigerator was retrofitted into the family house. They stand there importantly, to be the ones that witness God's first full words growing in Amn's chest. The words the first rotation of acolytes wasn't worthy of. The tools and accoutrements of furniture repair are everywhere around them here—the house's new life as a restoration workshop. Amn looks for his mother in the panes of the window, but all he sees is maybe how she viewed the smog. Something between her and the sun. Getting in the way of better ideas.

The bus stop isn't stone. It is, but it's ordinary granite or marble. The columns are, anyway. They lift annealed shingles at angles to keep the sun and the rain off the bus people when they wait beneath. There are copper seats bolted to the columns, which can sit a waiting person on each of the columns' four sides. Like cardinal sentries. The sitting of so many, each in turn at a time for bus after bus. Since independence. Their shared sitting has bodyoiled the silhouette of a torso and a head against each column, where they rested against it, taking a break from their heavy days upon the copper seats while they waited on this route or this route or this route. Making something Aeri, something human, of the foreign stone. The columns were somebody's gift from abroad, celebrating independence. The copper is polished to the color of evening sun from all the bodies upon it.

One of the silhouettes bears a vandal's spray paint. An outline around its body, and lines for an arm, where it would be—an uplifted hand, reaching for the next silhouette. Or perhaps just waving hello.

It's dangerous, creating graffiti.

Amn lifts his hand and waves back, and traffic passes between them in the avenue. His glasses whir with the deciphering of his actions, asking techs in distant lands who it is he's waving at—whom they're recording. Amn isn't sure what to tell them.

"Good evening," Suva says. This time she wears a white blouse and a string of spheroid stones around her neck. Her skirt is traditional, in all the best Aeri patterns, like she bought it from a tourist's shop in the city center.

"What now?" Amn says. His acolytes watch her on their phones.

She gestures with her hands, expansively, and her nails are manicured in some modern style. Amn doesn't think it's Aeri, but he doesn't know for sure with fingernails.

"I'm excited to tell you about the newest initiative from Home and Family Life," Suva says.

"Must I respond every time to prompt your next piece of information?" Amn says. He looks to his acolytes through the glasses for help. "Is this software that crude?"

Suva frowns in her occupied non-space in his chamber. "Would you like some help? I can respond to—"

"Please tell me about the newest initiative from Home and Family Life," Amn says. He thinks of other ways he's used this same voice to deliver blessings or name children or conduct service. He thinks about the similarity of all things.

Suva brightens. Her eyes are dark against her white blouse. "Project Daylight is our new effort to keep up with what you want to see in a safe and family-oriented Aer."

"What I want to see."

"We appreciate the many survey participants who so generously donated their answers to our questions about safety in Aer. Incentives will be distributed within eight days."

"Please tell me more about Project Daylight," Amn says.

Suva tilts her head. She is piqued by her own topic. "Project Daylight enables our dedicated police forces to get disruptive or disorderly citizens off the street without the considerable investment of a Registry hearing. Now, you and your family can count on orderly streets and prompt attention."

"You already do that," he says.

She rights her head and smiles. "Don't worry. We know everyone can have a bad day now and then, so administrative detention under Project Daylight will protect your every right so you can maintain your Registry status if things ever get out of hand. We're here to work together for a brighter Aer."

"I would not like to learn more about Project Daylight," Amn says.

"Thank you for your time, and may God remake you. Good night."

A car explodes in Fifth District, and Amn's glasses fill with streaming feeds of it. Its news and consequences and the interviewees who were nearly injured but weren't. No one was injured by the explosion, and Suva announces that climatologists are predicting an ozone alert today so to please do your civic duty and remain home unless you have essential business. She advises limited exposure to the sun, and the saying of it thins the day crowds by half. Screens and advertisements everywhere display the blinking eye Home and Family Life now uses to indicate a time for vigilance and reportage.

Amn moves with them along the sidewalk, and they leave him to his movement since they are looking at their phones or watches or the augmented images of their content glasses.

In passing buses they watch programs on the backs of headrests, and in the cars and upon the scooters they listen to streams of music and conversation. Building lobbies fill entrances with the programs and updates from State Radio. He brushes shoulders with men in this season's abatement wear and moves past older ones who don't care for fashion incentives and the information they must surrender or the tasks they must complete to receive them and instead move like representatives from the past, re-enacting the independence era for all the watching world. Women move by, girded against the sun, attired and wrapped and abated against their looming motherland. He sees so many healthy. He sees so many cleaned and painted buildings. He looks for the elderly, who mostly keep to their ascension homes, awaiting God, and he won't see them again unless God takes his hand from Amn's mind—if it is even there now. The elderly are what's left of the ascension. The infants and the children and the young parents will live forever. The dissidents who have taken over the plazas, with their demonstrations, will live forever. There is no danger to the imperfect form anymore—no engines of creation to evolve them into God's model. They have taken his tasks upon themselves, and they make healthy infants in the numbers they're allowed to, procreating correctly for the state, earning their incentives, and living for everyone outside The Wall. There is no threat to their existence, nothing to form an identity against. Only the conquering of an angry region and the quietude of its lethal millennia. He wonders if there is enough left of God to even lift the devout unto paradise. It doesn't happen overnight, after all. He wonders if God isn't out of things to say.

He maneuvers through the half-crowds and climbs a slowly spiraling avenue a district away from the city center. He walks on the stone cobblestones in the avenue, and the acolytes do their best to wave oncoming traffic around him. The texture on the newly paved concrete-and-stone composite sidewalk looks like skin to him—its uncountable raised grips like the standing flesh on someone's winter back. The color of the composite is close to the stone's natural hue. The map in his glasses leads him to the clothing dispensary he wants, and the foot traffic is light around him. It is the middle of the day, and the sun falls in even lines between the buildings. Ozone feels good upon his shoulders.

Inside the dispensary, he finds a clothier, who watches Amn like a cosmic event as he works his way between racks, trailing his acolytes.

"God remake you," Amn says.

The clothier stares at him a moment longer, then spares a quick glance for the acolytes, who are as uncomfortable with the situation as he is.

"And you," the man says. He has lost the hair on the top of his head, and the skin there shines from its days in the Aeri sun. He has a mustache, and he is shorter than Amn, with brown eyes. Amn imagines staring back at himself, seeing himself through this clothier's brown eyes, thinking what he thinks standing with one of God's next favorites. How blue eyes are more fascinating in the head of a priest.

"Where are the trousers in my size?" Amn says.

His acolytes take their notes, as if he is uttering the vowels of creation.

"Sir?" the clothier says.

"I am a little taller than you," Amn says. He takes off his glasses so the smaller man can see clearly. "So a size larger."

The clothier appeals to the acolytes with nervous staring.

"The clothes are for you?" he says.

"They are for God," Amn says.

The acolytes stare dazzled, like gazing at suns, struck by the nonsense importance of their hopeful saint's first supernova. They make notes upon notes—what they see and think around them, at this moment.

The clothier gets the trousers and a shirt in blue and white and sneakers that are comfortable for walking, when Amn asks for them.

"I need your card," the clothier says. "There can't be a deficit in the inventory."

"I have none," Amn says.

Amn sees the fear in the man's eyes. Some audit. Some overseer to report to. He's clearly Registered—this job is his hope for his children. Amn sees how alive this makes him.

"I understand what you need," Amn says. He bundles his hopeful's vestments into his fists and shoves them at the clothier. Amn walks back through the clothing racks to the doors.

"Sir, I *need* your card."

"I know you do," Amn says, leading his procession back into the day.

Amn follows a man who is talking on his mobile phone. Amn walks fast to get directly behind him, taking easy steps in his new sneakers. The man is younger than he is, but older than the acolytes. His clothing is fashionable—he has participated for his incentives. They pass a pair of women greeting each other elaborately before a shopfront. A police volunteer watches them from a distance that should be out of frame, if they are performing for a lens. The volunteer looks at Amn as he hurries through the frame, inches from the heels of the man in front of him, trotting acolytes only steps behind him.

"It isn't a problem," the man says into his phone. He moves around people by instinct, without even seeing them.

"It isn't a problem," Amn says, sideways over his shoulder, so his acolytes can hear him. One of them scribbles a note, while the other two steer him down the sidewalk with their hands on his shoulders.

"I'll be there when I can."

"I'll be there when I can."

The man turns to look at Amn, and he's startled to see him so close, so he hurries his step. Amn keeps up with him—he's in good shape.

"Hold on, there is some asshole here."

"Hold on, there is some asshole here."

He stops, and they all stop.

"What do you want?"

"What do you want?"

"Are you an infant? Why are you repeating what I say?"

Amn gives him the blue-eye. "Because they will write it down."

"Why?"

"Because it's important."

"Man, fuck off."

"Man, fuck off." It makes Amn laugh, and he lets the man go. The acolytes scribble furiously. They finally got a live one. Amn is happy for them. Simple young men, getting it completely wrong.

They take his new clothes at the common house and put him back into his vestments. His three acolytes don't participate in the effort, and they keep their eyes averted as Amn doesn't resist the redressing.

The next day, there are five acolytes, and they sleep in an alleyway Amn finds, rather than returning to the common house. He lets them get what they want from the dispensary window, and they charge his glasses with a plug in the window's kitchen. It isn't chilly anymore, and they are comfortable enough, sitting around each other all night.

She is easy for Amn to catch because she is so old. A warped thing. God's better image of a woman. He leans close while she steps along, and he looks like a missionary, in his plainclothes, an arm draped over her shoulders.

After he listens to her, Amn straightens up and turns to his acolytes. "My son is in this district," he repeats. "Can you help me?"

He leads them away from the woman.

"Get away from me, old man."

"Get away from me, old man."

Amn hits that one in the neck with his balled fist. He gives him something to worry about—a reason to be. The police aren't far, and they come when the man shouts for them, and they take Amn by his wrists, and the acolytes intercede.

"We can detain you in Daylight," Amn repeats, when they say it.

One of the new acolytes shows Amn how the glasses can stream State Radio. He sets it up for him, and the visual feeds on the lenses die, and Amn is left with just the sound of it. He listens to the updates from Home and Family Life, the weather, sporting scores from their international neighbors. He gets up out of this alleyway, and they shuffle to their grouped feet behind him, and they walk with the dinner crowds and the bar crowds and the family crowds toward the central plaza, past the groups of chanting youth who sleep now in the smaller plazas, under tarps and canopies they've taken for themselves. Amn has heard people talking about them. No one does anything. Suva doesn't do anything. Outsiders are watching, so the administration is, too. They sleep in the plazas, under those tarps, like the Unregistered. Like refugees, right here. Today, though, they look like they're getting ready for something. All of them. Like they're headed someplace soon. Amn doesn't say anything when he leads his acolytes past them but instead just listens to the radio.

His father hadn't liked the radio the way his mother had, and he'd been angry when Amn followed girls and comrades into the demonstrations. Work would save the nation, not marching in circles, and not listening to outsiders on the radio. There was honesty in masonry, or baking, or butchery. Amn's mother didn't listen to the radio when his father was home at night. She kept it on all day while he worked whatever job he'd secured at the labor lot. They had clocks in the house, but she tracked what time she had left with the radio by measure of the shadows between the buildings. Tracking the sun, as Amn's grandmother had done. And women before her, measuring their days beyond what was expected of their nights.

When Amn gets to the central plaza, police volunteers saunter around, not yet sending people home for the night but having a look at how many they'll be dealing with. There are more of them than Amn is used to seeing.

The radio feed fails, and the glasses suddenly light up with visuals, and the square around him is alive with tags and video windows and scrolling comments in languages he doesn't recognize. He sees the Worldview icon in the bottom of his visual field. Then it all disappears, and the radio resumes. He wonders how he could see Worldview like that. It isn't allowed, but he thinks seeing it would be good for the Aeri. It's what they need.

His father didn't beat him when he announced his intention to become an acolyte. He just left to see his friends in a café, and

Amn's mother turned the radio back on, and they had tea while the Angel of Death whispered the names of the ascended unto God.

There is a pair of abatement workers standing at the gate through the fencing around The Host. One of them is talking with the police volunteer whose job it is to stand there.

The night Amn's mother died, he listed to the radio alone at the table in their kitchen, and he tried to read shadows beyond the window. He was already an acolyte then, and he was waiting for the end of Belan's life. He spent the night of his mother's ascension awake, reciting dialogs to himself, surrendering his thoughts to the saints for succor. And the doing of it broke his sleeping for good.

He walks closer to The Host, and he thinks about climbing those sarcophagi, beneath all the restoration and abatement. He listens to the Angel of Death when she begins, waiting, as he did as often as he could, to hear her intone his mother's name for one of the other women who used it in life. He thinks about what the people need when she says Vesse's name.

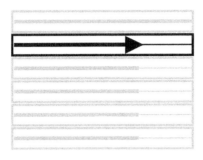

HELENA

Helena can hear her phone ringing, even over the sound of the shower, but she isn't finished. The digital timer in its waterproof blister beside the door tells her she has three more minutes before the water softener switches off and she can wash off all the additives and decontaminants. Helena is probably Bruce's last call for the day, if he's still in the same time zone. He never tells her when he's traveling, only after he gets there. She should have silenced her ringer so she could be in here in peace. She stares through the shower's small window. Another golden day under Aeri skies. Her skin feels slick when she fidgets, as if she's ready to make a mold of herself or tuck her body into a rubber suit. Things that necessitate easy release. Skin motion. The world smells plastic under the water, and she will be Aeri clean once the solutions have performed their work. She saw the instructional media recording for the new chemicals when it arrived in her phone. She watched it that morning so she could get media clearance on her phone. She is a contained world in here. A pure space with fingers and toes and a full range of movement. She contains multitudes.

The phone starts ringing again. She makes sure to keep her mouth closed when she turns into the water, following instructions.

▶

"No," Bruce says, "I can't get you more time."

"I'm making a difference," she says.

"With profiles on tattoo artists? An uptick in twenty-somethings with full sleeves is hardly shaking the zeitgeist."

She has an angry look for her phone. It sits unaffected on her nightstand, its screen hematite-blank, saving its battery while it picks up her voice and throws Bruce's back at room volume.

Helena thinks about how she doesn't want to continue the conversation.

"Come on," he says. "It's out of my hands."

"The tattoos was your idea," she says.

"It was good. Everyone likes the French in Aer. It's adorable. Especially when they come bearing tattoo guns."

"They're not 'guns.'"

"I rest my case."

"I'm not interested in human interest," she says.

"Not that I can grant you an extension," he says, "but if I had nothing better to do than hear this, what would I hear?"

She moves to the window and pulls the curtains away from each other. Their hidden metals weigh like entrails, and they have ranges of motion of their own. Her room is high enough that no one can see her from the street. Not in any way that matters. Her new abatement lotion is still slick on her skin. The application is thinner than standard cream, but it takes longer to dry. A clerk at the dispensary told her about it. She prefers it.

She stands there, drying. Following all the instructions in each of her daily washings and dryings. Ablutions for a day with the stone.

"They're disappearing people," she says.

"What, Registry criminals?"

"No. She's never appeared on the lists. I check every day."

"It's a big city. Project Daylight—"

"Project Daylight people get returned—it's just some stunt. But not the woman I'm looking for. They arrested her and took her away, and she hasn't returned, and I have footage. I interviewed her friend and boyfriend and family. Nothing. It's part of this whole fucking misogynist thing they're doing. And I know she isn't the only one. I think."

"So, what?" Bruce says. "Population and disease control in the most overcrowded city in the world is misogynist? And some woman got lost? Please. Put down the Kristeva. She probably made some kind of break for it."

Helena crosses her arms, and they stick to each other. She uncrosses them.

"There's more to it. I need more time."

"Look," he says, a tiny mechanical man in the room's scrubbed air, "I believe you. Instincts are good, but you're out of time. There are regulations. You can't just stay and cook for as long as you like."

"I'm hardly cooking. I'm drying a second skin as we speak."

"Then turn on the video."

"That's sexual harassment."

"I know. I'll get dinner when you're back."

"Jesus. About that Kristeva."

"Sorry. Hands are tied. Better package everything for one of the others."

"I'm not giving my work to another reporter. They're busy."

"They're supposed to be. And by the way, tech is complaining about long periods with your phone in your room."

"What, when I'm asleep? Give me a break."

"During the day. The workday."

"I like to take walks."

"I told you to drop the tunnels," he says.

"I did."

"Drop them."

"Have I sent you anything about tunnels, Bruce? Christ."

"I'm looking out for you here."

"*Eat a dick*," she says in Aeri.

"*That's* sexual harassment," he says.

"Tell H.R."

She crosses the room and ends the call. The screen on the wall runs a story about young people handing out flowers at checkpoints. The security contractors think it's nice. They have a hard job, and it's difficult responding to the reporters in Aeri. There's a B-roll of the flowers and people smiling in line. Some kids are rearranging abatement tarps in the plazas outside their conversions. It's a slow day.

▶

"Excuse me," the older woman says, "do you speak English?"

Helena looks at her and raises a hand to her headscarf without thinking about it. This one is sapphire-blue and gray, and its lead-fiber doesn't show as obviously as some of her others. She managed a sunburn on her scalp, along the part in her hair, straight through her white scarf. Its watery-red flower print didn't help.

She takes the scarf between two fingers and pulls it a bit over her neck. The older woman and her husband are only two of the clustered people in the elevator, up against the doors, alongside Helena, as fate would have it. The older woman has paid for slightly nicer abatement, as has her husband, whose ball cap bears pins from Machu Picchu and Niagara Falls. Helena doesn't spend the time decoding where the rest of his pins are from. He and his wife both wear networked watches, and what was probably once the woman's wedding ring is now a dinner ring. There are different-colored stones swirling around that central diamond sun, suspended by a white gold tangle of orbits. Stones for her children and grandchildren. Helena knows women who wear them, back home. The Aeri don't wear them.

Helena's own abatement looks even more urbane than this woman's. It's thinner, sewn of newer, denser fibers, and it affords her a plunging neckline, which reveals the cream-colored wedge of her blouse. It's comfortable at this time of year.

"I'm sorry, no," Helena says, with her best Aeri accent. She manages a demure smile.

The older woman pats Helena's arm. "That's okay." She starts looking for whatever it is she wants on her watch instead.

Helena thinks about these two back home, before they came, dutifully attending their favorite Worldview content, talking about the trip, how the Aeri really *are*, with their friends, with their concerned children. About choosing which visa package they should buy.

Helena is the first one out of the elevator, and they all smile at her, every one of the older women, packing the lobby with their husbands, eating complimentary breads off plastic plates. They're just so happy for her.

They sell hat pins of the Aeri flag in the hotel's gift shop. They're among the other things the tourists don't realize they can get for free out in Aer, included with the cost of their visas.

▶

She could've geo-tagged this content from her tablet in the room, and it would have layered itself onto all its predecessors in this precise location, and Content Management would have crawled the data and linked it out to the older content where applicable, and she could still be in her underwear thinking about room service, but Helena wanted to put it here in person. It's an interview with an open-collared young Aeri back from one of those preciously rare study abroad permits. He answered her questions with bright eyes and full-sleeve tattoos of Hawaiian fish—ahead of the French artists Bruce suggested she cover. The new skate park was all business behind him as he talked about the social reasons why he started it: his own little Germany, or Switzerland, or wherever he was abroad when he saw skateboards dazzle the social order. Previously, the park was only relevant to Worldview for its stories about the birds and the first permanently safe place for them to roost, once abatement efforts dropped the radiation levels low enough.

But Helena wants to actually put this story here, the last piece of it. Her week's work. She interfaces her glasses with Worldview, to see the park as the subscribers will, and she grabs the blinking folder of her content in her virtual drive space, and digitally lobs it into the face of an Aeri kid in a helmet and knee-pads, and his expression, coming down the half-pipe, locks him into the story—a cycling animation of his concentrating face is now the QuikLink to Helena's story, for everyone in their morning content scroll, dragging fingers across screens in bed or at the breakfast table or on the train, if they are subscribed to the streams in this area.

Helena puts the glasses away and watches the skaters at their stunts. There's shade here, under these trees, and what remains of their leaves shields her from the sun. She slips her headscarf onto her shoulders, and her flats make simple noises on the sidewalk as she walks. Her slacks catch light in the movement. She passes Aeri women, and they exchange glances, like light from dark places, and the first thing Helena sees on any Aeri woman, after all her time here, is the dark makeup around her eyes. A maneuver against the sun, a tradition preceding the smog. Helena begins every encounter by looking into the darkness.

She wears that makeup, too.

Helena doesn't know how much time she has left in Aer. Worldview assignments, when they come, come in fast. Even Bruce won't know until just before she is reassigned. She only had five days to get ready for the Aeri assignment. Who knows who she replaced, coming here, how long they'd had in the Aeri sun. Maybe too long. Helena had to put everything in storage and sub-let her apartment to take the assignment.

Worldview is expanding its networks in other cities. Recent negotiations with the Riau Islands are introducing the archipelago to the media network. Helena has not yet heard what concessions were granted for cultural sensitivity in private spaces, especially for the majority Muslim demographic. Reporters are being transferred from Brunei for early geo-tagging.

Helena might only have weeks.

She reads the geo-comments through her glasses on the digital space of this hair salon in front of her. She needs a haircut. A night at the club. She could fit into something now that wouldn't make the bouncers hesitate. It's all the damn walking, accidentally getting her into shape. She has replaced most of the clothes she brought with her. She could use a night off, maybe. Some proximity that's based on body heat and movement instead of content and reportage.

She reads the comments on the salon. The subscribers think this one is slightly behind the trends. They watch the streams of people leaving the salon to gauge hairstyles. They can't tell if the

Unregistered who come in each morning are actually styling hair or just sweeping it. There are 10,089 votes for camera installation inside, which is well below actionable numbers.

On the bus, she watches a program on the back of the headrest in front of her. A troupe of Dutch artists are doing an installation with projectors and buildings. Their first few pieces paint the sides of buildings with light and motion, near the city center. They can do abstract shapes and colors, right onto the architecture, as if it were built of stretched movie screens. At night. But in Aer, they're doing recordings of Aeri people, as if they're walking straight up the sides of the buildings, filmed mostly from stationary drones up in the smog, like some Escher painting.

It took her a while, earlier, to find a new flat iron for her hair. The one she brought with her never really liked the adapter she used to plug it in. It finally gave up the effort. Her hair is long enough now, when she irons it, that she can actually toss it over her shoulder. The skirt she picked out has reflective fiber, stitched in places through black fabric, almost like glitter, but something that will stick around. There are older people around her on the bus who don't use headphones, and their phones chirp and squawk at them as they tap through whatever they're watching. Everyone has to hear it.

Helena can see the line into the club before the bus even stops, but she gets off anyway. She could go to another one, but she moves onto the sidewalk and looks at them in line. A hundred or more, sharing things on their phones or laughing and finding ways to put their hands on each other. The man at the door stands without looking at them, like some kind shepherd, allowing them their time out of the pasture.

The bus pulls away, and Helena stares at the line. She thinks about the program on the bus. About drones, deadlines. Relocations.

They're all younger than she is, in that line. She walks on down the sidewalk. There's an observation post not far. It'll be better.

►

Helena doesn't finish pushing the number keys on the security pad beside the door into the observation post before the door opens from the inside, quickly, and swings into her arm. She takes an awkward step on the diamond-plate landing, and planting her foot for balance nearly twists her ankle. There is a peephole in the door they are supposed to check before opening the door for this very reason.

Jeannette rushes through the open door, and she gives Helena a quick look, and she extends an apologetic hand in an odd gesture like she's keeping Helena at bay, and then she turns to jog down the metal stairs. They move a little in their brackets against the building as she goes.

Helena steps around the door and watches Jeannette walk rapidly into the sidewalk traffic. Helena thinks about reasons why she doesn't like Jeannette. She isn't sure she actually had one before.

▶

There is still an active session on one of the two workstations. Jeannette hasn't logged out. Helena glances at the aerial maps on the screen, their random highlighted buildings and rotation routes. It doesn't look like anything. The camera feed from the drone she logged into shows only bus traffic. Its command prompt blinks its eagerness for something to do.

"Jeannette left her session open?" Helena says.

Zach doesn't look up from his screens at the back of the room. He has diagnostic software running, checking on his corners of the network. Including this one, so the reporters can keep at it. Like Jeannette.

"Said she had to go," Zach says. The room is dark except for the desk lamps and the lenses of his glasses, reflecting screenlight.

"Go?" Helena says. "In the middle of a session?"

"Said she'd be back."

"This drone only has twenty-three percent battery."

"Uh-huh."

"Where was she going?"

"A date."

"A date!"

"Uh-huh."

Helena taps the return command into the screen, and the drone shuts off its feed. Back to the roost. She logs Jeannette out of the session without saving.

"What is she even looking at?" Helena says.

"Big places. Conversions and things that don't rotate."

Helena thinks of the map that was on the screen. She thinks of buildings like boulders in the flowing city, resisting the current.

"Did she find anything?"

Zach shrugs. "She had to go."

Helena takes her shoes off when she sits down at the other workstation and surreptitiously undoes the clasp in the waistband of her skirt. It pinches her, designed for dancing, not office chairs.

Zach finally looks up. "Why are you here anyway?"

She watches her screen animate through her log-in.

"Nothing better to do."

She glances at panels of notifications. There are updates from technical producers. Nothing from Bruce. She clears them from the screen and pulls up the index of trending tags. Phrases and locations scroll steadily up and down the index. The userbase at work, deciding what's important in digital Aer. She picks through them—nothing worth noting.

She alters the interface and pulls up the tag rate instead. The content index reorders itself, and the entries start appearing and disappearing faster than she can note them.

"Oh, shit," Helena says. She leans away from the screen. "Are any of the servers refreshing content?"

"No. No outages all day."

"Do you see this tag rate?"

He taps his screen twice and watches what it has to show him. He isn't impressed.

"Tag show," he says.

He taps it away.

"Tag show?" Helena says.

"Did you read your updates?"

"No one reads those. Only you guys."

"Tag show," he says. "Content Management is farming the hits in real time. Somebody's performance."

"What the hell for?" Helena says. "This shit is unreadable."

"Gets the userbase more rewards points—all that content at once."

"So we're just giving away click-throughs," she says. "Marketing's going to love that."

"We can take the hit. It'll only drive down our rates for a little bit. Most of them are just going to cash in the points for extended accounts in the new cities anyway."

"Jesus," Helena says.

"Speaking of," he looks up, "you get your new assignment yet?"

She frowns and leans back into her screen. She pulls a head unit out of the cubby beside the desk. She slides it on, and it cuts him out of her world. The unit exchanges information with her workstation for a moment, then its interior screen brightens. She sees her hands as the tiny lens on the front of the head unit sees them. She watches her hands pull the wireless dongle off the side of the workstation, and she uses it to maximize her view. Her hands disappear with the room, and the scrolling tag rate index fills her vision. She pauses it and pulls up the tag coordinates with the dongle. The system offers her a drone. There are several that aren't in use, and when she accepts the offer, she toggles her screen, and the drone's view of Aer comes awake for her. She can't tell where it is right now—somewhere in the Seventh District? The plaza down there is too full of repurposed tarps and packed young people for her to recognize it—but the drone accepts the coordinates' new course, and the planes and ribbons of Aer at night start unspooling as it goes. People on rooftop terraces sit or stand still around lamps and tables of tea or wine. Car doors hinge open like gills, expelling round-headed Aeri with swinging arms and legs. Police volunteers stop people at check points. Helena looks as high up as the camera angle permits, and she can see the city lights glowing on the bottoms of low-hanging clouds. The drone flies her, and she watches the edges of the city and there are pinpricks of light in the dark towers beyond The Wall.

The drone finds the destination while she thinks about her next assignment, and she isn't paying attention, so she still doesn't know where they are in the city, but the drone hovers, stationary, cutting the thick air with its rotors, and the camera drags her closer, closer to the street, and she can see them standing in line, waiting to get into some venue. She watches them, in their clothes like hers, standing for their turns inside.

Helena pulls up a semi-transparent pastel menu. The people in line shuffle and stand beneath it, just visible through the menu pane. She navigates through the software's many suggestions until she isolates the interior camera bank for this venue. There are a dozen lenses inside—two are offline for maintenance. Helena thinks that's a lot of lenses for a place this size.

She starts with an overhead lens, up among the lasers and gelled house lights mounted to the ceiling. The lights paint stellar patterns onto the crowd, who are mostly shoulder-to-shoulder, and the sudden volume of the music fills Helena's head unit. She decides to leave it as it is. Loud. She decreases the size of the camera bank's interface menu, and she thumbs the unit through the lenses, watching everybody dance and bounce. The sweat of the place speckles bare shoulders and shaven cheeks. The club's lights dazzle them with colors they don't even notice, like living among stars. She recognizes the performer, who calls himself S.H.O.W., which doesn't stand for anything in Aeri. Content Management has been cycling through his junkets for weeks—the hundreds of similar answers he gives for the name's origin. It's something enigmatically English, and he says it only stands for him. He's half-Lebanese, the son of an aid scientist of some persuasion. Helena doesn't remember. His mother grew up an administrator's daughter. Their marriage is the product of family visits to discuss aid allocation, back when. S.H.O.W. is beautiful—smooth and ragged, rapping in Aeri while his DJs spin rhythm and effects, hypnotic things the crowd moves to. Helena watches him through the lens among the stage monitors. He's too young for her taste. She backs out of such a close view and watches with the dancers, packed, listening from the space she borrows.

The drone's icon effervesces into her field of vision, asking if it can move on to other tasks. She dismisses it, and it reminds her to pull up her main menu. She activates the back end of the Worldview interface, and the club fills with ghosts. Faces and tags and looping first seconds of QuikLink videos. Helena watches as Content Management parses S.H.O.W.'s lyrics in real time, writing them large upon the digital scene of his stage, and as he fires off his declarations and indictments—something about the rotations: spin, motherfuckers!—the words spawn related content links. They pull up anything the algorithms can find with keywords that match what he's saying. They pile and layer links in the digital space around him, faster than anyone can feasibly follow. Clickbait. Like spinning some wheel in Vegas. S.H.O.W. performs Worldview's Aer. The digital club is alive with the sound and fury of the users, affixing their comments and clicks to the storm of tags, existing too briefly to do anything but drown in the swell, earning reward points for clicks they're not even fully following. Being there for Aer in its times of need, like now. Helena toggles the user tags on the club-goers themselves, and it festoons the Aeri in the club with everything everybody has to say about them—about their clothes and dancing, the video loops they've recorded, memes already altered and pasted.

Helena toggles the users back off, and she pulls up one of the song's associated stories as it flashes past: a historical narration of one of the statues in the central plaza. She thumbs it away and pulls up whatever else she can, one at a time, as fast as S.H.O.W. shouts ideas at her, and the stories' windows fill her visual field until they are all there is for Helena to see of the place. She downloads them to her workstation and powers down the unit as S.H.O.W. and his posse tell her to go fuck herself.

▶

Zach isn't at his desk when Helena takes the unit off and puts it back in its cubby. His screens are off. LEDs on stacks of thin, dark equipment blink arrhythmically in their recessed shelves. He even turned off his desk lamp, leaving Helena in darkness with a unit on her head, without even knowing it. Her workstation screen brightens when she deactivates the unit's feed. She's seen colleagues come out of the darkness like this before. It can be disorienting.

Helena wonders if Zach was even supposed to be here. Maybe he was called in for one of Jeannette's stupid requests. Helena wonders if they're both just self-absorbed reporters, as far as Zach's concerned. She decides she doesn't care.

The content she opened at the show is mostly uninteresting. Things she's seen a million times—linked stories and interviews and data files that Content Management's algorithms grabbed from the archives like idiot children with reflexes in the nanoseconds.

She should go back to the hotel. They finished renovating the bar last week. She starts to just trash the rest of the stories on her screen, or just log out and let the workstation cleanse itself of her flotsam.

Instead, she drops the links to her phone, logs out carefully, and walks out before the screen leaves her really in the dark. She checks the peephole before she opens the door.

▶

On the bus, coiling back through the districts toward the city center, Helena sees that the glow has changed. The heart of the city, when she sees it downslope between buildings and along intersecting avenues, is no longer warm. The amalgamate amber hue, from so many lights in their varied wattages and tints, always comes back to that same sepia-toned haze. As if there is no color for gathered light but this one.

Now, though, there is frost in the spectrum of the city center. She isn't going all the way to the central plaza, not on this bus, but she catches angle enough at a traffic light to see that the new color comes from the massive LED screen that The Suva uses to lavish the youth with more and greater *freedoms*. Helena can't keep the localism out of the woman's name, now that she's heard them say it. *The* Suva. She's a piece of shit, all right. A polished state head with all the personality of a pharmaceutical rep. Bruce told Helena no when she asked to create a beat just to look into and report on this woman.

Aeri kids don't take a lot of chances, but Helena has seen some graffiti on some of The Suva's posters. And more than one insulting meme. Helena likes seeing it.

She gets off the bus before it starts its descent into the heart of the city. There are too many stops—too much traffic there. It's faster if she walks to the hotel, even from this district. She joins the pedestrian flow, and Suva's cyanotic screen-glow disappears behind a block of residential conversions.

Helena isn't sure if she should go drink at the hotel. She does often enough—most nights—but the staff talk too much because it's a nice hotel, so they're Registered, volunteering themselves in button-down shirts and bow ties for a nicer place or a shorter upgrade wait for the next phone. The Unregistered, on the other hand, mix drinks like monks. Helena prefers them. And anyway the hotel staff know she isn't Aeri, so she might not be able to avoid some grandma's story about the wonders of the rock garden, or the new art installation, or how the priests eat rocks.

Jesus.

She can go to Abao's or one of the other popular places downtown, but she doesn't feel like using napkins printed with traditional Aeri patterns or watching out-of-towners with expense accounts doing whateverthefuck they are for whichever firm, or agency, or interested foreign party. They get too *natural* in that environment, almost like they belong here.

She passes a corner dispensary, and there is a building abutting it deeper into a pedestrian through-way. It has a neon beer sign, complete with glowing palm tree, like some child learned to finger-paint with light. The OPEN sign is in English. She ducks out of the foot traffic, and the door to the place is stiff, misaligned with the sagging stone lintel.

She's the only one inside. Split-vinyl seats sulk around support pillars for the apartments overhead. There's barely any abatement wash on the walls, and one wall is lined with soot-stained stone ovens. Helena wonders how long it's been a bar.

The place is lit entirely by imported beer signs and a pair of screens showing the feeds on opposing walls. Tiny, blue B-lights on a green electric line frame the mirror behind the bar in that sagging, uneven fashion she's seen in any dive anywhere.

She loves it.

She takes a stool at the bar, and a square-faced man in a dispenser's cap and jacket comes through a swinging door and smiles.

"*What would you like?*" he says.

"I speak Aeri," she says.

"What would you like?"

"Nice place," she says.

"Thank you, it is."

His thanks surprises her. "Is it . . . yours?"

He switches back to English with another patient smile: "*Of course not. The bakery was my family's since before independence. I work it now to keep it our home, each rotation.*" He gestures with his head, so she might know there is an apartment *over there.* "*It's better as a bar.*"

"*That's new,*" she says. She pulls a notebook out of her purse and jots the information down.

"*No,*" he says.

She sees a fish move in a small glass bowl further down the bar. She thought it was some floating candle or something.

"You have a *fish?*" she says.

He looks at it, as if to be sure he's really seen it too.

"They put it here," he says, "for an experiment. It has a label on the bottom somehow measuring levels. People want pets again. So."

He shrugs.

Helena stares at it. She's done the same no-pets story as every first-timer in Aer, photographed the same old statues and murals with the same old dogs and the cats that used to live with the Aeri, before the Registry Act and the abatement agreements, when it became just too inhumane to keep pets in this environment.

She's also done the same story about the mass euthanasia the Aeri quietly carried out to comply. And then the reports on the animals that still somehow get in, and starve. Animals go where people do.

"What would you like?" he says.

She puts her notepad away. "Gin martini. But in a tumbler. I hate stemware." She smiles for him.

He gets to work, and she pulls her card out for the tab.

▶

The air doesn't move freely in the bar. Her martini sweats in its tumbler, and she starts to take off her abatement jacket, the way she does in an observation post or in the hotel bar, which is as abated as a fallout shelter. She looks at the thin application of wash on the old bakery walls, and she decides to leave the jacket where it is. Bruce could have a point. Aer still lacks full abatement equity—that story cycles through Content Management about every three months, and Helena has been unlucky enough to draw the assignment twice already. Maybe she really *can't* just stay here and cook forever.

She drinks from the tumbler, and the condensation is cold on her fingertips, but the gin tastes off—almost buttery, the way vodka gets with vermouth. The bartender is back in his kitchen or alcove—wherever he disappears to. Helena can hear State Radio broadcasting headlines, a repeated recording from earlier in the day. It sounds delicate, brassy and airy from whatever radio's under-powered speakers. Helena thinks it's quaint, hearing it like this, as if she's in the Great Depression or something, getting news with the family from the radio, listening for better times beside the fire. She thinks the recording is copper-colored, like everything else is—or was. The city is taking on new colors with its art projects and technologies and pigmented fungi. The screens on the walls, in this room, are silent. She can pair her headphones with them if she wants to hear.

She decides the martini is fine.

She pulls up the bank of content she copied from S.H.O.W.'s performance. Pending assignment transfer aside, she still has deadlines. She thinks about a piece for the tech columns. She can crunch some numbers on the tag show, track the content trails and feed some speculation about the algorithms. Their true secrets are verboten, even to her. They were especially so during her first month, when Bruce thought it was funny to throw her into the tech readers' lions' den with missing information about the algorithms during a particularly uninteresting systems test in the city. The comment grid had all kinds of conspiracies in mind for the algorithms, for the test, for her. Some were convinced that Aer's Content Management was not simply handled by programming routines but by a full artificial intelligence instead. These same users now think The Suva isn't real. They think she is a product of that A.I. and a next-generation animation studio with a motion-capture rig and a warm body. Helena found out the hard way that she couldn't dig her way out of the tech readers' pit with empty promises for more information. There wasn't any.

She pulls up one of the tagged articles on her phone. The algorithms dredged this one up and flung it into the digital clubspace when S.H.O.W. rapped "your fucking flag's on fire" in "Little Hiroshima." It's a reference to Flags for Fuel, when the administration offered *exported* bumper stickers of the Aeri flag, which they bought from a producer in Malaysia, in exchange for donations of gasoline to keep Aer moving during the last energy crisis. Two years ago, Helena thinks that was. She had one of the stickers back home, on the mirror in the bathroom she left to take this assignment. The stickers are still in every hotel lobby and cultural center in the city, where the tourists can get other free baubles for their visa fees and their time in the city.

Helena will have to look up the rest of the lyrics to "Little Hiroshima" later. The article it awakened is about the removal of most of the city's municipal decorations—all the red bunting and building-sized flags. The userbase liked it all for a little while, after the sabotage of the abatement crew on the scaffold, when the world stood behind Aer and governments made promises to take care of the Aeri, to preserve even them—especially them!—in the fight against terror. Who even wanted to blow up Aer? And why? And after the money came through for better security, people got tired of the garish flag all over the place, enshrouding the architecture like some tacky advertisement. The subscribers wanted it gone. Many of the flags were blocking their favorite lenses.

Helena scans the transcript. The thumbnail for the article's QuikLink is an image of a football goal. The netting is patched with a battered flag. Out-of-focus children chase the football away from the goal to the other end of the pitch, which is, in this case, a mostly open plaza between three or four domestic conversions. Helena doesn't care about the content's embedded video or even the live-stream at its coordinate geo-tag. She thumbs through all the permutations of *flag*-ness that the algorithms identified. Nothing here—not for any kind of story she wants to do.

The bartender takes a call on his phone and moves back into his little kitchen for the conversation. Helena hadn't realized he had come back out into the bar. She tries to hear what he's saying, but she only hears basso, thorax noises through the doorway. She looks at the fish, and it does a little twist in its bowl. She imagines it can't pass whatever test they're putting it through. Fish are barely alive in the first place. How much radiation can it really handle?

It reminds her to take another drink of her martini. She looks back at the phone, and she's going to close out the content, and she sees that she thumbed her way into the algorithms' search results for user comments associated with the flag article. The breadcrumbs linking back to the main article hang like a weak bulb in a basement. One wrong click, and she's adrift in the full, unmoderated darkness of the user-generated content grid, with its links and associations to other comments, commenters, conversation tracks, keywords, tags, sponsored links, account settings, and favorites—they all hang from the digital sides of the comment feed, like ligatures stitching it side-to-side with its nearest psycho-somatic neighbors.

Helena taps her way delicately away from the full grid, like probing a flesh wound, and she sees "she disappeared" in the first linked comment. Are they *sexualizing* the flag? *She?* Like, literally the flag—not the whole sexist Nation-As-A-Womb bullshit men have been throwing around for millennia as a good reason to either fuck or kill something, for the national interest. No, if it's the flag, this is some new fetish she could chase for the Afterhours column.

Helena reads the comment's excerpt:

> I watched her every day on the same route. Fucking delicious. Lens-to-lens until they put up the flag in 11th District that hangs beside the stairs down into 5th, and the fucking thing would flap over the goddamn lens, and she literally disappeared. I couldn't find her anywhere on the route…

Helena looks: the user has similarly topical statements in other comment feeds, as well as original content in the user-generated content grid itself. The algorithms stitch together the user's interactions in their progressive inter-relatedness, from content to content, grading the semantic distance from the original "flag" tag in a series of easily recognizable color shifts in the link icons. Helena taps herself deeper into the grid—follows the user one step farther into his own personal Aer.

She lands in what the algorithms think is the root content for the originally associated comment. Maybe they are an A.I., after all. Who knows? Helena checks the breadcrumbs, and she's in a sub-grid under FAVORITES. This one is called ROUTES, in DISTRICTS: 11.

Stitches to other user-generated content line the edges of her screen, indicating this user's proper place in the hivemind. This post reads "My Favorite Aeri." Helena notices there is an adult content filter active on the post. As if that means anything. Anyone can turn them off.

Helena pulls up the content's video. It's a Worldview recording, probably captured on the user's tablet or phone. A public lens embedded in a tree in what looks like a traffic divider shows a wide-angle feed of rows of domestic conversions facing each other across an avenue. This user—what's his name? 0837572oobaby—has laid music over the recording, something ambient and airy. In the feed, people come and go from the conversions in accelerated playback. Some come out and pray together—Helena imagines the call to prayer she can't hear in the recording. Cars, buses, and scooters rush in opposite directions down the avenue. Helena has never noticed how much they actually swerve, going seemingly straight down roadways. The accelerated motion reveals it. The playback slows down as a tiny figure steps out of a conversion and starts down its stairs. 0837572oobaby highlights the figure with a pale circle, turning the figure into a point of light tracking motion through the now-darkened background. By the time the figure draws near the tree hiding the lens, Helena can tell that it is a young woman. She wears full abatement over a traditional skirt. No headscarf. As she moves out of frame, the view cuts to a traffic lens outside the roundabout into a hospital. Helena assumes the young woman is walking sometime in the morning, based on the shadows. She makes her way along the walk tracking the roundabout, and the next cut reveals her face for a few seconds, passing a storefront, and Helena can tell she is beautiful, maybe in her twenties. She has large, luminous eyes and a strong chin. Thick, expressive brows, the way they wear them now. The music swells to accompany her eyes as she looks at the lens. Helena wonders where it is—if the woman can see it. Moving past the crematorium, she appears from behind, a drone-zoom; 0837572oobaby must have had enough reward points to rent some time with one of the public units. Helena still isn't used to so many of them.

When the young woman descends the stairs from Eleventh District into Fifth, a camera beside one of the newly abated pigeon-nesting platforms offers a quick view down her blouse, despite her abatement, and the video lights up with interaction tags. 0837572oobaby's perv friends, getting excited, no doubt. It intrigues Helena how often the woman puts her gaze on the lenses that record her close-up. She has an intense, exploratory stare, like she's looking for something too, watching 0837572oobaby's voyeurism. Wearing it, like leadcloth or abatement cream. Helena watches her at every angle, moving through the city, and 0837572oobaby's music picks up a rhythm, and it intensifies, climaxing when the angle shifts, and she's nowhere to be seen, and a bobbing lens that must be on someone's foot makes the world jump up and down, up and down until it comes to rest behind columns of standing legs—people waiting at a crosswalk, clustered, and the view slides forward, like a predator, and Helena wonders what the fuck this is, and it feels like dark content, like contraband export outside of Worldview's recording licenses and regulations, and the lens slides forward still, like it's stuck on zoom, and it stops between a pair of women's flats, and the buses move through the intersection like blocks of dark stone, and the lens angles upward—is it still on someone's foot?—and now Helena is staring up a woman's skirt, past the rounded territory of dark knees, and the exposure adjusts, and the darkness irises away from thighs, rounded away from each other in even arcs in the woman's crotch. The interaction tags light up the video, and the playback hangs for a moment on the hourglass of cream-colored underwear, and then there is a resumption of darkness, and the woman steps away, and the world goes white with the sudden exposure, and the music relaxes, and the camera doesn't move as its video-world becomes normal with the light, and Helena watches the young woman from behind and below as she follows the pedestrian traffic through the intersection.

How the fuck did this user get someone to take *that* shot? Jesus. Helena makes a note to look into it. She has a heavy, uneven feeling that it must not be an isolated occurrence.

Fuck, these grids need moderators.

The recording resumes following the woman—into a shrine in Second District, and Helena is left staring at the sign explaining the shrine's significance while the recording elapses until the young woman comes back out, and now she has a shoulder bag, and

083757200baby loops the same journey, from the same angles, over and over, tracked, coordinated—an accomplishment, day after day, playing back in increasing speeds until the Aeri flag appears beside the pigeon-nesting lens and it flaps over the lens—again and again, proving 083757200baby's point. A condemnation of the damn flag, and it reminds Helena how she ended up with this content, "My Favorite Aeri," and after the flag appears, there is a semi-obstructed shot of the young woman on the stairs, and two police volunteers ascending the steps in her path, and then the shot is fully concealed, and when the flag moves again, she is gone. The video ends.

Helena taps the video's comment prompts.

—I fucking love her. [083757200baby] I have to meet her.

—You fucking pervert! [bl00s.om]

—Whatever. It's kinky-romantic. [Divers5720]

—Did you ever see her again? Did they arrest her. [Zsmithwow]

—My boyfriend is such an idiot. He would never do this for me. [Divers5720]

—Sicko! Sick, man. [Abbyshere]

—Yeah, she came back like six months later, like nothing happened. Same route started all over. Shorter hair. [083757200baby] I lost her in the last rotation. Why do they even still do that shit? Isn't there enough abatement now?

—Nice vid, man. Check out my favorite. [Charlessssss]

Helena sets her phone down. Six months. Shorter hair.

Like Vesse, off the record but still Registered. Gone one day, back the next. But where? Out of Aer entirely? Who knows—smuggling or something. If the police took this young woman, and brought her back, it was for a point. To scare her? Or for incentives for getting rid of a problem. Handing her off to somebody else. They wouldn't bring her back unless there was a reason.

That's where fucking Vesse is. Disappeared. In-between worlds.

She finishes her martini. She has to find Hem. She has to get out there.

The fish does a twist in the bowl.

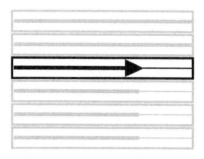

LEVE

Leve watches the abatement workers sweep the goats. The brooms have vacuums hidden within their bristles. The hoses come out the back end of the hollow-bodied composite broomsticks, and they give the workers about a meter and a half of slack and then couple with the vacuum units the workers wear on their backs. The broomsticks will accept all sorts of attachments: higher-powered, narrow-lipped wedge vacuums (which are handy for getting both standard dust and radioactive grit out of the seams in the sidewalks) or rubber-fingered mop heads (which don't mop at all but whose gentler touch is good for plants or clothing) or any number of other oddly shaped but useful modifications. Sometimes, they don't use any attachments at all and just walk around their assigned sectors hosing things up with the broomstick's sucking, uncoupled mouth. Leve supposes they're only called broomsticks right now, when there are broom heads on them. Ordinarily, they are "personnel vacuum units," which sounds like they're for sucking up abatement volunteers.

Leve has no idea what the bristles themselves are made of.

The workers sweep the goats and the horses and the dogs and all those species of birds on the zoo's squat façade. Leve doesn't remember how long ago they were chiseled or sculpted or precisely-what-methoded from the stone facing, but the building used to be some kind of administrative center for animal tributes, sometime when the empire thought it was important to collect animals for reasons other than food from the territories it conquered. The zoo's welcome app on his phone triggered remotely when he and Lana came within range, getting in line for admittance. It said something about "bas relief," which he supposes was the method in question. He thumbed the app away and put his phone in his pocket. He looked at children and their parents in line, ignoring the tourists around them who, in turn, were doing their foreign best not to impinge on the old Aeri tradition of standing in line. Leve wonders if Lana even consciously noticed the welcome app when it interrupted her social posting. She had already let everyone know they were here and had moved on to other pressing phone topics.

The zoo's façade has no abatement because the Ministry of Antiquities worried it would damage the animals. So, they sweep it once a day. It is the least they can do, and Leve never minded the task himself. He hasn't done field work since that day on the scaffold. He promised Lana he wouldn't, waiting with Belan for yet another decontamination shower in the basement of Central Maintenance. It was hard to have the conversation with her. She texted so much faster than he did. He promised his mother too. Dispatch didn't argue when he asked to work in the office instead.

One of the workers sees Leve in line, and he waves his broom. Leve can't tell who it is, behind the respirator and the visor. He just waves back.

▶

Inside, Leve doesn't pay much attention to the animals, what few there are—mostly different kinds of reptiles and a lot of insects in terrariums. There are some horses and a withered elephant in the large, rectangular courtyard. The building itself is just three long corridors intersecting at right angles. Whatever had been on the interior walls, back when they built the place, is long gone. What the walls lack in abatement outside they make up for in here, to protect the animals, Leve assumes. The elephant mostly stands in place and sways in its pen. Leve sees it on screens mounted to the walls now and then. There are special UV-filtering screens over the courtyard, and bright hydrogel tarps at creative angles around the viewing platforms give the area what Leve guesses is a playful, geometric feel. There are some alligators in a pond out there, too, and Leve pays half attention when the shuffle of bodies issues him and Lana past the huge, glassed-in water filter, which the placards and screens tell him is some kind of NASA-engineered reclamation system, originally designed for long-term space travel. It just looks like a system of tanks and tubes to Leve. Lana takes a picture.

Leve looks at the timer on his phone. Getting close. He is nervous. Is this too soon? But his mother said it wasn't. She cried when Leve told her, and she embraced him, and Leve thought she felt brittle. She complained of headaches, later, as they drank tea.

Leve keeps a grip on the wide leather belt Lana is wearing over her dress. It cinches her right around the middle, up above her hips. She's wearing one of her headscarves—a pink one with tiny threaded tassels—as a shawl around her shoulders, and it brushes against his knuckles. She didn't want to wear long sleeves. She keeps clutching it with her off-hand, holding its halves together against her chest. He can smell the perfumed oil she lathered into her hair this morning in the shower. The top of her head comes to just under his chin. Leve hangs on so they don't get separated in the crowd. It's nice out, as things go. She keeps taking photos and uploading them to the social hub. He happens to glance down as she takes a selfie, and there's his face over her shoulder, not smiling, not doing much of anything, bearded these days because Lana likes it. Everyone seems to. He sees beards everywhere now. He watched some talk show half-interestedly with Lana in bed last night, and the women on the couches talked about Aeri headscarves and how they're spreading. Knock-offs are everywhere, but demand is up for authentic ones from Aer, especially in traditional patterns. Women can even wear them in France now if they can prove they aren't Muslim. Leve didn't understand that part. American women particularly like them—the young ones. Leve stopped paying attention as they started taking the opinions of middle-agers on city streets who thought it was un-American.

He looks at a terrarium of toads as the throng stops. He watches them, their backs to the heat lamp as if they're making a point. Giving it the cold shoulder. One changes its angle with a little shuffle, trying to get the idea across. They just sit there, absorbing heat.

▶

"Why do we have to hurry?" Lana says.

Leve maintains a grip on her hand. He drags her more quickly through the crowd. He has to be rude about it, so he decides not to make eye contact with anyone. The tourists, in particular, are sorry they're inconveniencing him.

"I want to show you something," Leve says.

"Fuck, Leve—we'll get there."

She takes heavy steps, trying to keep up with him, her other hand clutching her shawl.

"No," he says. He looks at the timer on his phone. Almost there. He pulls Lana through the crowd at the end of the corridor, before the wall-sized aquarium. An attendant has roped off the viewing area immediately in front of the aquarium's glass, and the dark tile and textured walls here flash with blue-white water hues. Digital placards and app prompts glow like ornaments along the edges of the glass. Fish drift and wiggle and go important places in their NASA water. Leve guesses the zookeepers add the salt back in?

He shows the attendant the app on his phone, and the attendant lifts the velvet-looking rope and lets Leve and Lana pass.

"What is going on?" Lana says. She sounds embarrassed and angry.

The attendant lets a handful of people from the congested viewing mob past the rope as well. Leve hears him tell them to please enjoy themselves and sorry for the delay.

Leve stops in front of the glass and turns to Lana. He takes back his hand and taps the app, signaling his arrival.

Lana has both hands on her shawl now. She follows the other visitors with her eyes, but she isn't turning her head. Giving them the cold shoulder, too. Making a different point.

"Leve! What are we doing?"

He stares at his app.

"Just a second."

"Leve!"

It animates to a different screen, and he sees himself and Lana in it, standing in front of the indifferent fish. The lens recording them must be in the ceiling, over the attendant.

He puts the phone in his pocket. He swallows, and he takes both of Lana's hands in his. She lets him, and the halves of her shawl drift down across her breasts. Her eyes are blue-white, trying to read his.

"Leve?"

"Lana. It might be too soon. But I was thinking. I mean—"

"Leve—"

"What's the point? Waiting? We know this already. We know this. These months."

He lets go of her hands, and she lays her palms on top of each other, upon that skin bared by her freed shawl, just above her plunging neckline. She shuffles her feet, making a different point herself now. The crowd is quiet behind the ropes, and the people the attendant admitted have stopped wandering, and they look at each other, trying to figure out why.

Leve imagines it looks like a regular day at the aquarium, through the lens.

"I want you to marry me, Lana."

She inhales, and her hands go to her face, leaving only those blue-white eyes slick with pure, reflected water.

He pulls the jewelry box from his pocket, and he opens it for her, and that big diamond goes blue-white, too.

His mother didn't understand the ring when he showed it to her. Why did he need a ring? Was it some kind of gift?

Lana cries now, squinting behind her fingertips, and her face is wet with it.

"Lana?"

Shit.

"Yes," she says it so quietly. She moves her hands and she says "yes," and she puts her wet fingertips on his face, and she's shuddering with her tears when she wraps herself onto him, arms taut around his shoulder blades.

She hasn't even taken the ring from him. All the visitors applaud.

He pulls her away, and she puts her hands back on her face, and he pulls his phone out of his pocket.

"Here," he says. "Tell it you said yes."

Lana pushes the waiting button, and the Worldview screen flashes its congratulations.

▶

It's quiet around them at the café. The private dinner was part of the deal.

"How did you get this?" Lana says, looking at the ring. She's already taken pictures of it.

"It's a thing Worldview does."

"Why the aquarium?"

"Their idea," he says. "Part of the thing. The more you agree to, the bigger that diamond gets."

Lana has candlelight in her eyes now.

"What else?"

"Getting married in the rock garden."

"When?"

"I'll have to check."

"We'll be in the feeds," she says.

"I thought you'd like that."

"We should go out!"

"We are out."

"No, no. Let's find a party. It's been forever."

He drinks his wine. It cues her to do the same.

He gestures. "Sure. See what you can find."

She puts down the wine glass and picks up her phone. She taps away, searching for someplace to go.

Leve watches her do it. He watches that diamond. Her hair against her eyebrows. The cavities of her collarbones and the twitching of her neck, in that one spot, her pulse beneath all this flesh. He wishes they were back home.

"They want to talk to you," he says. "Dresses and behind-the-scenes and stuff."

She glances at him and smiles.

"Yes, of course, husband."

He smiles it back.

"Say that in front of my mother, I beg you."

"Never."

▶▶

Leve watches a program about the world's strangest animal species. It's narrated in English—British English, Leve thinks. It seems to take longer to say things in English than it does in Aeri. The script subtitling the narration gets its job done much more quickly than the narrator's rounded vowels and crisp, articulated noises. Leve can imagine this British guy actually owning all of these animals. Like maybe he's some manorial lord—like a *baron*. Leve thinks England has *barons*. Or it did, at least. This guy would talk to his creatures in this gentle voice, strolling his colonial holdings someplace, sweating and looking red for it—out of high-bred character and altogether wrong for his powdery complexion. Maybe a spot of gin and a nice shirt for the evening meal, dining alone, later. Leve has read novels-in-translation about it. It makes sense. The Aeri were doing the same thing, hundreds of years earlier. It's what you did to make sense of the world back then—you just took ownership of parts of it. Leve watches a blind lizard on the screen. It lives in a cave without any light, and it gets along just fine without even noticing the cameras and lights exposing its thin, thumb-colored flesh. Every episode is for a different animal.

"Leve, come here," Lana says. She isn't in the same room.

"What?" he says. He continues watching the blind lizard. How it catches blind insects. It waits a lot, to pull this off.

"Come here."

Leve doesn't want to get off their couch. His couch. The administration gave it to him after the attack on the scaffold. They gave him this apartment, too—last rotation. They have a clear view of The Host here, in the Second District.

He gets up, though, and he walks down the hallway. This apartment doesn't need abatement wash. Or it might, but if so, he can't see it beneath the smooth ivory panels that line every wall and countertop. The windows carry a slight greenish hue, because they are double-paned and filled with gas that filters UV radiation and sound. The apartment is much larger than he needs. He gave one of the bathrooms over entirely to Lana. He isn't even sure who her Sisters First! roommates are supposed to be. They never checked her in to her new place.

Lana is in her bathroom. She has curlers and irons and equipment on the ivory-paneled counter. Hairpins and sprays. Everything is plugged in and glowing and doing its best. She has her tablet propped against the mirror, and it is showing a picture of her own head, interaction bubbles and links and interface panes glow gently, semi-transparently, around the image of her. There is a glowing sphere over a portion of her head, above her left ear, and one of the interaction bubbles is filling itself with text.

Leve doesn't think her hair is really long enough for all this. The tablet is simultaneously playing one of the radio stations she likes to listen to.

"What are you doing?" Leve says.

"I'm going out for lunch with my mother," she says. She works on a clench of hair with her flat iron. She watches herself in the mirror.

"Am I supposed to go?" he says.

"No. We're meeting with some of the Worldview team."

"About the wedding?"

She glances at him now, like he's an idiot.

"Okay, okay," he says. "What do you want?"

"We got a message from Faith and Family." She taps her tablet and pulls up her email window. "It's signed by Suva. It says they're waiving our STD tests, for the marriage, because of your service to Aer."

Leve looks at the email. "I doubt she actually typed that."

"Who the fuck cares?" she says. "Now they aren't going to cram their things into my vagina."

Leve's neck feels suddenly hot. He thinks about it. Now they won't insert a swab into his penis either.

"Yeah, okay," he says. "That's good."

She brings back up the app with the graphic of her head. He watches her read the latest interaction bubble.

"Anyway, that's all," she says. "Good news."

"What is that?" he says.

"It's just a makeover app."

"You don't need a makeover."

She smiles at him in the mirror. "Shut up. They have good ideas."

"Who?"

"Everybody."

▶▶

The cats are no longer in the Christian Quarter. Leve stands there, shielded from the sun by the churches. He looks at where the cats aren't, and then he opens the tin of minced ham and leaves it on the pavement. He stands there a little longer.

▶▶

"I understand congratulations are in order," Dr. Taldi says.

Leve smiles. He smooths his beard without thinking about it. Dr. Taldi isn't Aeri, but he speaks it. Very well.

"Yes," Leve says. He watches the doctor tap prompts as they appear on his tablet. The screen indicates that the link is good. Whoever is managing the simulcast, at the other end of the connection, is doing a fine job.

Taldi holds up his palm to halt Leve as he reads the final bits of information on the screen. He turns to Leve and smiles. Leve hasn't bothered to find out where he's from. They told him not to ask Taldi questions during their sessions, only to answer them.

"I'm sorry," Taldi says. "One more time."

He folds his hands on his desk. Just to the side of the small omni-directional microphone.

"Good afternoon, Leve," Taldi says.

"Good afternoon, Dr. Taldi."

"I understand that congratulations are in order."

"Yes, I'm getting married."

"That is very good news. Sometimes, trauma can get in the way of leading a normal life. Even months afterward, it can linger, causing problems you don't even notice. You can end up leading an entire life in the presence of darkness without even knowing it."

Leve smiles. He is thinking about the lizard on that program. He likes coincidences.

"Yes, I imagine," Leve says.

"Moving forward, getting on with your life is crucial to recovering from something like a terrorist attack. I'm sure I speak for everyone listening when I say how happy I am that the event hasn't left you with a broken life."

"Thank you."

Taldi looks down at his notes.

"I'm sorry to say we can't say the same for your old partner, Belan. He hasn't been as fortunate, has he?"

"I guess not," Leve says.

"Belan still declines our offers for help. I worry that he may be lingering among the shadows you escaped."

"Yeah, maybe."

"The acts of one man may have caused permanent damage. And for what, Leve? How do you think Belan is doing?"

"I don't know. I don't see him much."

"Do you see him at all?"

"He still works in the field," Leve says. "I sometimes see him at the office, before he goes out. We don't say much."

"Why do you think that is?"

"I don't know. I think he's lonely."

"Belan's own relationship did not survive the attack, did it?"

"I guess not. I mean—"

"He is not engaged to be married. He doesn't have dinner or watch the feeds with a beautiful young woman, does he?"

"Well, no—"

"This is what trauma can do, Leve. This is why it's so important that you see me. This is what we're all learning."

Leve pauses. "Yes."

"Are you all right, Leve?"

"Yes."

"In our last session, we talked about your efforts to connect with Belan. Do you still try?"

"Not as much. I mean, I saw him—after. I helped him look for . . . someone, but we ran out of things to say. He just wanted to be alone."

"Well, we still hope Belan will accept our invitation. Belan, if you're listening, you don't have to live in the darkness."

Leve doesn't say anything.

"So," Taldi says, "I understand that you will be at the unveiling of the new rail line."

"Yes, Faith and Family secured seats for Lana and me."

"You'll be in some very important company," Taldi says. "We all know you don't want it, but you're something of a celebrity now, Leve. I think people will be very happy to see you on that train."

"Thank you."

"Last time, we talked about motivation. About understanding what causes our reactions to the events of our lives. Let's talk more about your attacker. What do you think motivated him to use you like that? How did you feel being an element in a terrorist plot?"

"I don't know," Leve says. "I guess he was angry."

"At you?"

"Something like me."

Leve's office tablet gets hung downloading its system updates. He leaves it on the worktable. Other clerks and managers sit around him, sharing the work space. Leve thinks of circles of druids or knights, creating order and maintenance in teams. Making mundane things sacred. Except in their case, it is the reverse. Keeping God normal in all these places.

Leve pours coffee at the station in the next room, where a pair of screens on the wall above the break table show different feeds. Global news, sports scores—one is running a feature on the orphans' league, which brings football to kids without parents. Most of their parents gave them up to the state to stay on the Registry. The kids receive state benefits as citizen-wards. They stay on this side of The Wall.

Leve has heard the story before. He processed most of the work orders for the new chroma-key abatement paint for their underground football pitch. The paint lets the producers insert audiences and advertisements from all over the world into the recordings of the games. For the orphans' benefit, or something.

The other screen shows fire and rescue crews at work on a domestic conversion in the Ninth District. The reporter, a blonde woman, identifies the building as only sparsely inhabited. Its apartments, larger than most, are part of a system of non-rotational housing for foreign dignitaries and official governmental use. The fire appears to have multiple points of origin, and witnesses report a complete AerNet connectivity failure in the area just prior to the sound of an explosion and the appearance of smoke from one of the conversion's windows. Workers on the scene are coordinating with system administrators and network engineers to investigate the possibility of a faulty server. Others are suggesting arson. Police are not answering questions on the scene.

Leve goes back to the worktable. His tablet finally finishes its updates. Leve doesn't care about the details. He swipes the update log from the screen and opens his routing and maintenance login. The program is slower now, after the update.

It lets him into the system after additional updates. He looks around to see if anyone else is having problems, but his fellow druids are all steadily at work.

Leve processes a number of work orders. One of them details the personnel and resources necessary for overnight abatement inspections on The Host. The order has his manager's clearance code already, so Leve adds his and forwards it to the crew manager. Leve doesn't understand why they haven't started overnight maintenance already, when people aren't worshipping or photographing the saints. Some restriction from the church, but the idea must be holy enough for operation now.

Leve notices Belan among the workers who have volunteered for overnight shifts. Leve looks at his name on the list. He likes seeing it in action. As if this is what Leve can do for Belan. As if Belan still asks him for favors, and this is one of them. Leve is pretty sure Vesse is out in the Unregistered Territory somewhere, but he doesn't say it anymore. It upsets Lana. Vesse wasn't very careful. She courted trouble, Leve's mother said.

He approves Belan's assignment. He gives the tablet a solid tap to do it, and it's slow processing the idea.

A courier brought Lana a string of polished stone beads and a set of matching earrings. Classy, traditional. They have a new abatement cream and sunscreen that they want her to wear. It creates swirls of metallic glitter, in places, so she is allowed to wear a dress without sleeves out in the sun today. They provided the dress as well. A slim, pastel yellow affair. As if she makes a better sun, a gentler, more useful one than the fireball up there constantly causing problems.

Lana combed a part into her hair, and she looks like an old American movie actress to Leve now.

He wears a linen-and-leadcloth jacket and a stiff white hat. He feels like an administrator—out looking suave with his fiancée on his arm. Inspiring confidence and service.

Police keep the people moving along the train platform. There are crowds of them, out in the streets, waiting their turns to shake hands with everybody—like Leve and Lana, their backs to the polished train cars. S.H.O.W. is supposedly somewhere farther down the line, with Worldview reporters at his sides. Leve can see the news drones hovering and moving around up over the building-tops. He shakes hands and smiles for pictures and answers questions about terrorists. Lana is demure and charming beside him. Her laugh is musical, like classical chimes—the kind ancient Aeri used in the old markets to identify different vendors at a distance, by tone alone. Lana isn't shy about putting her hands on people. Especially the elderly, for whom her outfit and jewelry are intended. To put them at ease. She puts her fingers on cancers and bad joints as their owners point them out to her—as if they're seeking her approval. Volunteers are giving away samples of the abatement cream she is wearing.

The protest is abrupt when it breaks out on the platform. The steady line stops moving, and people suddenly hold signs and banners—things they unfurl from beneath their abatement wear. The young women begin shouting about their bodies, their rights. SEX IS NOT A SIN, Leve sees. Lana stands motionless, watching the young women as if they're just queuing up for their own chance at a handshake.

The police start the shoving, and the protestors take it from there. An officer starts herding Leve and Lana onto the train with the other dignitaries and public figures. Through the windows, sitting in their seats as if they're merely awaiting an ordinary departure, Leve sees blossoms of tear gas out in the crowds beyond the platform, the ones waiting their turns in the streets. The protestors crowd against the train, and the susurrus onboard is calm. The train pulls slowly away, off toward the airport or some other, safer stop. Leve watches the faces watching him, and Lana is on her phone, posting updates for everybody.

Leve sees Vesse, among the protestors, up against the platform's edge, and she stares at him. Leve mostly notices how much her hairstyle looks like Lana's.

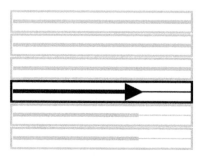

Jego

Jego stares at the massive stone vents atop the crematorium. It isn't far from the ascension hospital, which is only one concentric level down and a few blocks over from Jego's conversion. This building's engineer leaves his maintenance doors unlocked a lot, and Jego found the architectural plans for the conversion online, so it wasn't hard to figure out how to get around the original layout, between walls and along service mezzanines, up to the top of the building. Nedo keeps lighting cigarettes from a pack he found somewhere, but he can't finish one before they give him coughing fits and he puts them out. Dal's mother ascended a few nights ago, in the hospital down there, and today they're moving her to the crematorium, and she will cease to be through the third vent from the right, according to the official managing these things. Dal asked Jego and Nedo not to come to the funeral. They're recording it, the Worldview people who have a lens in his apartment so they can share one woman's path to ascension and the afterlives of her husband and son. Dal has an opportunity to study abroad, when he's older, as an incentive for his father accepting the lenses. The night his mother died, Jego saw on the feed from Dal's apartment, Dal stood in his hallway and threw his mother's antique stone forks and ladles at the lens until some network administrator shut down the feed. They suspended his AerNet access for it. All he has are regular phone calls and text messages right now, if he can get a signal.

He told Jego and Nedo not to come because they were going to ask him to explain his feelings when he was throwing the utensils, after the priest is finished talking.

She was stupid, and now she's dead, he texted. *How's that?*

Jego and Nedo saw the information about her cremation on the feed following her, so they are watching. There didn't seem to be many subscribers to her feed. Jego thought it was weird when they used Dal's mother's real name: Mira. The name of Mother's third daughter, who filled her womb with seawater and gave birth to the first twins. Jego thinks of Dal's mother as *Dal's mother*. Not as some woman with a name. He never really saw mothers using names. Not their own, anyway.

"One of these new saints says we're never getting out of here," Nedo says. "I saw it on his feed."

"The hopefuls?" Jego says.

"Yeah."

"You watch that shit?"

Nedo has a drag of his cigarette, and he pulls it off without coughing. "My mom does. We see it when Dad brings stuff up from the window for dinner."

"Which one of the hopefuls?"

"The really religious one," Nedo says. "Mom thinks he's the one God will choose. That other one is fucking crazy, living out in the street and shit."

"I saw that one punch somebody," Jego says. "Vidi watches him. It was funny."

Jego steps away from the stone barricade at the edge of the flat roof. Most of the radiotrophic fungus is dead and crunchy up here. Maybe cooked by the sun? Jego isn't sure if it works that way, but the stuff is still alive on the sides of the building. Jego thinks it probably isn't toxic anymore, when it's dead like this.

"This hopeful, though," Nedo says, "he says we're never getting out of Aer because God can't see us anymore. That we, like, barely feel him with all this shit all over everything."

"You believe that shit?" Jego says. He looks at Nedo's pack of cigarettes, but he doesn't take one.

Nedo shrugs. "The fuck do you believe?"

Jego shrugs. "Yeah, I guess so."

Nedo takes a turn watching the crematorium. The smog today makes it look dim, translucent, but they'll still be able to see Mira's smoke. They see other smokes all the time, on days worse than today.

"We just end up floating around Aer forever," Nedo says. "I guess."

"Like zombies?" Jego says.

"Yeah, I guess."

"Pretty cool."

They watch for Mira's smoke. It takes a while.

▶

Jego picks up another rock off the pavement. It is a piece of The Wall, in a segment that has weathered poorly and sheds pieces of itself in small chunks. From where he and Nedo are standing, The Wall here looks original. He throws it as hard as he can, and it clears the top of The Wall and vanishes soundlessly into Unregistered Territory. He looks down at the pavement to select another one. A guard with an automatic rifle watches as Nedo hurls a rock of his own, and it follows Jego's over The Wall. The guard turns away and walks a few paces away to monitor something else.

"Have you seen Siou?" Jego says.

"Yeah," Nedo says, throwing another. "What happened?"

Jego's next rock bounces against the rim and clatters down a few meters in front of them.

"One of her mom's friends saw us on the feeds, in one of the drone-shots. Siou was supposed to stay with her neighbors at the rally."

"Busted," Nedo says.

"Her mom suspended the net on her phone for a couple weeks."

"But that was . . . how long ago was that?"

"Yeah," Jego says, "but then she wasn't allowed to talk to me. Siou's mom started monitoring what she was doing."

"Fuck, just for being with you at the rally?"

Jego hurls two rocks at once.

"The drone saw me kiss her."

Nedo turns to stare at him. "No shit?"

"Yeah."

"Yeah, you're fucked."

"So what's she doing?" Jego says.

"School. Headscarves." Nedo shrugs. "I've seen her with some girls once or twice at the dispensary."

Jego nods.

"You just kissed her? That's all?"

"Yeah, on the forehead."

"The forehead? What the fuck is that?"

"I don't know." He tosses his next rock at Nedo.

"Don't throw that shit at me. I'm not the loser kissing Siou on the head."

"Whatever. You haven't kissed anybody."

"You're a fucking idiot." Nedo's expression becomes serious. "Of course I have."

"Yeah, who?"

"You don't know her."

"Yeah, right."

"She's fucking new."

"Yeah."

"How'd you like it?" Nedo says.

"Pretty cool. She smells really good."

"Yeah. You want me to tell her anything?"

Jego looks at the rock in his hand. "Yeah, just say 'hey.'"

"All right."

The guard comes over. "All right, that's enough."

He gestures them away with the muzzle of his gun.

Jego's father tightens the fit of his new hat—he pulls it down a little more snugly onto the ears. Its unbent brim looks stupid to Jego, like a flying saucer or something. Jego's mother adjusts the lay of her shawl. Vidi got it for her, but Jego has never seen his mother actually wear it as a headscarf, only like this, around her shoulders. It's blue and white, and the pattern looks like rivers to him. His mother kisses her fingertips, touches their parcel of exposed stone in its red approval frame, and joins her husband before the heavy front door.

"Get whatever you want from the window tonight," his mother says. "Jego, get something for Ad."

Jego starts to complain, by reflex, but his father shakes his head, so he stays quiet.

"We'll be in Seventh District," Jego's mother says. She looks over Jego's shoulder at the screen on the wall in their sofa room. Jego turns to see what has distracted her. The Suva is saying something, but Vidi has the sound muted. She has her phone in her hand, and she isn't paying attention to any of them.

"Call if you need anything," his mother says. "Vidi has study group, so look after Ad."

He lets her kiss his forehead, and his father gives him a look as he moves through the front door. When they're gone, Jego stands there for a moment. Ad moves soundlessly from the hallway into the sofa room, wearing the content glasses and his giant headphones. He sits on the couch opposite Vidi and ignores her.

"You're not going to study group," Jego says.

Vidi ignores him for her phone. She never talks to the boys in class—only to Samala, the girl behind her. They're always leaning close together and showing each other things on their phones. The boys try to talk to her, but the other girls actually talk back to them, so they leave Vidi and Samala alone, mostly.

"There is no study group," Jego says. "I've never seen it posted."

Vidi doesn't look up from her phone.

"So where are you always going?"

She looks up. Her eyes are bright and uninterested.

"There is a study group," she says. "You're just not invited."

"Why?"

She gets up, and he sees her run her palms over her arms. She does this before she decides to shave them.

"Too young," she says.

"But—"

"I have to get ready." She stands and stares at him as she walks out, like it's an insult.

▶

Vidi is easy for him to follow. She walks slowly, as usual. Jego thinks she does it so people have plenty of time to watch her. She isn't wearing study group clothes—not the way he thinks of them, like what Siou wore while they worked on their fresco presentation, which was mostly whatever she wore to school that day: shirts with prints of her favorite bands or flowers that don't grow in Aer. And jeans. Usually her hair in a ponytail. Sometimes she wore long dresses and bits of delicate gold jewelry on her wrists and around her neck.

Vidi wears leggings with a metallic shine to the fiber. She wears things like this all the time around the house, but those are just black or blue with whatever-color stripes. These, Jego thinks, their father wouldn't like. The way they shine, collecting overhead street lamps and flashes of passing screen-light on the sidewalk, they show somehow *more* of her—contours and movements that Jego watches on the other girls in class and tries not to see on Vidi. He sees the older boys watching her, when they aren't in their lessons or laughing at each other. Her blouse is white, and open real wide around the neck, so she has her headscarf looped over her shoulders to cover all that skin. Jego looks around for police. If her scarf slips, she could get in trouble for not enough abatement wear. If one stops her, Jego thinks he will run up and slap him, and keep running so the officer will have to follow Jego and Vidi can get away, or at least fix the scarf around her neck. Her hair is long, and she has brushed it, so it covers all of her back. Her shoes are bright blue, and they don't have heels so she should be able to run okay. He watches her tap at the buds in her ears, and she walks with her phone in her hands, head dipped forward, looking at it, like she might pray or start crying—he's seen her do it that way before. She avoids other pedestrians like magnetic repulsion, projecting her own field into everybody she doesn't want anything to do with. Jego knows all about rocks that do this, thanks to geology.

The traffic in the avenue gets heavier as they descend through the city. Buses roar past, making too much noise for the speed they're traveling at, which isn't very fast. Scooters swarm behind and around them, symbiotes relieving the bus system of some of its passenger load, and taking advantage of the larger vehicles' displacement in the stream of traffic. Jego knows about symbiotes now, too.

They move closer to their last neighborhood. Jego doesn't remember her going to study group then, either, but he wasn't in the same classroom as her then. Maybe she just misses her old friends. Jego understands.

When Vidi gets on a bus, Jego follows her, but she doesn't look up from her phone, so he moves past her in the aisle and sits further back. There is a police volunteer at the back of the bus, watching everyone get on and off. He looks like he doesn't care. Jego makes sure the officer isn't staring at Vidi, whose head he can barely see four rows ahead.

▶

She doesn't see him when she gets off the bus, either, but he isn't watching when Samala meets Vidi outside the breezeway between two conversions. Her hair is much lighter than Vidi's—blond—but it's just as long, and it moves in the same wind that pulls at a loose hydrogel awning and claps it against its building overhead. Jego notices Samala just quickly enough before she takes Vidi's elbow and turns her around, for having walked past wherever it was she was actually supposed to meet Samala. Jego just turns into the conversion's exterior wall and stares at it. He doesn't know what else to do, and the girls walk past him, uninterested. People bump into him as they walk past. They look at their phones, and he's just in the way. They don't take the same care not to bump into him as they subconsciously do with his sister and Samala. Aeri gems, he thinks, the way The Suva says. Things to be careful with.

▶

He waits a while when they walk into the colonnade—these rows of pillars holding up whatever's going on in the conversion above them. If there were ever exterior walls around the columns, they're gone now, and it reminds Jego of a parking garage, but there are no cars or scooters in there that he can see. No ramps in or out. Vidi and Samala just walk in between the columns, which bulge and contract gently in the warm breeze as the plastic sheeting banded onto them inflates and ripples in the air. Jego can tell the arches connecting the columns are all classical, and it doesn't look like the engineers have figured out how to get plastic sheeting to stay put up there, so it hangs in shrouds from its arches.

Jego sees Vidi and Samala stop just inside the colonnade, and three older boys join them, and Vidi talks to one in particular, and she tucks her hair behind her ears while she does it, and Jego sees her kink one knee, the way she and Ad do at home, on the couch, and she lifts that heel a little off the ground and stands mostly on her other leg. They talk for a minute, and the boy leans his head forward to be close to her ear, and Jego hears Vidi laugh, and Samala and the other two move off first, and it is a moment before Vidi and the boy follow. He takes a hold of her elbow a little bit as he finishes talking, and Jego thinks he's never seen Vidi stand that way, with her back a little arched. They go further into the colonnades, and Jego waits a while before he follows. He finds it pretty easy to follow them quietly, moving between sheets of gently clapping plastic.

He has to wait awhile again when they all stop to unlock a metal door implanted into the stone wall deeper under the conversion. They leave it a little open when they go through, girls first, and Jego stays mostly behind his column while Vidi's boy goes through last and looks around a little bit before mostly closing the door.

He can still hear them, but he can't see them when he goes after, so he uses his phone as a flashlight, and they're in a storage place with old apartment doors and buckets of abatement wash and mops. He can tell they engineered this place exactly how they wanted; in some places the wash-limed stone abuts artificial walls and doorways seamed together from pieces of yellowed abatement panels. Now and then an overhead vent pipes domestic noise from the hallways and corridors overhead. He can tell now that there are more people ahead of him, not just Vidi and Samala and the three boys. Samala's laugh is louder than Vidi's, and she squeals distantly.

After they go quiet, he finds a piece of abatement paneling that has been cut into a door. Someone has taken a knife or a razor to the metallic tape the engineers use to cover the seams between panels, and it created a makeshift swinging door. It's dark beyond, when he opens it, and he takes a chance with his phone's light, peering through, and there's an unabated stone stairway going down in front of him. There used to be something scripted into the arch, but it just looks like lines and curves to him now.

The stairs go deep, and the hallway at the bottom has water running along its flat floor. Jego thinks Vidi probably didn't like this part, in her blue shoes. He can see wet footprints in the somewhat-dry places along the edges, where the floor hits the stone bricks that climb to a low, vaulted ceiling. He hears Samala squeal again, and it echoes down here.

When he gets close enough to hear all of them—lots of them— he can smell cigarette smoke, and somebody's playing some music. Some of that dance club stuff Vidi likes, even though she's not actually old enough to get into the dance clubs. There are little rooms and things off the passageway now, and he steps into one before he gets too close to everybody. They have some kind of lights with them, in the places ahead, and it makes everything brighter for a ways outside, so Jego turns off the flashlight on his phone.

This side-place is like another hallway, a *perpendicular* one, which he learned in geometry. There are holes in the wall up against the ceiling, and the way all the light spills through from the bright area nearby makes Jego think that's probably what the holes were actually for, back when they did whatever they did down here. He isn't tall enough to see through them, but when he holds his arm over his head, he can angle his camera lens until it focuses on the people in the next corridor and gives him an image. He sees them drinking and smoking and kind of hanging on each other. Some of them stand in little girls-only or boys-only groups. He has to try a few holes before he actually sees Vidi, and he can't exactly tell what she's doing in the image, so he pushes the record button on his camera, and lets it run until she moves out of view. He puts his phone back in his pocket, and he goes back the way he came.

▶

They see him pretty easily, back in the colonnade, and these new arrivals shout at him, and tell him to get the fuck out of here, as if he's only just arriving. And some of the boys chase him. He isn't far from his old conversion, so he runs, and he doesn't check to see if he's lost them until he gets behind the drink machine and into the hidden corridors that, here, he has a stronger claim to.

▶

The recording is bright, here in the darkness, and Jego watches Vidi standing with the boy. There isn't anyone around them, and they're holding hands, and their heads are close together. The light makes her leggings look like steel, and he can see her muscles move a bit beneath the material as she shuffles with the boy. He has her headscarf in one hand, so Jego can see a lot of her neck and shoulders. The two of them stand like that until the boy looks up and waves at someone farther into the dark. A man comes close to them. He has a beard and a big jacket, and Vidi's boy says something, and the man shakes Vidi's hand, and she tucks her hair behind her ears again. The man pulls something dark and flat, like a book maybe, or a tablet, and gives it to Vidi, and she puts it in her handbag. The man shakes both their hands again—Vidi first—and he goes away. The boy is very excited, and he squeezes Vidi's shoulders, and he kisses her, and she kinks her knee again. They kiss for a moment before he leads her out of the camera's field of view.

▶

He checks before he goes, since he's here, but Vesse is still not in the apartment. Jego watched for weeks before he gave up, and then they rotated, but he never saw her come back. He thinks they broke up. They didn't make Belan rotate, probably because of the terrorism and the scaffold. Belan just called a lot of people and cried some and then watched feeds on his screen. For a long time. Jego got tired of seeing it. People came over sometimes, probably to cheer him up.

There is somebody in there with him now—another man. He has a dark beard, like the man in the recording of Vidi, but it can't be the same man—Jego got here too fast. He wonders if his dad ever grew a beard. Jego will probably grow one as soon as he can, like the older guys in the classroom. Belan and the man are talking, leaning close on separate couches, and Belan is mostly listening, but he nods a lot. The bearded man has a nice watch, and Jego thinks he should probably get a nice watch, too.

He goes home, before his parents get back.

►►

It is easy for Jego to find the device in Vidi's room. He checks the desk drawers first—opens them with his fingers carefully on both sides of the drawers to pull them evenly without creating the squeaks or groans or whatever-noises they may be accustomed to. The chipped paint is almost the same brilliant color as his classrooms always are, painted and repainted so often, in sedimentary layers, as if the building's engineer is trying to create stone himself. The desk fights him for the drawers, then relents, and Jego pulls them open with a quiet dragging sound. He checks all three drawers, but Vidi doesn't keep much in them—he finds a cigarette lighter, but he leaves it in place. He listens for anyone outside her door with one ear; he wears one of his buds in the other ear, which feeds him his phone's audio recording, where he left it on the floor outside the bathroom door so he will hear if Vidi is coming. The sound of Vidi's shower sounds almost like static to him. Like the noise his mother sometimes plays from the machine that helps her sleep. He had to listen to it a lot when Ad was younger and fussy, and the sound in their room is all that could calm him down and make him sleep.

Jego looks at her handbag on the bed, and he doesn't move for a moment. His mother told him to never look into a woman's handbag without permission. She was serious. His dad said not to bother even when they say it's okay. It's never worth it. The handles on her handbag are cracked and split, in places, from her hands' constant grasp, or the way she slides her arm through and carries it on her shoulder, and its shape is mostly flat, like some sort of preserved lung or a canopic bladder, which Jego knows from Egyptology. He still doesn't quite understand why the pyramids are such a big deal. Most of his friends don't either—or they don't care.

He pulls Vidi's handbag open before he changes his mind, and the device is right inside—smooth and light. When Jego looks inside, he sees mostly pens and sunglasses and tubes of lotion and cream. He tucks the holy items back inside and takes the device and flees Vidi's sanctum and leaves through the heavy front door in the first of the many movements and maneuvers it requires to get to the conversion's roof, where the day is clear and the smog seems mostly like an idea, hanging where it hesitates in its usual invasion of the city. The crematorium moves bodies unto God, over there in its place, and the city center sounds not unlike Vidi in the shower, an amalgamate susurrus loosing the secrets of traffic movement and the heavy machinery maintaining their cultural birthright.

Jego tucks himself into the shadow of what he thinks used to be some kind of observation post. There are stone scars under the dead abatement fungus, where other lookout spots look like they were shaved clean off the roof. He pulls the device out from under his shirt and turns it over in the light. It's plastic, most of it—black plastic and a few tiny chrome screws. There are unshining LEDs on it and a pair of simple buttons. Someone created a label for it with a piece of masking tape and a marker. Jego isn't sure what it says. It's in English, with some Aeri script, but there's a little drawing of a star on the label, inside a square, and it reminds Jego of the flag.

He pushes one of the buttons, and nothing happens. When he pushes the other one, he feels something click inside the casing, and it vibrates slightly with whatever it's doing. The LEDs come on after a few moments, blinking and stuttering in alternating red and green flashes until they settle into some kind of pattern they like that doesn't make any sense to Jego.

He flips it over and examines it again. It doesn't do anything else.

His phone vibrates a notification in his pocket, and he pulls it out with one hand, the other still confoundedly holding the humming device.

His phone informs him that it has linked to a new network, which irritates Jego because he has turned network notifications off on the damn thing a million times. It forgets every time there's an update, and he has to reset the fucking preferences. Except this network has a strange name, and his background apps are closing themselves down. Jego looks at it even more closely, and he can't read the network name any more than he can read the label on the device. It only takes him a moment to flip the device over again and examine the label and realize it matches the network. The LEDs blink their strange language at him. He sets the device down

gingerly and takes up his phone in both hands. It auto-plays through
a video of something that looks like news: chopped-up recordings
of The Suva and a woman out in the Unregistered Territory in
handcuffs, wearing a teal jumpsuit. She has short hair, like a boy,
and a pair of security consultant-looking men in body armor have
her by the elbows, and The Suva's talking about Registry crimes
and temporary detention—has he heard this speech already?—and
the video of the woman isn't very steady, like someone's zoomed in
on her through a phone, and when they cut to a different recording,
when her hair is longer, Jego sees that it's Vesse, and he nearly drops
his phone. He thinks this device might be the administration's, but
why does it have English on it? His heart beats faster, and what the
fuck is Vidi doing with this thing, and who was that man who gave
it to her, and he should probably tell Belan, right? But what if Belan,
like, turned her in or something. He might turn Jego in, too. The
video shows lots of other people in teal jumpsuits doing different
things, until the video says something about the *truth*, and it ends,
and his phone starts downloading a new app, and Jego decides he
should push the buttons on the device again, or maybe throw it off
the roof, but he recognizes the Worldview logo on the new app, so
he waits. It opens a series of search boxes, in Aeri, tagging content,
and Jego looks at it. Is this fucking *Worldview*? The *real* Worldview?

He stares at the screen, and he thinks about his father telling him
women's handbags are never worth looking into. He doesn't really
mean to start browsing the app, but his fingers start manipulating
it of their own volition, like they do with every other app he never
thinks about opening but finds himself looking at anyway. Images of
Aeri landmarks, rotation maps, performers, and pictures of people
he doesn't recognize. Everything blinks and animates, inviting
him further into the content and promising connections with
like-minded users everywhere. He has to keep dismissing prompts
to comment threads and user-generated content banks. It's all in
Aeri, though some of it looks weird, like it might be translated or
something. He thumbs away radiation maps and profiles of people
who have ascended, and he sees a flag with a data stream in the
corner of one search pane, and it tells him that there are three souls
in the crematorium right now, and Jego looks up, and sure enough,
there are.

Everything seems still. He looks over the barricade at the edge of the roof, but he doesn't see any police or anything. People are just walking and driving like normal. He doesn't even hear any sirens on the wind.

He sits back down with the app. He isn't sure what to look at. He pulls up a pane labeled "mass," and it suggests interactions with the protest at the train opening or data about the last rotation. He searches for "Suva's rally," and there it is—a world of things about that day in the central plaza. He searches again for "kiss," and he scrolls past the dozens of tiny windows that appear until Siou's red dress catches his eye in one, and he taps it open, and he watches the drone watch him kiss her, and he didn't realize at the time that the wind had moved her hair that way, and banks of archived data line the recording, and he sees interactions that call it romantic and sweet and pathetic, and a recorded voice says something in untranslated English, and he can hear people around that voice laugh, like they're an audience.

The Aeri recording, on the social hub, that Siou's mother saw, didn't have any of this extra stuff. It was just a recording, among others from that day. He stares at it while it replays, and they laugh over and over, and he wants to see Siou's hair move that way himself, next time, and there would be—there would have been—a next time without the recording that got Siou in trouble. That fucking drone. He was going to kiss her for real. He was going to see if she would unbutton her shirt sometime, somewhere alone where he could hold onto her, after they'd gone together for a while.

Fucking Worldview. Watching Dal's mom die. Watching him kiss Siou. He wonders if they've watched Vidi do anything. What if they saw her get this thing? Jego decides it's better that he has it. He can get away from cops better than Vidi. She doesn't move fast enough, and he doesn't want his parents to see her in a jumpsuit behind The Wall someplace.

He follows a prompt deeper into user-generated content, and he sees long write-ups and montages of particular people doing things in Aer, like they're being followed, and he goes deeper, and he sees some porn links and window recordings, and he'll probably check those in a second, but he gets down to a phone search with lists of known Aeri numbers, but there aren't that many listed, and he realizes he's not in the Worldview app anymore but some kind of custom browser, and it keeps masking the addresses in its navigation bar, and he can tell it's wiping its cache and probably swapping out his network I.D. because it keeps flashing as it reloads, and Jego already has some apps that do that for looking at porn and stuff.

He types in his own number and searches, and he sees a double-layered window showing the results he's found, which are the results he's found. He's looking at his phone as if he's eavesdropping on himself. As if he's hacked his own screen. He quickly types in Siou's number, and the app searches for her, and the results show a game on her phone flashing through different bands she can listen to, and he knows that game, and he knows which band she will choose because he knows her favorite, and he watches her choose it. And she gets a notification for a message from one of her friends, and it is somebody asking if she's going tonight.

Jego watches her read it. Going where? Going where?

The image closes on itself, the customized browser animates away, and Jego watches the app uninstall itself, and it finishes with coordinates and a timer counting down. They learned coordinates in geography. He puts them into his nav app, and it's the central plaza, right at The Host, and his calendar shows him which night it's counting to, and he creates a reminder for himself and checks his history, his downloads, his active apps for any trace of anything, but there's nothing. He looks at the device, and it isn't blinking anymore, and it doesn't vibrate inside when he lays his fingertips on it to check.

He thinks about Worldview. He thinks about that site, watching Siou's phone. About how he can see what she's doing and there's no record of it. How she could see his, maybe, too, if he showed her how, and her mother wouldn't be able to see evidence of it on Siou's phone. Will the device reactivate for good, or is it only temporary? Does it really matter, as long as it keeps telling him when it will come on again? They could create a schedule, a special time just to watch each other. Maybe send messages. He looks at the device. Some kind of piece of Worldview, beyond AerNet. He thinks about its timer and he'll have Nedo get Siou to the coordinates on time.

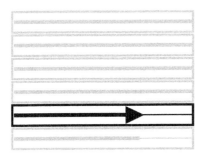

SALMI

"Who are you?" the woman says.

Salmi holds the tarp into her apartment steadily aside. It creates a triangle of space between her and the woman standing in the corridor. Owia is laughing at something next door, and the noises of the feed on Owi's screen sound like underwater voices.

Salmi looks at the woman. She isn't Aeri, but she almost looks like it. Her hair is dark, and she wears it short, like the Registered women she sees in magazines, but her skin is the color of pale tea, and her accent is Western. The woman looks at her phone and glances past Salmi into the apartment.

"Jesus," the woman says. "You're lit up like a Christmas tree."

"Aeri don't say Jesus," Salmi says. She doesn't think she could get past the woman and away from here without being grabbed, if she needs to. If this has something to do with her story. What she's seen.

—Keep her talking, Salmi. I'm trying to figure out who she is.

Salmi looks at the scarf around the woman's shoulders. "What are you doing here?" she says.

"Can I come in?" the woman says—Salmi thinks they're about the same age. "I just want to talk."

"Not yet," Salmi says.

That seems to surprise the woman. She holds up her hands, as if Salmi has a knife or a gun. She has her phone in one hand. Her nails are painted.

"There was another flare yesterday," the woman finally says.

"I know." The woman in her earpiece told her this morning.

"When that happens, Worldview engineers have to do signal sweeps to reconnect to many of their devices."

Salmi doesn't say anything. She holds the tarp steady.

"I know how to do that, too," the woman says. "My produ—someone showed me how to do it."

—Her name is Helena Villarreal, Salmi. She is a Worldview reporter. She isn't supposed to be here—she's transferring out soon.

"You're not supposed to be here," Salmi says.

"No, but I don't think you are either."

—Let's see where this goes.

"You're trading signals with Worldview satellites." Helena's hands are still up. She points at her phone with the fingers of her other hand. "I can see it. You're all alone out here."

Salmi makes room for Helena to come in. "All right, come in."

Helena lowers her hands slowly. "I'm not alone. Just . . . just in case you're thinking of taking measures."

"*You* came *here*," Salmi says. She doesn't really want Helena standing in the corridor any longer.

"Yeah, still. There's someone who can get the word out. If necessary. If something happens to me."

"Where is she?" Salmi says.

"He."

—Tell her to come inside, Salmi.

"Where is he?"

"He's around."

Salmi thinks this is odd. "Why bring him up if he's not here, too?"

Helena cocks her head. "You don't watch many feeds, do you?"

Salmi gives her a flat stare.

—We should get her out of the corridor.

"Well," Helena says, glancing around, "if you did, you'd know to always leave your whistleblower behind, in case you don't show back up."

"Okay," Salmi says. "You should come in."

"That way you can't get us both."

"Come in, Helena," Salmi says.

"You know my . . ." She takes a breath. "Jesus."

▶

It only takes Helena a few steps to explore all of Salmi's apartment. Salmi doesn't say anything while she explores. Helena glances at her. "You don't wear abatement," Helena says. She looks at the small rack holding Salmi's books and magazines. Salmi has nearly filled it. She started buying them when Sarah started giving her trade credits.

"I have some," Salmi says. "But we don't need it as much, inside. These buildings are metal and concrete."

Helena picks a book up off the rack.

"The Wall," Salmi says, "is abatement, too. The new parts of it. It keeps God mostly in the valley. Did they tell you that?"

"No."

Helena looks at the bookmark in the book. "You haven't finished this?"

It is Salmi's father's book. Sarah got it for her because the American feeds will probably ask her about it.

"No," Salmi says. She gestures for Helena to sit on a thin cushion.

"You should," Helena says. She sets it down and sits. "It's important. It's why I first became interested in Aer. In college."

—Go ahead and tell her.

"I know," Salmi says. "My father wrote it."

Helena exhales quietly. "Oh my god."

Salmi doesn't say anything.

"You're Salmi?"

"Yes."

"And you're linked to Worldview?"

"Yes."

"Why?"

"I won't be here much longer either."

"I don't understand," Helena says. "Is . . . Worldview sending you someplace?"

Salmi waits, but her earpiece is silent. She glances at the spotted girders in her ceiling. "How much do you want me to tell her?" she says.

Helena's shoulders tighten. "Who are you talking to?"

—Anything you like, Salmi. This is your story. We have Helena under control.

Salmi gives Helena her attention. "Worldview are doing a story."

"About . . . you? Here? They're watching you *here*? Fuck." She stands up, but she doesn't move toward the corridor.

Salmi points to her collar. "There is a lens here. The story is about my emigration."

"They're recording out *here*?"

"Everything I see. Before it's time to go."

"And right now?"

"Right now."

Helena squares her shoulders. Salmi wonders if she will run.

"Does Bruce know I'm here?"

—Tell her to sit back down, Salmi.

"They think you're ruining the story," Salmi says. She gestures to the cushion. "Please."

Helena lowers herself onto the cushion. She looks at Salmi as if there is a disease on her face.

"Why did you come here?" Salmi says.

"Jesus, we aren't supposed to *be* here. It's in the international charter." She slides the scarf off of her shoulders and bundles it on the floor. Her skin looks polished to Salmi, bare. Like stone.

"I think they have permission," Salmi says. "There is a charity who are helping me move to Texas."

"Texas? But why—"

"There is a man in Texas who has sponsored me, for administrative reasons. Anyplace is fine."

Helena uncrosses her ankles and leans back against Salmi's wall. She bends one knee and drapes her wrist over it. "Well, I'm fucked. Being here, on your lens. So, what the hell—I might end up in Texas, too."

"Do you know Texas? A city called Frisco?"

"Everybody knows Texas. It's huge. I think I have cousins down there. But I've never heard of Frisco."

Salmi doesn't hear Owi's screen any longer. She wonders if they're trying to hear her conversation.

"I see. And you work for Worldview?"

Helena sighs. "I did. I don't know anymore. They don't like it when we break the law."

Salmi looks away from Helena. "Do you think she is unemployed now?"

—She is part of the story now.

Helena cocks a slim eyebrow.

"I think it's up to me," Salmi says. "Would you like some tea?"

▶

The flame from Salmi's can of gelatinized cooking fuel is thin and blue. Her teakettle is the only piece of stone she owns. It is inlaid in the handle. It was her mother's.

She offers Helena one of her cigarettes.

Helena looks at her for a moment before it makes her laugh. "A cigarette in the Unregistered apartment of Salmi, Samu's daughter, over a pot of tea. Anyone in the world would kill for this story."

"Not anyone."

Helena takes the cigarette and Salmi's lighter.

"I should be recording this," Helena says.

"You may if you like."

Helena coughs. "I was kidding."

Salmi taps her collar. "I have worn one of these everywhere—even to the toilet. I have gotten used to it."

"I think your recordings will be heavily edited," Helena says.

"So I don't care what you record with your phone."

▶

"I came because I am looking for someone," Helena says.

"How did you get here?"

Helena adjusts the angle of her phone, pointed at Salmi.

"There are tunnels. Less trafficked anymore, it seems, but you can get in and out. Slaves used to move through them."

"Oh, those. I thought they were closed."

"Some of them," Helena says. "Worldview doesn't want us talking about them, but, I mean, we've been trying to get out *here* for years, and now here you are. A walking, talking exposé. Who knows? There could be tunnel tours in a month."

"The administration will tell this story," Salmi says. "They're doing something for a famous activist's daughter to improve their image. I'm sure it won't be an exposé."

"Then why do you cooperate?"

"It's just part of the arrangement. It is my role to play."

"What was it like, growing up with him?"

Salmi takes the kettle off the flame and sets it on the concrete. She tucks the puckered lid back onto the can, and it snuffs the flame.

"He was opinionated and talkative. But I didn't grow up with him."

▶

Salmi stands and rolls up the tarp over her window to let some of the cigarette smoke out. She hears a helicopter somewhere. Owi taught her to recognize the sound. The air is dry, and she pulls her long hair into a fist and lifts it off her neck. The film of sweat on her skin feels good now.

"Who are you looking for?" Salmi says. Her earpiece has been quiet for many long minutes.

"A young woman," Helena says behind her. "Someone the police abducted."

"For what?"

"I don't know exactly. Official reports are hard to get. Probably for being young and angry. For being a young and angry woman."

Salmi turns around and settles her hair over one shoulder. "Why would that matter?"

"You need to get out more."

Salmi stares at her.

"It's—sorry. It's just an expression. A joke."

"Not a good one."

"No, not a good one."

"You think I know where your friend is?" Salmi says.

Helena studies her. "I've seen recordings of her—and others— out here."

"Yes. They bring them sometimes."

"My friend," Helena says, "the one waiting for me, he knows where some of their buildings are—where they take them."

"Yes."

Helena looks down. She studies her painted nails in her lap. "There are people out here—foreigners, I think—who are creating their own net. A real one that lets Aer out of its cage. It shows people things, about Aer—things they don't know about themselves. That the rest of the world knows. I don't know what their plan is, but they're getting into the city, into the demonstrations. They're getting their signals and stories out. I think some of them recorded her. There are things that people like them can do, with a signal like yours."

Helena looks at Salmi's collar. "They can tell the truth."

"You think they are around me," Salmi says.

"They can find you. Just like me."

Salmi thinks about everything she's seen. Everything she's shown them. All the images and lives she's taken ownership of with her lens. With her constant companion, following her everywhere Salmi thought to go. Everywhere she went to get them out—to get their story out. Beyond The Wall. Beyond Aer. As far as Canada, where her father told his own stories, which aren't her stories. As far as Texas, where they're ready for her. She thinks about the eyes she carries. An inhabited body. A way to put lenses where Worldview couldn't get them before. A way to get a new story, for their watchers. The people that pay them to pay Aer.

"What will you do if you find these people?" Salmi says.

"I want to tell her story. Outside of this place. I want to find out what happened to her. What happened to Aer. I think these people can help me get that story started—they can help me get the userbase asking the right questions. Lots of questions. It's the last important thing I can do here."

"They already found me," Salmi says. "I thought it was a coincidence."

"Worldview creates coincidences, Salmi."

"What was this woman's name?" Salmi says.

"Vesse."

Salmi touches her neck. She rests her fingertips in the hollow of her throat, so close to the lens in her collar. A piece of equipment the size of an early-stage tumor that she keeps warm and secret while it develops its story.

"Many of them probably carry that name," Salmi says.

Helena stands and joins her at the window. She takes Salmi's unpainted fingertips in her hand. "Have you seen any of them?"

"One of them."

"Will you help me?"

Salmi moves to the small chest near the mat where she sleeps. She pulls out the device the American gave her, the day she told him about Vesse in the building. She never returned the device when its lights stopped blinking.

▶

Helena and the American speak English too rapidly for Salmi to follow their whole conversation. But she stands with them in the gathering dusk, and the American keeps looking at her, and she understands that the new device he gives Helena carries a date inside it. A time when Helena must be at The Host, if she wants to get her story out. She can send most of her material about Vesse to the device beforehand, in case there is a technical error as Helena gathers her conclusion. The American promises Helena that she will find her missing friend.

▶

Helena embraces Salmi outside the old building, where her escort will take her back underground and into the city.

"I'll look you up in Frisco," Helena says. "We have more to talk about."

Salmi smiles, her arms at her sides. She feels as if the embrace is not hers to return.

"Your story will be more important than your father's," Helena says.

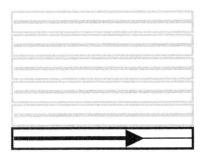

ASHA

Asha leaves the kid standing by himself, apart from the other onlooking demonstrators in the plaza. The kid can't be more than sixteen. He stands dutifully while Asha walks back over to his commander. Other demonstrators cast sidelong glances at them, but they've stopped their yelling for now, and one of them with some speakers—big ones, like something borrowed from a club—turned off the music when the commander marched unflinching into the plaza and yelled at him to shut it off. They all stand around now, watching the police and posting things on their phones. Like Asha and the others have broken up a party and not an ongoing protest.

"Well," the commander says, "take off your helmet. I don't want to record this."

Asha pulls the new standard-issue helmet and visor assembly off his head, and he switches off the camera that streams what he sees to . . . wherever. He's glad to get it off for a minute.

"The kid doesn't know much," Asha says. "The victim apparently sexually assaulted a woman at another demonstration in a different plaza. The attackers were female, about ten to fifteen of them. No one tried to stop the assault, and no one even seems to have any photos or recordings."

"That makes them all accessories," the commander says. He looks down at his tablet and tracks his finger across what looks like a map of the plaza and the surrounding avenues. Asha watches the other volunteers in his unit as they move around and talk to the demonstrators. A few are recording the surrounding alleyways, their hands clamped on the sides of their heads, palming the lights mounted on the helmets to life so they can see who's doing what in the darkness.

"The women apparently shouted about justice," Asha says.

"May have been," the commander says.

When Asha's unit left, to answer the call, there were twenty other demonstrations in motion at plazas around the city. They had doubled, and it had only been a couple of months, it seems like.

"Anyway," the commander says, "where'd they get off to?"

"The kid says they ran in a group down that alley."

The sergeant looks and consults his map. "That one doesn't go anywhere. Dead end."

"No one's inside the building."

"That's because they're under it. Or were. Motherfucker."

"Sir?"

The commander slaps the tablet against Asha's chest, who takes it reflexively.

"Put your helmet back on. Fuck, we need to change the plan. After we get him to the hospital, anyway."

Asha follows the commander over to the victim, who is laid out in loops of his own blood and teeth on the pavement. Asha can't tell if the sound coming from the man's gaping throat is breathing or choking.

"Asha," the commander says, "pick up his jaw."

▶

They pass two more plazas, each with its own demonstration, on their way to the hospital. Asha watches them through the darkened window as they roll along the avenue. The siren, mounted somewhere up among the ambulance's emergency lights, bleats at the motor traffic, and people in cars move lazily to the side, wherever they can find someplace to pull over—onto the walkways, mostly. The scooters don't stop. They pull away from the buses they have been swarming and weave their ways through the pedestrians on the sidewalk. They do it in streams, tire-to-tire in line, like a burst vessel or a busted valve, flowing along the path of least resistance. The domestic conversions towering over everything flash in the emergency lights, like some festival strobe, like they do downtown sometimes. The new digital screens on the sides of the buses paint the conversions' lowest floors in slow, fluid shades of light, glowing their advertisements and programs onto the bleached architecture—brilliant white, when the sun's out, with some new abatement Asha isn't even keeping up with.

The demonstrators in this plaza watch them go by, their faces clownish and staring in the colored light. Eyes upon eyes that flash in the darkness, staring at the ambulance as if they're starving. Some of the young men are shirtless. Asha sees bare women's arms everywhere. The thuds of their music reach him beneath the siren. They've pulled down hydrogel sheets and abatement tarps from somewhere, just like all the others. They've created walls and enclosures throughout the plaza with them. It's theirs now. Some of them sleep in there, in each tarped-off freeholding around the city. Doubtless, they know who's in the ambulance. Word travels fast.

"Commander," one of Asha's coworkers says, "should we pick up a couple of them? Take them with us?"

Asha doesn't know this one's name. He's new—young. Someone else with the connections it takes to get into service.

The commander looks up from his tablet. The assault victim bleeds on his gurney between them. He isn't making much noise beneath the oxygen mask they cupped over the chasm of his broken mouth. The commander doesn't look at the victim. He studies the demonstrators.

"No," he says. "Not at random."

"Sir?"

The commander goes back to his tablet. It makes his face glow when he looks down. Dispatchers deliver clipped squelches of information over the radio. Asha watches the radio receiver's readouts, up on the dashboard, slip between digital and analog operation.

"Worldview is watching a lot of them," the commander says. "Ever since the train opening. It's this 'Stand With Aer' thing. Users pick demonstrators and follow them through the drones and . . . all the other lenses. They rack up points. They make a bunch of noise if theirs gets in trouble. We have to ask IT who's arrestable."

Asha's young coworker spits on the floor. He scowls.

"Fuck's sake," the commander says. "Don't spit in the *ambulance*."

"How are they tracking them?" Asha says.

The sergeant taps through the reports on his tablet.

"Phone numbers, we think."

"How—"

"Do I look like fucking Worldview to you people? Just . . . *sit there*."

Asha sits there.

▶

There are new murals on the side of the Civic Center. They are giant portraits of old Aeri emperors, painted with shades of some reactive paint that glows in black light. All of the floodlights along that wall have been replaced with bulbs that make the paintings light up. During the day, they just look white and gray, like the sculptures the artists used as models.

The commander scoots out of the van first, directly through the assault victim's blood, where it is still warm between the grooves in the rubberized flooring. He ordered Asha's young coworker to follow the victim into the hospital and report if he found out anything. The kid took the task seriously.

"Thanks," Asha says to the driver, who didn't have to give them a ride from the hospital. It was out of his way to Central Maintenance, where they could properly scrub the vehicle.

The driver lifts a hand to wave, but he doesn't turn around. He's looking at something on his phone.

Outside, Asha watches the other volunteers in his unit shuffle away, toward the city center. He doesn't envy them the walk.

"Come on, Asha."

▶

The commander unlocks an aluminum cabinet door recessed into the hallway, and inside Asha sees at least a dozen shotguns. Their barrels look a little shorter than he's seen on the feeds, and there are small, tubular lights affixed to the undersides of the barrels. The commander pulls out two and hands one to Asha.

"Give me your helmet," the sergeant says.

Asha hands it over and watches the commander tuck it into the cabinet. The commander shuts the door, and it beeps as it locks. The hallway is lined with identical cabinets. A hundred at least. Down here, in the mezzanine under the Civic Center's primary basement, Asha can't hear anything except the flow of air. Even the overhead lights are silent.

Asha looks at the shotgun.

"Don't worry—they're nonlethal rounds."

"Why?" Asha says.

The commander gives him an odd look. "So we don't kill any of them. At least not on purpose."

"No, I mean—"

"Because they're getting too far underground. Come on—you'll see."

Asha follows him down the hallway and then down a half-flight of stairs into a sub-basement. He recognizes the area where he watched them examine Vesse for her baseline data, back . . . whenever that was. He would need to look at his duty logs. They pass rooms with chemicals for outbreaks and what looks like an emergency hospital room. There's a wing full of unopened doors, and he recognizes a radiation symbol on the lintel over the entryway. The open door looks like it's about thirty centimeters thick.

The commander leads him past dozens of uninteresting rooms and offices, until they reach the end of a hallway, and a door flanked by a pair of caged work lights stops them. The commander punches a sequence into the number pad, and it unlocks for him with a thud. He turns on the light attached to his shotgun, so Asha does too.

"Here," the commander says, reaching, "different channel."

He changes the settings on Asha's receiver. It doesn't make any suddenly new sounds. It hasn't made any sounds in a while.

The commander adjusts his own receiver, then leads Asha through the doorway and into a stone corridor. It's old. Empire-old, Asha thinks. A pointed vault gives him just enough room to walk fully upright. The apex, though, brings the stone close to the sides of his head. There are more caged work lights at hip-height about ten meters ahead. The stone floor is flat and dry, and metal conduits carry cables, he assumes, at different heights along the walls.

The commander moves past him, and they walk in silence. The rubber soles on their boots don't make much noise on the stone, and it's a while before their receivers chirp with news about an arrival. People in locations with operational names Asha doesn't recognize give status reports. Everything seems to be all clear, according to the conversation.

The commander stops at another locked door recessed into the wall. Asha can see where the stone was cut to accommodate the new hardware. The adjoining arched vault indicates that some kind of passage has been here much longer. The door opens on heavy-duty hinges, and the commander steps aside.

"Check for activity," he says, gesturing with the barrel of his shotgun.

Asha looks at him for a moment. He isn't used to patrolling or investigating without knowing what he's getting into. He walks through the dark doorway, gun-first, and there are no lights on this side. The stonework looks the same, but there is a trickle of water running underfoot. He looks as far as his light will reveal, in both directions, and then steps back into the original corridor. He is aware of his heartbeat, and he doesn't think he's as tactical in his movements as he's seen on the feeds.

"Nothing," he says.

The commander reports no activity into the ghostly communication channel, and they move on. They find no activity at six more junctions, each just as far apart.

"What are we looking for, sir?"

"Anything."

The final doorway, after Asha has become fully bored with this assignment, leads them onto a metal stairway that descends into a large chamber. Stonework pillars support a bank of vaults in the ceiling, and metal service doors, like those they've seen already, plug passageways on every wall, at the tops of staircases and beneath them. A semi-circular passageway the size of a bus gapes in the largest adjacent wall, and Asha sees traffic stripes painted onto the floor in here. There are at least two dozen other police volunteers milling about the pillars, some standing and smoking, some looking at phones that don't seem to be working, and some that look just as clueless as Asha. He doesn't recognize anyone.

"Wait here," the commander says. He goes to talk with a cluster of officers all tapping and staring at the same tablet.

Asha waits there. His receiver tells him arrivals are inbound.

He hears the vehicle approaching before he sees the spill of its headlights. It sounds as loud as the train, tossing its noises around inside the tunnel. Everyone in the chamber turns to look as a black SUV emerges slowly from the tunnel in the adjacent wall, tucked neatly between the traffic stripes. A foreign security consultant in black body armor gets out of the passenger seat and confers with Asha's commander and his group. He has two pistols strapped to his belt. He nods when he's satisfied with the conversation and goes back to the SUV. The commander waves Asha over.

"We're going to escort the administrator and his family back to their home," the commander says.

Asha doesn't say anything. He stares at the tunnel, and he thinks about how far it has to go before a car becomes necessary to get through it. Back to their home from where?

A middle-aged man gets out of the back seat and speaks with the security consultant. He's wearing beige slacks and leather shoes without laces. His arms are tanned under his white shirt, which has a collar and short sleeves. He wears a nicer watch than Asha has ever seen. A woman gets out behind him. She is younger, maybe thirty, and she slips a thin abatement jacket over a shirt with finger-thin shoulder straps. Her shoulders are as tanned as the man's as she covers them, and her hair is trimmed close to her ears, the way all the young women are wearing it now. Her jeans are tight against her legs, and the rings are large on her fingers. She reaches back into the SUV, and Asha looks away as she bends over to retrieve something. It takes her a while, but she comes out with a toddler—a little girl—she situates on her hip. A young boy bounds out after her wearing neon green shorts and rubber slippers. He has a towel around his shoulders, and he's clutching a phone. He stands behind the woman and begins immediately tapping the screen.

"Let's go," the commander says. The SUV is loud as it pulls out behind them and heads back down the tunnel. Asha's receiver says something else about other arrivals, but he can't hear it over the noise. They move through a doorway and into a corridor that is lit warmly by overhead steel fixtures. There's soft music in here, piping in from somewhere.

Asha follows the commander. Behind him, the administrator's phone rings.

"Yes," he says, "we've just arrived."

Behind the administrator, his wife tells her son to keep up.

"I understand," the administrator says, "but listen: how recently was the pool cycled? We were just taking Juro to the beach. They have a nighttime thing, with lights, that brings crabs out or something. I promised him a swim."

Asha wonders how long ago it was when the empire was large enough that it contained beaches.

▶

Asha hears the crowd long before he sees them. It sounds like they walk directly beneath them and through another door and up a staircase onto the bottom floor of a conversion. The tile here gleams, and there are other police volunteers standing around and at least six security consultants standing at the reinforced glass doors that lead to the avenue. Asha doesn't see any of the crowd up against the doors, but he sees them out in the street. They're standing around differently here—not the way they do in the plazas.

A balding man in a suit, shorter and older than Asha, walks quickly up to the administrator, and Asha and the commander follow the family into an elevator.

The small man whispers into the administrator's ear, who listens dully. The elevator is lined with mirrors. When the administrator finally nods, the small man leans around him and looks up at the woman.

"I'm so sorry, madam," he says, "but the directive came down. We've had many of the shades pulled, and all the screens have been on for months, but there are drones in the crowd, and we need them to think to see that your family is living here in Aer."

She smiles at him. "It's all right, Ad. I spoke to some of the other wives. We understand."

They step out of the elevator, past a number of other brass-numbered apartments, and Asha goes last through their front door, into a luxury hallway of paintings and brushed-nickel fixtures. The family moves off and into the noise of an apartment seemingly occupied. The small man turns to the commander.

"Thank you. That will be all."

The commander gestures Asha out. Asha can finally hear the crowd's chant. They say *Rotate!*

"Plenty more where they came from," the commander says. "Not a word."

"Well," the senior clerk says. He closes out Asha's file on his tablet and folds his hands on top of it. "I think everything here is in order."

Asha smiles at him. The man has vivid red veins on his nose, and his teeth are stained the color of corn. The odor of his last cigarette hangs in the air. The one he smoked during the interview.

"Excellent," Asha says. "Thank you, sir."

The man pulls off his glasses and wipes them with a handkerchief. "Please understand it will be some weeks before everything gets processed."

"Yes, of course," Asha says.

"You mustn't stop volunteering for the police. An interruption in your service record could be disastrous."

"I understand."

"In that case," he extends a hand—Asha sees spots on his knuckles that are already mapping the man's ascension—"please give your father my best."

Asha shakes his hand, his fingertips along the man's cancerous future, like some sort of fortuneteller. "I will, sir—thank you. I look forward to getting started."

Asha leaves, past the senior clerk's burdened book shelves and over-decorated walls. He moves away from pre-revolution photographs and trinkets from times before anyone measured their radiation. Asha looks back, and the clerk is smiling in his tomb.

The secretary doesn't look up from her tablet as Asha moves down the hallway. The door to the office has a frosted glass insert, and Asha thinks it looks like a private eye's door, and he thinks about working here, like putting himself into a time capsule.

Outside, there are demonstrators in the small courtyard. This one is smaller than others Asha has seen. The young men kick a football between them, and the women sit around a stereo, smoking and sharing their phones with each other. A few are having a discussion, and one of the men is saying something loudly with a book in his hand. Asha can smell the remains of their lunch in a pile of discarded dispensary cardboard. None of them look at him as he moves through and onto the avenue's walkway.

He goes through a checkpoint with only one guard, and the young man doesn't even ask for his identification. When Asha gets off the bus, outside his conversion, he stops in the dispensary on the corner for a few bottles of beer and a chocolate bar for Nisa. When he thinks about it, he can't think of anything other than the assault on the rapist that's been much bother in the last few weeks. They haven't blown up any more cars. The rapist probably deserved it. Asha feels glad he didn't survive. He thinks about Nisa and Mir. Fuck that guy.

With everybody watching so much now, Asha wonders if they'll even start enforcing the Domestic Return again. Nobody's bothered since they all took to the plazas to have arguments and give speeches and talk to the Worldview lenses. Asha has even seen Worldview people going to meetings in the Civic Center.

Anyway, being a clerk will be better. He can't take many more curb-stompings, and he doesn't want to be the one to eventually kick everyone out of the plazas.

The screen on the fridge tells Asha that Nisa has turned Mir's monitor over to the net. The app briefly fills the entire screen and shows him Mir's temperature, heart rate, and other numbers that he hasn't learned to decipher yet. The tiny adhesive pads Nisa adheres to Mir's wrist to collect and transmit the data are in a drawer next to the sink. Mir's fever is gone now, and the app tells him she's asleep, so Nisa actually pulled it off. The app blinks Nisa's profile image at him, identifying her as the one who handed the monitor over to the net, as if absolving itself. Then the app minimizes away. His program resumes on the screen. A program on the engineering marvel of an Aeri rotation—the planning and schematics and software support behind it all. He scrapes the last of their evening meal out of the dispensary's cardboard, into the waste basket. The cardboard has to go in the recycling bin. But not until he rinses and collapses the containers. There are bright, graphical stickers on the recycling bin reminding him to do so. He might have a beer when he's done. Nisa is probably with her phone in the bedroom.

"Hey," she says, behind him.

He turns, and she has a thin, lace headband across her forehead, keeping her hair out of her eyes. There is a small stone pendant in the center, and it looks at him like a little eye. He hasn't seen this before. She has drawn shadows around her eyes with a makeup pencil, and her lips looks a little chalky beneath their gloss with its stone glitter.

Asha lets the container rinse itself, and he hears the tiny compressor in the filtration unit under the sink whir awake, on duty. He looks at Nisa's garment. It doesn't look Aeri. It's black and sheer, and he can see through it but also not. He sees the teardrops of her breasts, their altitudes over her ribcage, but he can't see her nipples through the fabric. The straps across her shoulders are just strings of small stone beads, but that's okay. It probably doesn't weigh very much, and it only reaches to her hips. She isn't wearing anything else, and he lets himself stare at the packed mound of her pubic hair, pressed into shape by a day beneath her underwear.

"Whoa."

She smiles. "Stop washing the containers."

He stops. She comes a few steps forward, and he can see a silver adhesive pad on her own wrist. She touches the screen on the fridge, and his program disappears into Nisa's health profile. Her heart rate is slightly elevated. She taps at the displays prompts until it pulls up a calendar, and one of the days—today, he guesses—is blinking. A few days before are glowing gently, too. She points at it and turns a coy expression on Asha.

"Know what this is?" she says.

He closes the space between them and puts his hands on her hips. "Today?"

"Ovulation," she says.

He lets go of her. "You want to get pregnant? Again?"

"Don't you?"

"Sure," he lets her press herself against him, "but the whole administration seems to be hung up on cutting it out."

She kisses his chin. "That's not for us, babe."

"What?"

She drops her voice a register. "That's for the other women. Not volunteers' wives or administration families."

He doesn't fight her. "That's not true."

"You know it is."

She leads him into the living room. The screen on the wall lights up, transferring Nisa's health profile, trying to be helpful. She presses the pad on her wrist, and the screen goes dark again. Only the amber city lights through the window light the room.

"Is your health profile up on Worldview?" he says.

"Who cares?"

"That's . . . private."

"It's just numbers, Asha. People help you plan things."

"Did they plan this?"

She gets on the couch and rolls her eyes. "Are you kidding me? Get the fuck over here."

He pulls off his shirt and walks to the couch.

"I mean it," he says. "They might not let you keep a baby."

"Yes, they will," she says. She opens her legs on the cushion. "Why do you think I put my numbers online?"

He pulls off his underwear, and she points at the window. "Close the curtains."

"No one can see us."

"Don't be indecent."

He closes them. Their abated weight brings them heavily together. "I can't see."

"You know where I am."

He gets to the couch, and his hands follow her as she climbs on top of him.

"We need a lamp," he says.

"No, we don't."

She lifts his penis into her, and he thinks, somewhere, that she might have used a lubricant.

"Is this. The best position?" he says.

He gets his hands back onto her in the darkness. After a moment, the dim light from the screen's standby indicator on the fridge glows onto the stone on her forehead, and it's all he can see of her.

"It doesn't matter," she says. There is a breath between them. "We're just getting started."

Asha can hear them, but he can't see them yet. They're working their way toward the city center, from the adjoining districts. The other volunteers report in from farther out, tracking the crowds as they move—serpentine flows of protestors. A slow human avalanche collecting everything in the street and streaming it in Asha's direction. He listens to the updates on his receiver. Suva has been able to keep their demonstrations out of the central plaza so far, with tepid support for their peaceful demonstrations, as long as they stay in the smaller areas, away from most of the monuments and traffic routes. Suva's threats of arrest in the central plaza have not been empty. This is Asha's third shift in a row, collecting those who are bold enough to bring their protests into the tourists and the old people going about business as usual around The Host and the common house. He's handed more detainees over into the backs of vans during his last few shifts than he has during the whole of his time as a volunteer. Security consultants and extra police volunteers move around at the edges of the great plaza, ostensibly to keep them all at the edge, when they get here. Asha doubts it will work. It sounds like *a lot* of people. The first of the evening's violet shadows appear in the corner-of-the-eye places around him, between faithful on their knees, praying, and on the shoulders of rented abatement jackets protecting foreigners who are busy experiencing Aer. They seem undisturbed to Asha. He looks at his watch, measuring the time until they floodlight The Host, and every task down here gets harder.

▶

He is distracted by a pair of dancers, in third dynasty traditional dress, who are performing for a small, hovering quad-copter with a pair of too-bright spotlights for something its size. The dancers are pulling clapping onlookers into their routine, and there is some kind of coordinator in modern, black abatement collecting donations in a handwoven basket. Asha doesn't know which conquered territory gave them baskets, back whenever they conquered it.

The abatement workers surprise him when they appear at his post—the gates in the fencing that surrounds The Host.

"Whoa." He stops them. "What's going on?"

The one in front extends a small tablet in his gloved hand. They are both wearing full abatement suits, with respirators and visors. Asha thinks they look like deep-sea divers, or astronauts. He takes the tablet and taps at the work order it's glowing at him. He glances at the workers. The one in front looks around the plaza, like he's bored. He shifts his toolbox from one hand to the other. The one behind him stares at Asha. Shorter. Maybe a woman.

The work order details inspections of abatement housings on some of the lower levels of the Host.

"Doing this right now?" Asha says.

The respirator's speaker crackles. "I guess so."

"You don't need a priest up there?"

"I guess not. Just checking the bolts and stuff."

Asha hands the tablet back, and the worker kneels and opens his toolbox before Asha even asks. He's done Host work before, this one. Asha takes a look inside—nothing but tools and tubes and bits of things that look useful. Same in the woman's toolbox. He toggles his communication channel by pressing one of the buttons on the side of his helmet.

"Dispatch, this is city center patrol. Can you confirm an abatement work order with Central Maintenance?"

"Copy, city center. Standby."

Asha stands there. The first of the protesters are getting in to the traffic in the great roundabout. Some of his coworkers are encouraging the tourists to get back to their rooms, encouraging the old to get home.

Asha points at a cluster of priests grinding stone, cross-legged in the shadow of the soaring Host.

"You won't be interrupting them?" Asha says.

"No, they're fine."

"City center, this is dispatch."

"Go ahead, dispatch."

"Work order confirmed. Just looks like maintenance."

"At night?"

"Affirmative."

"Do we know why?"

"Negative. But it checks out. Who knows?"

"Copy, dispatch."

Asha waves the workers in. "Well, be careful in there."

"Will do."

▶

It doesn't take long for the demonstrators to move past the extra police volunteers and security consultants. Nobody does anything to stop them. Those were the orders. Their presence is just a bluff. The crowd moves in slow circles, concentric rings with different velocities out in the roundabout and in the plaza itself. They move like they're rotating. Some of them chant about rights and bodies. They aren't wearing abatement. There are arms and knees and anklebones everywhere on the move. Asha just stands at his post and watches people move in toward The Host. He doesn't stop them at the gate, and a few of them shout at him. They get in there, and they rotate around it, too, talking to each other, taking pictures and posting things to the social hub. The priests take a few accidental knees, sitting there, before they collect their stone and get up. Asha thinks about Belan's famous directive. To be disturbed. Well, there it is. No one is saying much of anything over the communications channel. What is there to say? Orders were clear. There are drones overhead and lenses everywhere. This is just today's big news in the ongoing Aeri demonstration. Asha's superiors don't want volunteers to *be* the news—any of them. This will settle down. Suva is on the massive municipal screen on the far side of the plaza, but Asha can't hear what she's saying. Her stone earrings are the size of small cars up there, and they are very still, hanging from her lobes as she keeps calm and explains whatever it is she thinks they're doing.

Asha thinks about the abatement workers, crawling around in The Host. He thinks about the ones that were nearly knocked off that scaffold. About all the copper and hydrogel that the protestors have been dismantling to make their camps in the plazas. He doesn't think they're going to be very popular with this crowd.

His phone vibrates in his pocket, and he shouldn't check it, but Nisa might be watching, and she might be worried. He looks, and there is no message. It's letting him know that it has joined a network with some gibberish English-Aeri name. Like the ones beyond The Wall. He scans the crowd rapidly, but everyone just looks like people. Many of them are staring at their own phones, getting Suva's message on the go. Or are they getting new networks, too? Asha hears reports across the channel of other volunteers discovering weird networks. Dispatchers put them on standby as information goes up and down the chain.

He moves into the circling crowd, and he takes a few shoves as he gets up to The Host and finds the access point in its abatement superstructure. He gets himself into the darkness inside and activates the light on his helmet, and the flesh-toned sarcophagi of the saints wake up to it. He follows the cautionary tape that weaves him between and around the reinforced gaps. It is a tight fit, and he ducks and turns sideways and gets himself up the narrow aluminum rungs that normally ascend the preservationists and abatement workers and priests and scientists whose tasks are the taping and labeling and reinforcing of God's forgotten favorites. Asha's phone buzzes again as he climbs, and he can't get to it, sliding between a pair of masterpiece stone lids and along a thin passage just beyond the outermost abatement layer. The path is a series of symmetrical steps, spiraling upward, created back when they decided to align the saints neatly for a time—Asha steps on the tops of the sarcophagi to make his way. Once, The Host was only *this* high. And there is nothing but abatement board and sheeting between him and the fall to the ground. It should be about time to for the floods to come on, outside.

The crowd gets quiet, out there, below him, and all he can really hear is the thunder of their mumbling and their herdsteps and the honking of the desperate vehicles, caught in the swarm like flood victims.

He looks at his phone, and there is some kind of data stream of the crowd—some are still moving, some aren't. The stream on his phone is recording of them, a live one, from—fuck—up here. From someone staring down, recording down. They stare back, down there. They watch themselves on their phones, and Asha taps the audio into his helmet.

"God remake you," a man says. "Questions are the basis of God on Earth. What has God for you today?"

Asha tucks the phone back into his pocket. He keeps climbing. Where are they?

"What is your name?" a woman says.

"Amn."

"I have two cousins named Amn," she says.

"What is your name?" he says.

"Vesse."

The protestors are still listening, out there, below. He doesn't hear them moving anymore. He only hears himself moving now. It has to be her. It has to be *that* Vesse. Is this the same recording? The one that got her into trouble in the first place?

"My mother was named Vesse," Amn says.

"I wish to hear Ad's Second Dialog on the Mountain," Vesse says.

Amn clears his throat. "Usv tells us in the Second Dialog how Father brought God's paradise to Earth. How he and Mother, carved of God's holy stone flesh, inhaled his divine breath and moved upon Aer. Father worked by day upon the mountain, grinding fragments of God against each other, and the wind carried the dust to the reaches of the Earth, so that we might walk there, too."

Asha stops long enough to look at his phone again. He is covered in stone dust, and he is sweating beneath his uniform. She isn't recording the protesters anymore, in the video stream. She's showing them her face. Vesse's face. She isn't wearing any gloss on her lips, nor powdered stone around her eyes. The scar on her forehead catches the light like an adornment. She stares at them, and he feels her staring.

"And by night," Amn says, "he and Mother made children, so there might be people to ponder the face of God and the cosmos he created in the First Dialog to bring form unto the darkness, light unto the void. So that the universe might have consciousness to think upon itself."

Asha climbs again, and when he finds them, they are at the end of a tight corridor. They have created a hole in the adjacent abatement board, and they have bolted two of their work lights onto the trusses of the superstructure, and their toolboxes are open a few meters ahead of him. Their abatement suits are a cloud-colored pile in the path. She stands in the light, and he is laying at her feet, in the darkness. There is no light for him. Asha feels her look at him, looking past her phone in its spot on the truss, where it is recording her. She stands with one arm at her side. The fingers of her other hand are on a zipper at her neck, and Asha watches her pull it down, parting the halves of a teal Project Daylight jumpsuit. She is naked beneath it, when it comes away, and there are no creams on her skin, and there is a device of square metal plates and wires around her belly, just reaching her pubic hair, which is a triangle creeping near her belly button. It almost favors the color of the hair on her unshaven arms. The device is too big for her toolbox. Asha sees that it is bolted together. She wore it all the way up here. He thinks about the weird networks. About the bridge beyond The Wall. About how long it took him to get up here and how long it will take to get back down. About how he only checked the toolboxes because that's what he's supposed to do.

Vesse's partner is naked below her, Asha sees now, and Asha looks at his phone again, and the recording is zoomed out to show her, pale in the light, a shadow with an erection at her feet. She lowers herself onto him, and it takes a minute, with a hand behind her, to adjust him. Asha thinks about Nisa in the darkness, how she became nothing but a glinting stone in the darkness. A contained woman. The programs and rules she was right about. Who she can get away with being. What it means to her to be Aeri and naked and decent in their apartment.

He backs away from Vesse, one hand before him, as if she is too bright.

"And Father worked—" Amn's voice says in Asha's helmet, "those eons—bringing down the mountain, bringing Aer down, grinding stone against stone in his meditations upon creation, and when the Earth had been filled with the soft places for his children, Mother gathered the dust and fed it to her daughters, so they might know creation themselves. And in his work, Father came to understand the whole of the cosmos, and everything that would befall the Earth and the Aeri upon it. And when the mountain was no more—

Asha hears them yelling, down below, and there is a new thunder of movement, and some of them are screaming, but most of them, a unified chant, raise Vesse's name in the night air. Asha flees wildly between the saints.

A timer chimes in the audio feed.

"Your time is almost upon us," Amn says. "You may re-enter the queue if you would like me to finish—"

"Thank you, Amn," Vesse says.

"God remake you."

"And you, Amn."

SALMI

"I understand," Salmi says.

—Most of the abatement on The Host was destroyed. The equipment holding it in place collapsed.

"Was The Host destroyed?"

—Parts of it were.

"I see."

Salmi lies on her mat in the dark. She listens to sirens on the wind. They're quiet, this far out, as if she need not concern herself with their songs.

—They're grounding flights, so we won't leave tomorrow.

"When?"

—Soon. You can go ahead and turn on your new tablet. No doubt Sarah will want to contact you.

Salmi sits up and unzips the luggage that Sarah brought her. She moves her fingers carefully through the new clothes, folded to fit in all of the pockets and packing spaces. The tablet is smooth and unyielding when she finds it. She wasn't supposed to turn it on until they left Aer. It wakes up to her touch, and her apartment fills with its blue light. The Worldview logo animates across the screen as the machine powers up, and it transitions into a languid glow, slow and brilliant, gently rolling a digital image of the flag.

STAND WITH AER it tells her.

DONATE TODAY.

The stacked and blinking content panes of the Worldview interface replace the image of the flag. The donation prompts minimize to line the sides of the screen. Subscriber interactions climb in their tickers as if racing for new digits without names. Advertisements pulse meekly in their embedded slots, abutting the news with useful and interesting products. There is a large pane in the center of the screen, and it has a picture of a woman's face—a pretty woman, with dark hair and stone jewelry. The English under her image says SUVA SPEAKS, and Salmi taps it, and the woman starts talking fluently in desperate tones about record need in Aer, and terrorism, and how to get everything back on track, and how she has never needed your help more, and she is so grateful for all the help they've received in these important first hours, so soon after the catastrophe, and how much Aer owes Worldview for its careful and thorough coverage, and how she knows the world stands with Aer against terrorists who wish to destroy Aeri treasures—global treasures—and tears begin to slip from her eyes, dragging glints of her eye makeup across her nacreous skin, and administrators have all been escorted to safety, and they will even be checking on the Unregistered, whom they suspect are behind the attack. And there's an audio stream for supporters to call in for information, and Suva reads a statement by a terrorism survivor called Leve, who is taking questions just outside the cordons that the police volunteers and security consultants have set up at a safe distance in the city center from the central plaza. Suva's content pane provides a QuikLink to Leve's. Survivors can tell him their stories.

The other content panes jitter for Salmi's attention with looping recordings of the explosion at The Host. The sudden white of day, like a private dawn, there in the central plaza. The people look like supplicants as they fall in the brilliance, and Salmi has never seen so many so reverent, and The Host looks so thin without its abatement, an upright idea in all the smoke, and there are saints and pieces of saints out in the plaza now, lying next to people who share their names, as if there is meaning to the any of this. Salmi looks, but she doesn't see it.

Darin holds a B.A., an M.A., and a Ph.D. in English Literature and Theory. He has taught courses on writing and literature at several universities and has served in a variety of editorial capacities at a number of independent presses and journals. He lives in Texas with his wife, where he dreams of empty places. *Totem* is his third novel.

CPSIA information can be obtained
at www.ICGtesting.com
Printed in the USA
LVOW04s0431080916
503578LV00001B/1/P